DEATH OF A KING

Massan Gow and the Hounds of St Andrew

Volume I

By

GEOFF HUIJER

First published in Great Britain in 2012 by Ritadore Publishing
First published in paperback in Great Britain in 2012 by Ritadore Publishing

A CIP catalogue reference for this book is available
from the British Library

ISBN 978-0-9573899-0-8

Printed and bound in Great Britain by
Ink Shop Printing, Cumbernauld

Cover design by Kit Foster
www.kitfosterdesign.com

www.facebook.com/MassanGowAndTheHoundsOfStAndrew

DEATH OF A KING

Massan Gow and the Hounds of St Andrew

Volume I

In loving memory of my mother
Doreen R Douthwaite
World renowned archery champion
including five times Scottish Archery Champion
& Scotland's First Female Master Bowman

CHAPTER ONE

Edinburgh Castle, Scotland, 18th March, 1286

It was twilight and the Council was over. They had eaten later in the day than usual as the meeting had overrun. The usual grand feast had made way for what could only be described as a light buffet consisting of legs of pork smoked over the kitchen fire, roasted beef, salted venison, salmon, and eel, along with figs, nuts, and spices which had been brought to Scotland by ships returning from lands reported to be bathed in constant sunshine. The King had thought of these climes many times today as he gazed out the window of the great hall at the town struggling under the weight of the relentless snow. He had also thought of Yolande, his beautiful wife of five months, who was in early pregnancy and who was effectively alone in their small castle at Kynkorn in Fife. She had had difficulties before whilst trying to provide him and Scotland with a son and heir so he was determined to be with her this night, the night before her birthday. In recent years the King had lost his three children to illness and Margaret, the 'Maid of Norway' and his grand-daughter, was now the only surviving descendant in the direct line, and as such had been acknowledged as heir presumptive to the Scottish throne on the 5th February at Scone by the country's magnates.

Alexander, King of Scots had made up his mind and would not be swayed. He would journey to Fife this very moment to see his wife whether the meteorological conditions signalled the End of the World or not. In fact, as he had announced to his flock of advisers, it gave him all the more reason to be by Yolande's side. The King had already ordered four horses readied for his departure and he made his way across the courtyard bowed against the driving snow that swirled around him and the various counsellors attempting to keep up with him. One of the men, an elder statesman unaccustomed to chasing after his liege, pleaded with him.

"Sire! I beg thee return to Fife on the morrow. The night shall be wicked in the saddle with the storm easing not."

"Enough!" Alexander turned in his tracks making the small group almost collide over one another. "My decision is made and I shall not be swayed, not even by

1

such men as wise as thee, my Lord Chancellor. To Fife I go, God willing, and ever-mindful that speed makes way for sure-footedness this eve."

The King then mounted his impressive grey steed, nodding as he did so to his three waiting squires who only just caught sight of his signal through the white haze. He then pulled the mount round in a half-circle and slowly the four riders set out through the pend towards the gates of the royal fortress and beyond. The clatter of iron-shod hooves could still be heard despite the blanket of snow now covering the stone-slabbed courtyard. Consequently, the horsemen barely heard the chorus of well-wishing from the Lord Chancellor and the other statesmen as they started out on the first part of what was to prove an eventful journey.

As they moved out into the quiet streets of Edinburgh the weather and imminent arrival of darkness conspired to give the impression of a ghost town awaiting some terrible fate. Perhaps the prediction by True Thomas, who was understood to have the gift of prophecy, fuelled by assorted friars countrywide that today was Judgement Day, had pushed the townsfolk indoors into the relative safety of the little, single-storey structures that lined the snow-driven streets. Perhaps, on the other hand, it was just the miserable weather that had cleansed the streets, terraces, alleyways and narrow backland plots of their populace. After all, these End of the World predictions surfaced from time to time. Whichever, Alexander still thought the scene as eerie as he had experienced in all of his forty-five years, man or boy. The howling wind was the only sound to be heard as the little band made its way past the last few wattle houses and out towards their first scheduled stop in Cramunde.

At length, the men spotted what appeared to be a woman heading also in the direction of Cramunde. As they drew closer, they could see that it was in fact a small man bent almost double against the elements. The top of his hood and his shoulders carried enough snow to suggest that he too had come from Edinburgh. The King recognised the red cross on his dark grey habit that identified him as a Redfriar.

"'Tis folly indeed, good friar, to be venturing out in such conditions."

Startled, the little man turned and peered to see by whom he was being addressed. Recognising his monarch a smile lit up his face.

"Aye, but I am near to my lodgings which although humble and unfit for a King are always open to thee, my lord, especially on a night such as this."

"And most welcome they are, my good friar, for a King is but a man in conditions such as these when an impending byre is worth more than any castle or fortress that cannot be reached. Your hospitality is most welcome."
At that the Redfriar inclined his head.

"Then I beg thee follow, my lord, for we are but only a short distance from the shelter and warmth of the Redfriars of Cramunde." Without waiting for any further response he turned, and pointing the way with his staff he shuffled off, once again bent double against the elements. Little did any of this inauspicious party know that this day would forever be thought of as the key that opened the door to one of Scotland's most cataclysmic periods in her history.

*   *   *

The main gate to Abirdaur Castle had been closed since the early part of the afternoon. The snow had killed off any chance of there being visitors today, although being on the main pilgrimage route to St. Andrews one could never discount the occasional traveller seeking refuge. On a clear day the castle's tower could see out across the River Forth to Edinburgh and its own castle sitting on the rock overlooking the town. Tonight nothing. Even the outer bailey, which was no more than a stone's throw from the tower, was obscured by the relentless flurry of snow and it was testament to the gatehouse porter there and his alertness that he even saw the lone horseman approach.

"Wit's yer business, stranger," he shouted. No reply. "Name yersel'."

He had had no visitors since his shift started at midday and certainly hadn't expected to see anyone now as the weather worsened. As the rider drew up to the outer gate the porter, recognising him through the gatehouse fissure, swung open the portal to allow him immediate entry. This caller was someone he had not seen for some time and he was the happier for it. He had been in this man's company only twice, fleetingly, as part of the Earl of Fife's staff and although his feudal lord seemed to like the stranger well enough, there was something that made him feel uncomfortable, even fearful. Fearful. Yes that was it. He was fearful. Something about this man, now dismounting, made him fearful. What was it? The way he always seemed to address him in Gaelic? He must know that a native Fifer, a gatekeeper who had barely travelled anywhere outside the burgh would have no understanding of the Celtic tongue. Maybe it was the man's appearance. His Highland garb of kilt and plaid that had the colour of ripe wheat and late season birch leaves seemed to be assaulted by the functional black brooches that held things together. Black. Like his heart, he thought. This most unusual outfit which was pulled up over his head to form a hood was finished off with a dark otter-skin sporran slung to one side, low, open-toed ankle boots, and remarkably long, almost sword-like dirk which swung loosely to the side making him look like he was in a constant state of readiness, but ready for what? The porter was sure that trouble followed this barrel-chested beast around. His lank, red hair flowed out from under the hood and he could see now that this man had known trouble before: his right eye courted a scar across it. His left was perhaps more unusual bearing a Celtic swirl inked round it in black and stretching out to his temple.

That's it! Black-eyed, the Fifer thought, his name's the Celtic word for black-eyed. Och wit's his name? And suddenly it hit him.

"Dubhshuileach, sire! Let us tak yer mount. I'll hae her look'd efter up the stable. Yer drenched, min! Come, come inside to the fire and warmth. Food, drink, anythin' fir yersel'…"

"Take her," he grunted, dismounting. "MacDuff at home?" He waited for no answer as he strode up towards the tower's main door.

Even his horse is black, thought the porter, grabbing for the reins as the big horse reared uncomfortably. Finding none he realised the big man rode in the Pictish style: mainly using his legs and knees. Bloody teuchters were all the same: backward.

The heavy door swung open as the big man reached out to rap on it.

"Dubhshuileach! A pleasure always, yet more so when I can warm your feet by my fire, warm your belly with my porridge and warm your veins with the finest ale this country has to offer. A night to be indoors I declare. Come eat, drink."

"Duncan MacDuff, *deagh* Earl of Fife, unless you have beer from the Redfriars of Cramunde then it is I who has the best beer in the land." And he produced from behind his back a large pigskin flagon which he tossed at the earl. "*Air do shlàinte!*"

"And to your good health also, my friend." The weight of the vessel almost knocked the young boy over for indeed the earl was only that: a young lad. He only knew certain phrases from the Celtic tongue having had them explained to him by his guest in the past, and as his visitor only used those familiar to him, he felt a sense of importance that Dubhshuileach should honour him in this way.

Dubhshuileach hugged MacDuff warmly and patted the earl on the shoulder as he started up the steps to the main entrance hall. It was not lost on him as he climbed the steps that few guests would have the door opened by the Earl of Fife personally, especially when he, himself, was a man with no royal blood and no title of importance. His reputation meant doors were opened for him, he mused: by the gullible, the scared and the weak. He glanced back at the earl who was now following and allowed himself a smile.

There was no onlooker but had there been, the grimace that distorted the flame-haired man's face would have sent a shiver down the spine and to the tips of the toes.

*   *   *

It had been a good day's fishing and mussel collecting for Massan Gow out at the Black Rock despite the weather conditions. The snow was lying on the sandbank around the cluster of rocks that lay a considerable distance from the beach at Pettycur Bay. Local legend had it that The Binn, which was the imposing, extinct volcano overlooking the bay, had once literally blown its top, spewing out these blackened boulders into the sea. Of course, that was all years ago: The Binn was really just a big hill now.

Can't recall seeing snow out this far, he thought, especially lying on the sand. Can't even see The Binn.

It was up there, near the ridge in a slight hollow surrounded by some trees, where Massan lived with his mother and his sister, Aibhlinn. He smiled as he thought of them and clutched the boar-tooth that his mother had given him on his very first fishing trip. It was tied to a thin piece of deerskin which enabled him to wear it around his neck.

"For luck," was all she had said but he knew there was more to it than that. His mother had carved an intricate Celtic symbol onto it with an incredible precision and care, painstakingly reproducing the one that she had made for her husband years ago; the one that Aibhlinn now wore constantly with pride. His mother had a skill people admired, she had a keen eye for design and he had always wondered why she

4

had never sold her pendants, brooches and the like at the market: she could certainly make far nicer things than some of the jewellery they'd seen being sold at the market.

Massan had glowed when she had presented him with it. He had always felt a slight twinge of envy that his sister had been bequeathed the original. Now he had an identical one of his own. Like Aibhlinn, he now wore his all the time.

Binn Village only consisted of around twenty houses that sat astride a main street but proved to be both a friendly and busy place to bide. They lived in the last house on the left. It was a small structure made primarily from timber although the walls were reinforced with clay, dung and turf which provided good protection from the weather on days such as today. Sand from Pettycur Bay was used for the floor along with straw, heather or grass, depending on the season. Massan's mother, Christina, was in her early thirties with long black hair and a pale complexion which always looked as though she had just scrubbed her face; her skin was incredibly soft, however, for someone living in such a cold climate. She sported two little moles on her right cheek and had a dainty dimple on her chin. House-proud, she would sprinkle herbs throughout to give the place a clean, sweet-smelling atmosphere. There was a small plot out the back that housed a couple of geese and some chickens. The family had a relatively comfortable life: they certainly were not rich but neither were they poor. Each family member had a strict routine: three times a week Massan, now fifteen and a man, fished from the Black Rock for eels, cod and mackerel.

"Got a richt guid catch today!" he shouted into the wind. "And a fair few mussels an' aw. That'll keep Aibhlinn happy! They're her favourite!"

Her task was to watch the chickens and geese: quite a task for a six year-old.

"Watchin' the birds is the most important job in the family, Aibhlinn. It lets yer brother fish and it lets me work too." Christina provided a decent income for her family by preparing wool and flax for spinning and she was always telling her children that their jobs were essential.

Nearly everyone in the village had some association with textiles, which meant that the residents had become very close over the years. They all depended on one another in some way. She felt protected like never before.

Christina had come to Fife from an island off the west coast of Scotland after her husband had died, it was thought, of leprosy. She had blotted most of her memories of that time out of her mind: a time of sadness but also one of love. She could not, however, erase the vision of her husband dying, covered in lesions, pock-marks, scars, wounds, sores, call them what you will, his face twisted both in agony and shame. This image she still awoke to, bolt upright, in the middle of the night, sweat pouring down her face and soaking her back.

She still felt resentful that the Lord had not helped her husband.

"He would help if He could," she had said, "so why nothing? Does the Lord care nothing of us – we who worship and follow His word?"

Her neighbours on the island seemed more upset by her outbursts against the Church than by the slow death her husband endured. They said she had become heretic, tainted by Old Nick – the leprosy was a sign – and they no longer wanted her company. It was made clear to her that she should take her family and leave before it was too late. One night she gathered up what she could carry and with children in tow, set off in search of a new life.

Her wanderings had brought her here by chance and she now felt at home even though she missed hearing the sweet, singing lilt of her native tongue. She felt safe near the sea and often wandered down to the beach with her children to breathe in the fresh air, to close her eyes and to listen to the familiar sound of sea birds as they swooped down onto the water.

Although she was used to Massan being away in all weathers and on occasion even overnight, she felt a little uneasy at him being out in such horrific conditions. She was right to feel strange for she was not to know that when she waved Massan off that very morning she would only ever see him once more and by then their worlds would have changed forever.

CHAPTER TWO

The *Merle* merchant ship, Yarmouth Harbour, England, November, 1275

The angry sky scowled over the tightly-packed ships and boats which sought refuge in the harbour, the greyness belying the fact that it was nearly midday.

"Let me speak with yon bailiff!"

The booming command came from a big lad in his mid-teens who had almost knocked over the skipper of the ship in his eagerness to get to the starboard side which competed with the harbour wall. He had a large patch covering his left eye concealing a heavy swelling. He spoke with the unmistakeable lilt of a Highland accent, recognisable even through the rage.

"I say, let me speak with yon bailiff!" he shouted once more, but the words were swept up and away leaving a small crowd of puzzled faces on the quayside staring up at his gesticulations.

He turned to the bosun, a man in his fifties, as the skipper headed ashore.

"Tell me again."

"We have been accused of piracy and are not being allowed to leave the harbour."

"Piracy! For the love of…I do *not* believe this…will not! And who exactly speaks such nonsense?" He never gave the boatswain the opportunity to answer. "Bailiff!" His scream was heard this time on the dockside but contemptuously ignored by the bailiff who was in animated discussion with the first mate. "And you cannot release any of the ship's cargo?" he addressed the bosun again.

"No sir, everything is being covered by the port authorities."

"Port authorities? Pah!"

"Aye. Port authorities. King Edward's newly committed taxing and formalising of England's ports means that we have near enough an army on our doorstep and a shitload of paperwork to remove before we can set sail."

"But piracy…?" The lad looked confused.

"Skipper thinks it is a way of gaining more monies from us. So, seeing as our liege Lord Alexander doggedly dodges Edward's proposals that he should pay him homage for Scotland it means we are to be played like pawns in the King's big chess game."

"Alexander already *does* pay homage to Edward of England. He does so knowing Edward almost as kin – his first Queen was Edward's sister…"

"Aye son, you have the rights of it. Almost," replied the older man. Our King of Scots pays homage to Longshanks but only for his lands held in England – Tynedale, Huntingdon and Cumberland. He has never bowed to Edward's attempts to have him pay homage for Scotland…even as a child-monarch he had to fend off Edward's father before him. The Plantagenets have ever had a keen eye on Scotland."

"Which leaves us where?"

"It leaves us here with nowhere to go," sighed the bosun. "All it takes is an accusation and we have to stay put. Piracy is an accusation not to be laughed at, we face death or imprisonment. King Edward does not mess about with pirates."

"But we came in only to confirm our journey's transactions and receive the completed papers. Mere formality. We are no more pirates than I know not what…it is absurd!" The big lad was looking exasperated.

"Aye laddie, but it is politics. The wool we obligingly agreed to deliver on the outgoing voyage is the thorn in our side. Some Englishman has accused us of having stolen his wool and he requests the bailiff detains us until truth is out."

"That wool was duly processed…"

The two men were disturbed by shouting below on the quayside and watched as a crowd of soldiers helped the bailiff pull two men apart who were clearly intent on doing damage to each other.

"May I suggest you go below and wait things out," said the boatswain. "We will not be allowed near the ship's stores or even to disembark whilst matters are being dealt with."

"Aye and how long will that take?"

"Oh, maybe an hour, maybe a week…"

The big lad let out a sigh and turned, heading below deck.

"Well make sure and tell me what is going on when you know," he demanded as he headed off, looking an English official up and down as he deliberately bumped past him.

A few hours passed when word went round the ship that the shipmaster was gaining ground in the negotiations. The important fare-paying passengers – only five of them on this journey which comprised the young Highland lad and his clerical companion, two white monks heading back to Derbyshire and a herald returning to Canterbury from abroad – were gathered in the skipper's cabin to hear details of the news, sketchy as it was with no-one being allowed ashore. The bosun had secured an information line (shouting from ship to shore) which proved their only source of news however unreliable. Currently going the rounds was that the skipper, Shaw, was nearing agreement with officials. He had been asked to agree to all the ship's stores being laid out quayside for inspection by His Majesty's representatives. This, he had steadfastly refused, whilst managing to negotiate a deal which allowed an inspection of the ship itself by the authorities; news that had the big Highland lad flying into a rage. "All the cargo, say you? There is no need to inspect all the stores! It is a ruse…a trick…to rob us! Or to tax us!"

The first mate, whose name was James, tried to reason with him.

"It cannot be…we are newly arrived back from Flanders and Sevilla. We have the documentation to prove so. Our exports are exactly that: exported. We have the paperwork to confirm our exports and for those we bring back. We have nothing to hide."

"'Tis duplicity I tell you. A swindle...call it what you will but I smell a rat."

"We have no wool," said James. He let the sentence hang in the air a while before continuing. "Oranges, olives, purple dyes, spices we have…but no wool. It is trickery yes, but to gain a payment to smooth our passage, 'tis all."

"My luggage is mine own and not for the likes of any fool to rummage around in. My priest travels with me and agrees," said the young Highlander with an air of panic creeping into his voice. "I have important documents that are not for prying eyes," he added quickly, eyes darting round the cabin.

The priest stood up.

"I concur. Private luggage should remain private. It bears no relevance to the ship's stores and any wool or documents or monies relating to wool." He sat down.

The Cistercians remained silent but nodded gently in approval. Clerical bonding perhaps?

"We shall see when skipper Shaw comes back," said the first mate. "Methinks the inconvenience caused to us of searching the ship will well suit our eager bailiff."

"He shall not have my trunk to rummage in!" The patch on the lad's face had peeled off near his ear revealing part of a tattoo that was still tender-looking and only recently done. It had been done with a dye or ink that was black but it was still raw and bloody by his temple enhancing the appearance, which was the edge of a Celtic knot design. "By the rights of it he will not invade my personal belongings…"

"Come now," the bosun stood up with his palms held out, "we needs must await the skipper. He will put our needs first to yon bailiff."

At that the shipmaster returned, followed by a dozen soldiers and three other men, presumably bureaucrats.

"It appears that the paperwork we have for the wool exported is inaccurate," skipper Shaw started glumly.

"And proves wholly my assumption of illegality," continued a short man with a hook-nose sporting a close-cut black beard and short curly hair. He wore a long, blue, woollen, ankle-length over-tunic and gold chain and looked down his long nose at his audience as he spoke.

"Sire, I beg to differ. The whole shipment for export contained fifty-six sacks of wool, the Gatacre part of that being six sacks, the Cistercians had fifteen sacks and the rest – thirty-five sacks – belonged to Leonard de Ludlowe," Shaw looked exasperated. "Furthermore, the Gatacre entry in the port's log has been altered to thirty-six as the ship's documentation proves…"

"Ah! Proving my lord Gatacre's point exactly, my good skipper. Your paperwork does not agree with ours so cannot therefore be genuine."

"Bailiff, we have just discussed this – the seal on our paperwork is yours along with the seal and signature of the harbourmaster. How can it be forgery?"

The shipmaster's retort left the room in silence before the hook-nosed man spoke.

"Sire, we aim no harm to you and yours. The paperwork is not in order therefore I require monies to compensate the loss of my wool. Monies you undoubtedly have aboard this ship, yourself having agreed that fifty-six sacks of wool have been delivered – sold – in the low countries…"

"Flanders, yes," said Shaw.

"Now, by the good of His Grace Edward, King of England whose laws needs be adhered to lest we all be pirates, I insist by right of those laws that *I have compensation!*" Gatacre's face had been gradually turning redder and now looked purple enough to suggest he was having some sort of fit. "*My right, you hear!*"

"My good skipper," the bailiff put his arm round Shaw's shoulder and turned him away from the assembled crowd of silent onlookers, Gatacre seething to himself amongst them, "Good sense is required here, see you. Fifty-six sacks were collected by your ship not three weeks ago; fifty-six sacks have been sold. You agree?" He waited for no reply but Shaw was nodding his agreement. "Now, what matter to you whose wool has been sold? All that matters is that you go on your way; you complete your journey; deliver your foreign wares back to Scotland and see your passengers right, is it not?" Shaw still nodded. "Now, let us be the judge of paperwork. We can clear it all up without my lord Gatacre becoming too…how shall we say… obstinate? Pay him the monies for thirty-six sacks, the white monks have monies for their fifteen and Ludlowe gets the rest." Shaw rubbed his chin, mouth and face continuously with a clammy hand as if trying to wipe away dirt. The bailiff continued, "That done and you can be away by morning." He let the whispered words hang in the air for a moment. "Think on it. We will return later for your answer." He took his arm from Shaw's shoulder and turned to walk away, stopping briefly. "The choice is yours, my good shipmaster, and it seems it is one between freedom and piracy." He turned and headed for the door.

"Come!" Gatacre gestured to the guards, and to Shaw, "you know what to do Sirrah! Think on it well!"

At that the bailiff and Gatacre left followed by their troop of men, leaving the skipper's cabin in silence, the occupants just blinking at one another.

The silence was broken by the bosun.

"Exactly what has that man Gatacre got to do with the port authorities in Yarmouth when he is a wool merchant from Salop?"

"Good question," replied Shaw, "he is kinsman to the bailiff and a sheriff in Salop, so a man of importance. I believe he has Edward's ear also. He obviously is not a man to miss a moneymaking opportunity when he sees one, legally or otherwise. This is a man who likes things his way – Sir Leonard of Ludlowe will testify to that having had to turn tail and leave at the request of Gatacre's men."

"So what next?" the big lad wondered aloud.

"We let them search and we pay and leave," replied Shaw. "I do not intend to have my Lord MacDuff have his vessel harried any longer than necessary. My thoughts are that I must make to Fife with haste, but a charge of piracy cannot be wiped clean so easily..."

"I will not allow a search of my possessions," started the lad, only to be silenced by a motion from the priest.

"Well that is as may be son, but we must return to Scotland with purpose...I have goods to deliver and further voyages to make, not least my lord needs must know of his friend Ludlowe's treatment at this port and it seems that we could be here for some time despite proof of our innocence. I have sent message to our liege-lord and King Alexander to ask for his support via Edward. This delays things meantime."

"Good, we can but wait then..."

"Aye, replied Shaw.

It took eleven days for an answer to come back to them on the *Merle* and when it did it was not what they expected. MacDuff had been informed and petitioned the King, assuring him of their innocence; however, Alexander would seem to not have pushed Edward overly forcefully which was understandable given the tender political climate. He had certainly denied their being pirates (which Edward accepted) but had suggested that as he knew his vassals had nothing to hide they should allow a full search of the ship and all the belongings thereon.

"We have no desire to interfere with the running of one of his Grace and Lord Edward's ports and offer a full search of the said ship which no doubt will prove fruitless," King Edward agreed.

So it was that the search took place and darkness had fallen by the time Gatacre returned with his men to conduct it. A brief discussion with Shaw and they were rummaging their way through the ship, confirming as they did that the guards left on board had allowed no-one to interfere with any of the stores, food and drink having been supplied gratis for the last ten days by the harbour stevedore. The customs guards searched their way through the ship, working their way methodically towards the stern where the skipper's cabin and small private quarters were. They went about their work with relish but not uncaring, making efforts not to break anything or damage any of the ship's stores or wares. The more they worked their way through the ship the more the Highland fellow seemed agitated. He consulted his clergyman constantly and was overheard on more than one occasion.

"But…my father…I promised him…first mission."

The cleric managed to quieten him down at first but as the *black gang* – Edward's customs officers who specialised in the searching of ships – worked through the vessel the more worried he began to look. Unfortunately for the young Highlander all this meant was that he had protested to such an extent about how he would not allow inspection of his trunk he only served to create huge fascination as to what it concealed. His clerical companion again attempted to calm him, and indeed to silence him, but to no avail. Gatacre became agitated, curious, fervently so now. His composure had remained with him as he and his men shadowed the *black gang* as they searched the ship inch by inch, but as they neared the stern he urged them to examine the trunk. They refused to be told their jobs by this arrogant upstart, the leader telling him politely words to that effect.

Eventually they were outside the skipper's cabin. Gatacre motioned to the leader of the *black gang* to remain where he was, at the same time giving him a stare which indicated it was a non-negotiable order, not a request. He stepped into the room with his men.

"Last chest…" Gatacre motioned towards the northerner's trunk.

"No, Sirrah! I will not allow it!" He stood up to his full height and although he was only of young age he was a big lad, both broad and tall, muscles filling out his arms which burst out from his dirty, sleeveless vest. His bark would most definitely match his bite. Gatacre stopped.

"I have the rights to search all this ship," he said calmly, "and I intend to do so, young man, whether we gain your consent or not. Moreover, as a representative of His Grace, Lord King Edward I have law on my side. Knowest you English law?" He did not wait for an answer continuing, "Your co-operation is not necessary – we will search your trunk…"

"You will not! I forbid it!"

"Leave us," Gatacre turned to the assembled crowd in the cabin; the same crowd that had witnessed the discussion earlier with Shaw and the bailiff. "Leave us!" This time his instruction was louder, more assertive. They started to file out in silence, including the lad's priest who waited for a confirming nod allowing him to go. The lad gave it; the priest left. Shaw paused by Gatacre. "I expect you also to leave us to do the King's work," he said matter-of-factly to Shaw who turned to the lad and shrugged his shoulders before leaving. The lad was now alone. He was cornered by Gatacre and a dozen soldiers. "Step aside," Gatacre commanded.

"I will not!"

The lad stood tall, sweat now starting to glisten on his forehead, fists clenched, ready. Adrenalin pumped through his body – he was not afraid, merely psyched up. He could not remember feeling scared, ever – not even three weeks previously when his father had given him his task and then asked him to plunge his *sgian* into his heart. He had done as his father had asked without as much as a butterfly in his stomach.

"I shall ask you only once more, lad. Step…aside…"

"No…"

"Do it!" Gatacre turned and at that the lad smashed his fist upwards into the nearest soldier driving the bone in the nose upwards into his brain. The man crumpled to the floor, face grey, eyes lifeless a red mess where his nose had been. The crunch stopped the others in their tracks momentarily, giving the Scots lad time to swing round and slash another foe across the throat with a blade drawn from his waistband; the very same blade that had dispatched his father. His speed and agility seemed to catch his adversaries unawares. Again, they all stopped, Gatacre watching agog from the safety of the cabin door.

"Come on then!" The lad was red-faced now, veins in his neck bulging, gesturing knife in hand with blood splashed across his vest. The room was silent with the soldiers not quite knowing what to do, each one hoping that another would make the next move. Their two colleagues lay dead on the floor, pools of purple blood slowly spilling out from them. Gatacre looked shocked. What was in that trunk that was worth all this? He felt quite excited by it all and motioning to his reinforcements outside, stepped out of view to allow them to stream into the room.

There were over thirty men in the room when the big lad decided enough was enough. He acted fast, knocking over the two oil lamps on the table next to him, sending flames across the floor whilst simultaneously unlatching the shutter behind him and leaping into the darkness. A remote splash was all that was heard of the Scotsman.

"Quick! Get him!" Yells went up into the air and confusion reigned as the men fought back the flames threatening to engulf them. Gatacre charged back in, pushing his way past a young soldier who was backing away from flames rapidly. "Grab the trunk! Save the trunk!" Gatacre paid no heed to the two bodies on the floor as he shoved the lad back into the flames. "The trunk…grab it!" he yelled.

The flames were soon doused and Gatacre sat alone in the smoke-filled cabin, lit again by oil lamps, nursing his prize. He sat for some time just staring at the large coffer. He marvelled at the workmanship – it was made of *cuir bouilli*, the leather soaked in oil which thus became waterproof and supple. The top of the trunk was curved to allow rain to run off easily and the whole structure was reinforced with iron strips and fittings which were secured on the face with a lock which required a key – a key which he did not possess. Unlike the impedimenta he was used to this box reeked of quality, and despite his keenness to discover the treasures within he did not wish to have such craftsmanship violated by simply it ripping it open. No, he thought, I will keep the trunk as well as the contents. So, he got up and walked to the door of the cabin opening it to find, as expected, one of his men.

"That lad been found yet?" he snorted.

"No, my lord…"

"Well, see to it," he snapped, adding, "Fetch me someone who can break into this box without damaging it. Search Yarmouth if needs be and hurry to it." He closed the door and sat down once again to examine the coffer.

A few hours later he was disturbed by a knock at the door which turned out to be a master locksmith who had the wherewithal to safely unlock the padlock on the chest. Gatacre waited until he was alone before thinking about opening the lid. The Scots lad had made such a fuss over his trunk that Gatacre could not resist having it. He had become obsessed with it and could only imagine what it contained therein: gold, silver, crimson jewels, diamonds and exotic silks. He almost drooled at the thought and found himself shaking as he prised the lid up slightly.

It creaked like an old rusty door hinge and he needed to put a little more effort into opening it up. He put his shoulder against the top of the chest to force it up and it seemed to give way, allowing him to pop it open all the way. He sniggered aloud to himself like some sort of ancient alchemist discovering that he had found the secret of turning metal into gold. Rubbing his hands he peered into the darkness of the chest.

It was too dark.

He grabbed the nearest lamp and held it over his treasure. He peered in again to see…another chest! This one was also rectangular in shape and about two feet long, fitting easily into the larger, better-made coffer. It was a dark wood, polished highly and very smooth. This must be olive wood, he thought, running his fingers along its length: he had heard of it but never seen any for himself. The Highland lad had packed his clothes tightly around this box to secure it within the bigger one. Gatacre rummaged through the clothes: vests, a couple of grubby tunics, a Highland plaid which was all of thirteen-feet long when he finally pulled it all out of the trunk, a pair of open-toed boots made from deerskin, a sporran made from the same, and various other garments, all of which he threw over his shoulder wildly. Underneath all the garments was a pair of table knives with crystal handles which he grabbed, rolling them round in his hands. They were of exceptional workmanship, almost certainly from the Holy Land and so were worth something, which had Gatacre drooling once more. Valuables, he thought. But not as valuable as the main prize, he thought also. He lay the knives down by his side and knelt up to examine the smaller box more closely. He held it up into the light and as he did so a rat shot out from under a table shooting across the room and jingling over the knives as it did. Neither rat nor man paid any attention to the other – they were both absorbed in their own worlds.

Kneeling, Gatacre set the box down and used one of the table knives to slit a wax seal, which held it shut. It opened easily and he turned it into the light to illuminate the contents.

His jaw fell open.

"No…" he murmured aloud. "It cannot be…"

He looked inside again to check that what he had seen the first time was true.

"I…do not…understand…"

He spoke slowly and as he did he put his hand into the box and pulled out a small, foot-long piece of wood: it appeared to be part of an old olive branch…

14

CHAPTER THREE

The Holy House of the Trinitarians, Cramunde, 18th March, 1286

With exception of the King, none of the men sitting at the long table, which glowed with the warmth of the roaring fire, wanted to venture out again into the blizzard. The combination of warm porridge and wonderful beer made them feel that they should honour the Redfriars by staying the night.

They had perhaps had a little too much ale, although even the King had remarked that beer as good as this was hard to come by. What was it that made the Redfriars such good brewers they had wondered? Perhaps they had picked up tips from various poor pilgrims that they had helped over the years. They must see many people, sited as they were on the main pilgrimage route from the south to St. Andrews. Perhaps some of the many captives they had ransomed had brought back new ideas from the Holy Land, a place known for its bizarre ways but one that had embraced beer for hundreds of years, according to the Redfriars. Whatever it was, the beer was good and the more they had drunk of it the less they had felt like travelling on to Kynkorn, especially with a ferry ride to negotiate as well.

The Redfriars had been very hospitable. There were only six of them and it seemed that the little man whose name they discovered was Callum, was actually the prior. Two of the other men it seemed were priests and the other three were lay brethren. Although most of the talking had been left to Prior Callum, what little the others had said suggested that they all knew how to brew good beer, taking it in turns as brewers on a weekly basis.

"I am of a mind that my lord King visits not to discuss the merits of beer, my friends, but to have peace, rest and warmth on a journey which must be of enormous importance to have to be made on this very night."

"Aye you have it. A prior with eyes that see men inside and out." The King stood up and as everyone else followed suit he gestured to them all to sit. "Sit, all. Callum, my good Redfriar I have done you a great disservice. It is right I tell you of our visit and the importance of our journey."

"My lord, I meant not to pry…"

"No offence meant. No offence taken." Alexander continued. "I shall tell you my reasons. They are no secret. It is my aching heart you see. I am but married one hundred and fifty days and the love I have for my queen is strong. It shall not be dampened by rain or by snow in my quest to be reunited with her. Nor indeed shall distance be a barrier to me. My heart has an ache which needs must be cured by the sight of my Yolande, her with child and whose birthday demands me by her side. This my reason and reason enough I feel." The last was said with an emphasis and a sideways glance to his squires which betrayed his feelings of anger towards those that day who had tried to sway his mind from his journey. He recognised this and with a change of tone and of subject he went on, "Young Andrew it seems is rather the worse for your good brew, Callum. His eyes are as pissholes in yonder snow. Ha! Ha!" His laugh was hearty and genuine. Andrew, the youngest of his squires, now held his head in his hands, leaning on the table not only in shame at having let the drink get the better of him but because if he didn't assume that position he might have slumped across said table. "It looks like you may well have a lodger for the night after all."

"It can be a strong brew for those unaccustomed to it, my lord. I fear the blame lies with me as young Andrew widnae ken its strength…"

"Nonsense!" Alexander laughed. "I know the beer's strength and I also know Andrew. It is his liking for *lots* of ale that is to blame and not how strong it is. It is not the brew that is wicked, my good friar, but the thirst that some have for it."

At that, one of the brethren was helping the young squire, who was now beginning to mumble incoherently, to his feet.

"I shall put him to bed to sleep it off. With your permission, my lord," he said.

"Indeed, and this episode put to bed with him. I shall hear no more talk of what went on here this eve," he announced to the room in general and no one in particular. "We leave now." The matter was ended.

The journey to the Queen's ferry was arduous in the driving wind and snow and barely a word was said by any of the three travellers save to indicate directions. King Malcolm's wife, Queen Margaret, had dedicated the ferry back in the eleventh century to allow travellers safer passage on the pilgrim route to St. Andrews, hence the name. A busy route, as the shrine of St. Andrews was one of the most important pilgrimage destinations in the whole of Western Christendom, for only two shrines,

St. Andrews and the golden, granite town of Santiago de Compostela (Saint Jacques) in Galicia, could offer contact with a martyred apostle of Christ.

On arrival they dismounted and entered the bothy.

"Good eve," the King announced, giving the ferryman a start as he had his back to the door, warming his hands above a little fire.

"Oh! My lord King!" the ferryman exclaimed as he turned, and standing continued, "I was expecting no visitors on this night, Sire. Let me get you some..." He leaned over to pick up some fleeces.

"Well, visitors you have and indeed over anxious to get yonder to Fife. Your offer of hospitality is noted, alas we cannot accept. Your services to aid us to Fife are all that are required."

"My lord this eve is not one for boating to Fife – the danger of such a crossing would be great."

"My lord, shall I..." started one of the squires stepping toward the boatman, only to be hushed by Alexander who continued to the ferryman.

"Well a boatman you are but one that has not mastered his art if boating in darkness and snow is deemed over dangerous. I needs must take the boat on my own to save you worry from danger. Your father ought not to have wrapped you up in woollen cloth at a young age as comfort seems to be your life now." At that the King turned to leave followed by his squires, saying as he did so, "Nice fire..."

The boatman reached out to grab the last of the squires with a shout.

"My lord King! I err with caution indeed, however to share in the fate of thy father's son is an honour not to miss. My caution is for my King. I will not see thee travel alone whilst I sit here. Thou shall be taken and with God's will arrive in Inverkeithing none the worse for the experience. Come, the ferry awaits..."

The ferryman had redeemed himself after the King's accusation of cowardice; an accusation that got the desired result.

*   *   *

Dubhshuileach was an oddity in more than just his appearance. Not only was he a vassal of the young Earl of Fife, he was also a landowner in his own right: his father was given the castle at Rossend by the current earl's father for whom he had worked as Procurator Fiscal; this was now his. Even more unique, in Scotland, was that he had inherited regality also from his father who had eventually moved overseas to warmer climes because of ill health. Regality meant that the immediate hamlets served by Rossend Castle, which included Kirkton and the Binn Village, came under his direct jurisdiction rather than the earl's justice to whom a landowner would normally submit. Regality was a jurisdiction given by a King. He was still technically a vassal of the Earl of Fife but his peculiar situation meant that MacDuff was not only respectful of him but wary of him too; the feelings were not reciprocated.

Dubhshuileach, the smooth-talker, had run the evening laughing and joking with the earl, plying the young man with ever more drink, showering him with flattery. All the time he carefully watched the earl drink himself into a stupor and eventually standing up he leaned over the snoring MacDuff, listening: heavy breathing. Pathetic, he thought. He then moved across the great hall to a wall that appeared to have a hole in it, and shoving his hand in, he rummaged about. Soon he stood looking at a large key. Beege has observed well and instructed better, he thought to himself. He slipped it into his sporran and headed towards the stairwell that led to the lower kitchen glancing back at the earl as he did. He stopped just before the stairwell by a flagstone red in colour. It almost called to him from under the carpet of straw. Again he glanced over to the sleeping figure and on bended knees counted out four stones to the left towards a small shuttered window.

"Now, one step to the left," he muttered to himself, and bending down, drew his dirk.

Suddenly, there was a loud groan and Dubhshuileach looked up in horror. His expression lasted mere seconds as he watched the earl's head loll to one side and the groan turn into a gush of brownish liquid splashing down his left arm and onto the floor.

"Now, easy does it..." His tongue hung out in concentration, working round his lips as he worked the dirk round the edge of the flagstone, digging it in deeper as he did. Suddenly it succumbed to his efforts moving slightly and letting the dirk slide in with ease. He lifted up the stone with the tips of his fingers and peered into the hole. Staring back at him was a neat row of bags: four scarlet silk bags embroidered round the edges with gold thread. From the Holy Land, he thought, knowing that MacDuff's father had travelled there. He took the first one and opened it.

"Shillings!"

He shocked himself with his exclamation and looked up quickly to check on the earl. Nothing. No stirring. All he could hear was the wind outside whistling as it banged on the shutters trying to get in.

Could do with some fresh air in here, he thought. The smell of vomit wafted over from where the earl was slumped; the fire at the far end of the hall was now starting to fill the room up with smoke, coughing up large puffs in bluish clouds.

He put the bag down to one side and replaced the flagstone, rubbing any loose scrapings and dust back into the edges. Once done, he picked up the bag and went down the stairs into the kitchen. MacDuff had already excused the scullion earlier in the evening so there was no danger of bumping into him: he slept down the passage in a room with the other kitchen staff. The kitchen door on the far side took him out into the yard opposite one of the stable blocks: he knew this would be where his horse was being kept as it was used exclusively for visitors. He crossed the yard, checking both ways to make sure he was not being watched, and crept into the stables. Right enough his was the only horse in the block and taking it firmly by the mane led it quietly south towards the outer wall. Here he found a small door that he knew he could squeeze his horse through, and taking the key from his sporran, opened the door. He locked it behind him, mounted, and trotted off into the darkness. If it hadn't been for the storm a gentle chink of shillings would have been all that was heard.

*   *   *

18

The ferry crossing had been remarkably uneventful considering the conditions and it had not been long before the King was conversing with the master of his saltworks in Inverkeithing.

"Lord, how often have I told thee that these journeys at night shall do thee no good? Our house is yours till morn when the storm will have tired itself out."

"My only need is for a fresh horse and two good local guides to further me on to Kynkorn," he laughed, almost exasperated by his people's constant concern for him. "My men can rest here till the morrow and I can be happy they will be warmly looked after, knowing as I do your hospitality."

"As you please, my lord."

Presently the King was on his way again, riding into the teeth of the storm. He was an accomplished rider and at times impetuous so it wasn't long before he found himself ahead of his guides. His horse kept to the worn paths instinctively so he was unaware that on nearing Pettycur Bay, when the route forked, he was taken off to the right: the wrong way. Shortly after, his guides reached the fork and knowing the way took the path to the left, increasing their pace a little, which was difficult what with the poor visibility.

Unbeknownst to Alexander he was now alone. He was also lost – and frozen. He kicked into the ribs of his steed, urging it to go ever faster into the gloom. Branches clawed at him as he rode down the narrowing path, pulling at his fur surcoat and at one stage drawing blood on his cheek.

"Mercy of God!"

The King's stallion reared up in fright as he almost careered into the young boy. Massan had been alert and stepped deftly to one side. He was less shocked than horse and rider.

"Easy," he called, grabbing the reins and calming the steed down. Then on recognising the rider bowed quickly. "My lord, I meant not to scare you..."

"Indeed, young lad, but alarm us you did. Pray tell what such a young man does in such darkness?"

"I head for home, my lord, after a long day at the fishing," he said, still gripping the reins of what was still a very nervous horse. "But, *I* am on familiar ground good King, not far from home. I fear *you* are not and without companions..."

"Aye laddie, you have the rights of it. Pray tell the way to Kynkorn and I'll be off. I needs must be there soon. I fear the cold is getting to me."

"Not far, my lord," said Massan, "and I can guide you. This path leads to Kynkorn for sure but is a winding route with many twists, hills and narrow passes. It is in truth uneven and not a track to be racing at. Yonder path," he continued, pointing up the steep cliff face, "is the swifter and by far the straighter."

Of course the King could not see any path high above but realised his mistake.

"Your offer is kind but as you say this path does lead me to Kynkorn and that is enough to know. I shall need no guide; especially one who needs must be home at this hour and in this weather. I'll be away now and have reason to insist you do the same..."

Massan still held the reins tightly as the King prepared to move off.

"My lord...for luck." He reached out and handed the King his boar's tooth pendant.

The King smiled and as he was about to refuse the gift shivered suddenly with cold. He wiped his bleeding cheek and taking the leather cord answered, "Bless you."

At that the King was off, this time at a pace more suited to the conditions.

"Bless you, my lord," Massan whispered as he watched the King disappear from sight into the blackness.

* * *

Steam was now pouring off the beast and its mouth was beginning to foam. Dubhshuileach knew that it was foolhardy to be riding so hard into the jaws of such a storm but was also acutely aware that he had only limited time to complete his task.

Not far from the cave now, he thought as he ducked under a grasping branch. Only a couple of more bends to go. The horse thundered round the next turn with its rider using his knees to guide it and clutching its mane firmly. It tempered its speed to accommodate the sharpness of the corner and accelerated once through it.

Massan had heard nothing in the gale and as the horse glanced at him he was thrown spinning into a bank of snow. He landed with a soft thud.

The horse and rider were gone in seconds and Massan knew not what had hit him.

"Oh, what in God's name was that?" he moaned up to the night sky as he lay on his back. His mind raced. Had it been a boar? A stag? He checked himself and found nothing broken but he was now sodden and needed to get home with God's speed. He pulled himself up, and checking to make sure which way he should be going, thought no more of his experience and set off with a little more urgency than before.

Dubhshuileach knew he had clipped something. Indeed, he was fairly sure it had been *someone*. It concerned him not as he had far more pressing matters to deal with. He had to get to the hiding place and then back to the Castle before he was missed.

He was not cold despite the weather. Beads of sweat poured down his face and it was as much for the worry of getting to the cave, as it was the hard riding in ridiculous conditions.

He slowed down the pace to make sure he did not bypass the cave and as he did so spotted it a few feet from the path behind a large beech tree. He stopped and dismounted. He looked around to check that he was alone. He was.

Well planned, he thought, and as he made for the cave to hide his booty, he stopped dead in his tracks. What was that? Someone shouting? He listened but could hear nothing over the howling wind. He turned to make for the cave again and as he did so heard it loud and clear this time. It came from towards the cliff edge.

"Help! Mercy!"

Suddenly Dubhshuileach was cold. Frozen, in fact. A shiver ran down his spine. What now, he thought. Am I caught? Should I look? His mind raced.

"Help!"

"Help is here my friend!" he shouted into the night as he walked toward the cliff edge noticing the snow on the ground had been disturbed dramatically.

"In God's name! Help! I fear I cannot hold much longer and my arm is broken."

Dubhshuileach kneeled down to get a better view, noticing as he did so some sort of talisman by his right hand. It stared up from the pristine white bed in which it lay. He picked it up and held it close to his face; he recognised the symbol as being Celtic. Tucking the boar's tooth into his sporran he peered over the edge of the cliff and again a shiver ran down his spine. Clinging to the root of a small gorse-like bush was Alexander, King of Scots.

CHAPTER FOUR

Kynkorn, Fife, 18th March, 1286

Yolande had been pacing up and down the room most of the night and now she just stood gazing out of the bedroom window. Snow fluttered in occasionally and a big flake even landed on her bare foot causing her to shiver and close one of the shutters. He should have been back by now. She knew that. He would not have let his advisors dissuade him from coming. She knew that more so. Their love was strong and Alexander had promised to return for her birthday. She stood to the side of the open window just out of reach of the grasping wind and stared out into the curtain of snow that seemed to be flapping at her; she felt a surge of emotion burst through her. Her eyes welled up. She grabbed her herself to avoid fainting, and clutching the wall, slipped down the wall onto the floor. She knew. She didn't know why but she knew. Like a flash she saw her and Alexander riding on their horses across the sands at Pettycur Bay. It was a beautiful summer's day. They had the beach to themselves. Her King had seen to that. They had splashed in the water like giggling children with not a care in the world. He wooed her in her native tongue, slipping into a French accent as pronounced as any she had heard. He was perfect, she thought. They ran up the dunes together hand in hand and fell into the warm sand in each other's arms. She could hear his laugh. She felt his skin up tight against hers as he gently removed her underclothes, his warm breath on her cheek. She could feel his strong arms around her and she could smell him. Clean yet with sweat. Gentle yet potent. Her naked body gave itself up to him. His lips were all over her. She felt him inside her.

The shutter slammed against the wall so violently she snapped out of her wonderings and realising she had wet herself; she began to cry.

*   *   *

The silence was eerie, thought Massan, as he reached the clearing near the top of The Binn. It was nearly dawn and usually even at this hour there were animals stirring. Tonight nothing. The terrible weather had gradually abated and there lay a thick, ankle-deep blanket of snow over the clearing. The moon, although not full, shone down now from the clear sky and enabled Massan to realise what it was that made the scene look so weird. No animal prints in the snow. Wildcat, badger, deer. All were known to favour the hours of darkness and pre-dawn. It was safer then with less chance of being disturbed by humans. He must have travelled this route home dozens of times by moonlight and he had always seen some sign of life. Although he had seen signs of life this eve and some fairly strange ones at that; the stag or boar that had collided with him earlier, he still felt the hairs stand up on the back of his neck as he viewed the surreal scene. It must have been a stag he thought, as it was surely too big for a boar. He remembered his chance meeting with the King not long before and how he found it strange for the King to be travelling with no guards or guides at such a late hour and in such adverse conditions.

"Shit!"

He looked down and realised his fishing catch for that day was gone. He must have dropped it when he was knocked over by the beast. He'd lost Aibhlinn's mussels, the eels and the couple of crabs he'd spent ages catching. How could he have lost his catch so easily? He'd spent the best part of the day making sure that what he took home that night would be top quality and he'd gone and lost it! Stupid. Should he go back and look for it? He knew the answer. It wouldn't be there. Some lucky fox would be tucking into what should have been two days' meals for his family. He knew that no matter how quickly he got back down to where he dropped it he would find nothing. Never mind, he mused; at least I can go and get the bag the fish was in. Nothing will have eaten that. I'll get it in the morning on the way to doing some more fishing.

Just then an owl swooped out from the line of trees to his left. Massan caught a glimpse of it as it glided across the clearing. It was a wood owl, a big bird, handsomely marked with dark and light streaks. He watched transfixed as it checked its flight and headed down into a snowdrift, plummeting straight into it with talons grasping. It stopped momentarily as it hit the snow and then it was off again, flapping its wings to give it momentum to climb back into the air. It arced round and disappeared whence it came. The leveret had not seen it, had not heard it and certainly had no idea that the owl was there until its talons pierced its back, lifting it into the night and off towards the trees.

As he gathered his bearings and made sure he was heading off in the direction of home he thought again of the King and what a strange night it had been.

*   *   *

Ewan was only seventeen years old but had served MacDuff as scullion for almost five years. His family had always served the Earls of Fife for as long as he could remember. There was a certain pride in being associated with the Earl of Fife as that particular title was held in high regard and was traditionally one of the most important positions in the whole of Scotland. It was their purpose, and only theirs, to place the Crown on the head of any new monarch. The holder of the title 'Earl of Fife' had always crowned the Kings of Scots throughout the ages. It was the way of things. Ewan knew not why. He cared less, although he had always felt a sense of importance being in the service of Duncan MacDuff. It didn't stop him from looking after himself however. Well, a little bit of beef here, a bit of bread there, some ale, who would notice? The earl was rich enough and after all, he only did it now and again. Tonight was one of those 'now and again' nights.

He could not be called a simpleton but certainly he was no genius either. This was borne out by the fact that he always managed to blank from his mind that the result of such thievery would see his head separated from his shoulders or his body hanging limp from the nearest tree or castle rafter.

Ewan sat up in bed peering through the darkness and listening to hear if any other servants were awake. They usually weren't. The others were mostly a fair bit older than him and everyone in the household worked hard which meant that they almost always slept soundly. Old Adam who was bedded nearest to Ewan a few feet away always slept not unlike the dead. Ewan smiled as he thought of how Adam usually burped, grunted or omitted a loud fart when going through disturbed sleep or about to wake up. Adam had worked here for years and only had grey hair and a limp to show for it. His age of about seventy accounted for the grey hair. The fact that he was useless and managed to drop a flagstone on his foot when helping repair the courtyard, thus crushing three of his toes, accounted for the limp.

"Pathetic, old fool," Ewan whispered to himself as he knelt up from his pallot, legs creaking out the stiffness. He quickly stood up onto the cold stone floor. The fire in the corner glowed slightly and he could now see that everyone was sound asleep. He peered over to see where Rory's bed was – he was an odd lad, sometimes staying awake into the middle of the night. Tonight however, like the others, he was sound asleep. He smiled to himself and threw his woollen topcoat on over his nightshirt, fastening it with a leather belt. Picking up his ankle boots he headed out of the servants' quarters into a long corridor that led to the kitchen. He stopped in the dark to let his eyes adjust and then put his boots on. All was quiet. He knew his way around as he had done this a few times. Tonight, he thought, I'll have some of that porridge that had been made earlier. Oh! He remembered the ale that had been dragged out for the earl's guest. I'll have a wee bit o' that too.

The door to the kitchen creaked a little as he lifted the latch and eased it open. He scanned the kitchen and noticed a couple of flagons sitting on the table in the centre of the room. It was a large room befitting one that had a minimum of six workers in it each day, toiling to feed the staff of this moderately-sized castle. Unusual then, given the empty floor space between Ewan and the table, that he should not notice the wet floor. Wet with footprints leading from the outside door back to the stairs which led back up to the great hall.

Ewan crossed the kitchen to the table, and lifting up the flagon to his lips, closed his eyes in anticipation of the nectar hitting the back of his throat. He slurped, gulping two or three mouthfuls down, eyes closed. He let the container drop back to the table with a gentle slosh and he opened his eyes just in time to see the hand come from behind him and clasp firmly round his mouth. Cold steel at the back of his neck quickly made him realise that he was caught and he should not resist. It was strange because the feeling of the dirk's tip on his skin made him relax rather than how he imagined he would feel when he got caught, which would be scared. He always knew he'd be caught; he almost welcomed it in some sort of perverse way. Now he was caught he was no longer fearful.

He was spun round in one quick, almost violent movement and found he was staring into a black, burn mark, the size of a man's fist.

"Laddie, yer first mistake wiz stealin' frae MacDuff. Yer second and last wiz to be in the wrang place at the wrang time."

"Sir, I wiz jist a wee bit thirsty. I didnae think it'd do ony harm…" stumbled Ewan now looking like he'd seen a ghost. He was now scared.

Dubhshuileach spun his captive back round whilst grabbing him by his hair and pushing him towards the stairs.

"Aye yir caught fair 'n' square, laddie and fine ye ken it. We'll see wit yer master reckons to yon thievery." His voice was firm but not much more than a whisper.

"Ye cannae dub me in, sir… ma job, ma life, ma…"

"Wheesht! I'll hear no more o' yer wingein'. Come." He tightened his grip on Ewan's hair, causing him to wince and forcing him onward started up the steps to the great hall. Once there, Dubhshuileach marched Ewan straight over to the smoke-filled room to the dais where he had left MacDuff earlier. He was still slumped in the same position; the vomit down his arm had now dried, although the puddle at the side of his seat was still wet and fetid.

Ewan let out a little squeal as the big highlander twisted his hair and forced him to stoop over his master.

"Shoosh laddie," he snarled into his ear. The man's breath made the scullion shiver, but Ewan knew that silence was his best policy. He also knew that this brute could hurt him a lot more if he was not to hold his tongue. He knew that when he thought of the dirk still digging into the back of his neck. "A shillin' fir ye," whispered Dubhshuileach as he let go of the scullion's hair. "Stay ye still mind!"

"What…?"

Dubhshuileach held out the coin in front of the scullion's face and as the servant grabbed it through the thick smoke drew his knife with one swift movement from just below the lad's ear round his throat to the other side. The blood burst out from Ewan's neck, splashing the coin and soaking the earl who was still slumped unconscious.

The splat as the red waterfall hit the flagstone floor should have been enough to wake MacDuff but as it was he was oblivious to the world outside of his drunken dream.

There was no scream from the scullion. It was over too quickly for him to scream. Besides, his captor had let go of the coin as Ewan had clasped it and pulled the back of his head back as he simultaneously slit his throat. Instant death. No screaming. No twitching or flailing. No sound. No life.

Dubhshuileach, still holding the scullion over MacDuff, stepped back a little as he didn't want to get blood over his boots. They were open-toed after all and he had only got them a few weeks back.

The pool of red around the two limp, lifeless figures mingled with the vomit on the floor creating patches of murky brown. Dubhshuileach eased the scullion's body to the floor taking care not to pull the head off; it was barely hanging on such was the force and skill of his assault. He then turned, stepped off the dais and sat down near the fire, pulling his hood up over his head.

"*Air do shlàinte!*"

He raised his goblet in toast to the corpse and set about finishing off the remainder of his beer.

*   *   *

"We travel on the morrow to St. Andrews," announced Callum, startling the others by shattering the silence so suddenly. The King had left some time ago and it was now late and with a few more ales in them the Redfriars had sat down to discuss their rotas for the next week. It had seemingly been settled with duties being a mixture of prayer, horticulture, political science and of course brewing.

"With God's blessing of course and an easing of snow." Callum sat at the top of the table now and was silhouetted against the backdrop of some ten large candles near the shuttered window. He inclined his head towards the large crucifix in the corner of the room and seemed to be addressing it directly. "I needs must meet with our lord Bishop of St. Andrews as instructed today in Edinburgh."

After a short pause Malcolm of Scotlandwell, one of the lay brethren, stood up. "My good Prior, I shall be honoured if you should allow me to accompany you."

"That you can, Malcolm. Good company shall make light of the distance." Standing, he moved over towards the crucifix, hands behind his back and head bowed as if deep in thought. "Seemingly Bishop Fraser has chosen we Trinitarians for a mission of sorts." He paused as he got to the corner of the room, and turning, continued to his audience. "Of importance to him I presume. A ransom to pay perhaps? Why else the Redfriars?" Turning back to the cross he continued as if to himself and alone. "No matter. We can theorise on our walk."

At that, he snapped out of his near trance and announced to the room. "Sleep now, my friends. We rise early for St. Andrews Cathedral."

CHAPTER FIVE

Kynkorn, Fife, 19th March, 1286

The songbird in the wicker cage in the corner of the bedchamber had been singing merrily away for some time when Yolande finally opened her eyes. The room was bathed in the early morning sunshine which accentuated all the beautiful colours in the room; the mural of bluebells that she had had arranged across the south facing wall, the red and gold shutters which had already been opened by one of her attendants, the floor tiled as it was with Celtic swirls in green and yellow. She had an eye for colour and design and as she sat up the entire room soaked up the sunshine, mixing it up into a rainbow of beauty. It smelt fresh with a slight saltiness to the air that she so loved. The birds outside sang back as if in response to her songbird.

Then she remembered. She remembered the King's guards coming back alone, their faces wracked with panic when they realised that he had not returned. She remembered screaming, crying and shouting. There had been a lot of shouting and even more tears. She had cried herself to sleep.

She now sat bolt upright in her bed thinking of the search party that would be out there combing the area for her Alexander.

"Isabella!"

Her attendant burst through the door. She had obviously been standing waiting for her Queen to awaken. She was followed by another two maids who immediately busied themselves, one picking up a bible, flicking to a marker and reciting from it, the other laying out a long, flowing dress on the bed and picking out jewellery from a silver chalice on the chamber chest. Isabella started to comb her Queen's hair.

"My Queen, do not fret. You have my sorrow with you but the King shall be found. He is a strong man and shall be hidden from harm. The day is bright. It is a happy day I feel."

"Ouch!"

The comb had snarled in a knot and tugged Yolande's head sharply.

"*Mon Dieu!* I am clumsy! Forgive me!" Isabella stumbled. Clearly she had been affected by the night's events, her mind wandering.

"I know he has gone, Isabella, I can feel it in my heart. It is broken and I…"

"My lady! Do not think such. He shall arrive soon…"

"'Tis kind of you, my sweet. You think of me, my broken heart. Alas it is not to be mended I fear. And I with child…" she started to sob again and her three attendants stopped what they were doing and sat on the bed consoling her.

After what seemed an age there came a knock on the door, making the Queen break from her maids and jump up onto the cold tiles. She slipped a cloak on.

"Enter."

The messenger opened the door gingerly and stepped into the Queen's chamber. He was a thin, weasel-featured lad in his early teens at a guess. He sported a couple of large pimples, one of which was on the end of his nose shining bright red. It was the only colour in him. He was ashen-faced.

"Er… my Queen. I…er… have news," he stumbled.

"Out with it, lad!" She was firm now.

"My Lord King is dead."

"Leave us."

She turned, moving slowly to the window. Gazing out over the brightly lit, snow covered landscape she could see May Island clearly in the distance. The sea was calm.

And such a lovely day, she thought as her eyes began to well up again.

*   *   *

Massan had woken with the birds and was already on his way to the beach remembering to look for his bag on the way. He trudged over to the clearing where he had seen the owl and tried to figure out from which way he had travelled the night before. He took a path to the left of an old oak tree figuring that he had been in front of that tree when he had seen the bird fly out from the left

Shortly he came to the spot where he thought he might have dropped his catch. The snow was beginning to melt but he could still see different tracks left in it from the various animals since the bad weather had ceased; foxes, badger, boar, birds and most unusually there appeared to have been more than a few horses heading in both directions.

Strange, he thought, looking up and down the track. It was a beautifully clear day and he could see some way down the track. He saw no one but did spot his bag halfway up a little embankment near what must have been a foxhole. He went over and picked it up feeling rather pleased with himself. At that he headed off down the track to the point where a path led off down the steep hill towards the beach.

Coming out of the trees and bushes onto the sand he noticed a large crowd feverishly working away along the beach.

"Good fellows! Can I be of help?"

None of the group registered, carrying on with what they were doing.

"What gives? Can I be of assistance? I know the land hereabouts…"

"Laddie!" one of the guards shouted back suddenly looking up from bended knee. He looked to be the man in charge. "Come thither. You needs must be of aid on this black day if not only to firm us of your whereabouts lately."

Black day? thought Massan. Whatever is the fellow gibbering? As beautiful a day as has long been seen, even with snow covering most.

"Well…?" challenged the guard as Massan finally approached the group which he could now see were fussing over two cloth-covered lumps in the sand. Clearly these lumps had been dragged some distance as the tracks led back to the rocks at the bottom of the cliff.

"I have come this morn from the Binn Village." Massan pointed up towards the top of the old extinct volcano that dominated the scene. "And you? You appear to be the most unusual site on this beach. Fishing is reason for me, not for you I wager…"

"Fishing for trouble with such a tone, young gelding! Your King lies dead and the only soul for miles around his broken bones is a lad with an attitude and a fishing line for an alibi…"

"The King dead…but…no…it cannot be. I saw him alive and well and headed for Kynkorn. In the night… What happened?"

Two of the guards now grabbed Massan by the arm to prevent him from leaving the scene such was the suspicion aroused in them now. They held him firm causing him to wince.

"Easy lads," said the head guard. "We needs must find out the truth from this wee poltice. Come young fella…" he said, tugging Massan away to one side. "You say you saw the King last night. Where? When? Did you speak together?"

"Sir, indeed I saw our King. He seemed cold but otherwise fine. He was on the low road and alone so I pointed him in the direction of Kynkorn. It was late and we near collided. His steed was nervous of the conditions, but otherwise all seemed fine."

"Together you spoke?

"We did, sir. I offered to be his guide, but he refused."

"And this was where?"

"I gave him a tooth," Massan replied absentmindedly.

"And your meeting with the King was where, laddie?" repeated the guard.

"Oh…er…it was yonder." Massan pointed a few hundred yards down the beach in the opposite direction from Kynkorn. "What happened?"

"I fear a terrible accident, such that horse and rider have died. You say his steed was of a nervous disposition?"

"Aye sir. It seemed that way. I held the reins such was its excitement. What happened?"

"You needs must come to Kynkorn to recount your story to our Earl of Fife. We shall summons him when we return with the King's body. Come…"

At that, the sombre group of guards, along with Massan who was no longer being manhandled, made off east along the sand towards Kynkorn.

"I gave him a boar's tooth," said Massan.

No one was listening.

*   *   *

"Alarm! Alarm! Murder!"

The young Earl of Fife had woken up to the stench of his own vomit despite a fresh wind blowing through the hall which still failed to waft away the earl's own contribution to the scene. Dubhshuileach had opened the window some time ago and still stood by it looking out to sea. Being sick was not particularly unusual for Duncan MacDuff but the spectacle that he awoke to this morning was one that he had not expected. At his feet lay the body of his scullion, Ewan, pale and motionless, head lolling to one side being held on only by tissue and sinew. A large black pool of blood covered the earl's feet spilling off the dais and onto the flagstone floor.

"Murder!" he continued not noticing the figure by the window.

"My lord, all is well."

"Dubhshuileach…"

"My lord, all is well. There is nothing to fear…" It was said nonchalantly as if discussing the weather.

"Of a Mercy what is this?" The hysteria in the earl's voice was less now but nonetheless still wavering and shaking. "You say nothing to fear! I have butchery at my feet and you say nothing to fear."

Suddenly the door burst open and three guards and two kitchen hands burst in.

"My lord! Treachery! Young Ewan…" It was Old Adam hobbling through the doorway. The first guard was now standing over the corpse agog as the other two scoured the Hall.

"Leave us." It was Dubhshuileach who spoke. "This floor needs a clean for sure and our assassin and thief needs be removed, but later. I needs must discuss this treacherous villain's demise with Fife." His voice was assertive. Commanding.

"My lord?" The guards looked to the earl for confirmation, which was given by a slight inclination of the head.

The earl and killer were then left alone.

"Have you done harm to this lad?" The question slapped MacDuff out of his trance. Its bluntness caught him off guard.

"Huh?"

"Have you done harm to this lad?"

"Have I done harm to this lad? My good friend Dubhshuileach you ask of me something I understand less than the carnage around me. I see a body almost without head. Blood, sick, piss and filth floods my dais and you ask if there has been harm done? I know not…"

"My lord, I ask only if in past you have maltreated this lad. Would it that he mislikes you?" continued Dubhshuileach calmly.

"Mislikes me? Riddles…you talk in riddles, Sirrah!" MacDuff was still struggling to comprehend the awful scene that he had awoken to. There was now a slight anger in his voice, no doubt borne of frustration; frustration at the scene around him; frustration at this questioning.

"Sire, I surmise as to why one of your staff should want you dead. Why one of your staff should want to rob you."

The earl's face froze as he started to realise all the implications and as his guest continued he fixed his stare on the lump at his feet.

"I find I cannot sleep with howling wind, with belly awash with fine ale. I find myself pacing your great hall eyes streaming with smoke. I sit near this window." He sat down by the window demonstrating and continued. "The smoke does not let up so I go downstairs and outside to breathe fresh and cold night air." The description was acted out like a Palace entertainer such was his animation now. "Sire, a noise behind me makes me come back inside and back up to your hall. I arrive in time to see yon thief and near killer of Fife preparing to send you to the angels. He is over you and I have no time. You die, My lord. Or he dies…"

"He prepares to do murder…?"

"Evil murder. He kills you while you sleep." He was now at a near whisper and almost into the earl's ear so close he was now. "I slayed him I admit. I have no regret Sire, else we never could have this converse today."

The colour was coming back into MacDuff's cheeks now. In fact as the full implication of his guest's supposed actions dawned on him he went into a full blush, cheeks burning.

"How can I repay such action?" he said rhetorically.

"My lord I am at your service always and as such no debt has been given, no debt earned. I wager you needs must choose staff a trifle careful in future! Ha!"

"Rob me…?"

Banging on the door cut the earl off mid-sentence. Banging again, urgently this time.

"Enter!"

A small man stepped into the Hall and marched quickly over to the dais ignoring the corpse on the floor.

"My lord. Urgent news." He looked over to Dubhshuileach. "For your ears only, Sire."

"I go to arrange a clean up for in here."

As the door closed behind Dubhshuileach the messenger bent down onto one knee.

"My lord, our King is dead. You are needed in Kynkorn. At once."

*   *   *

31

St. Andrews, Fife, 19th March, 1286

It was a crisp morning as Christina arrived on the southern outskirts of St. Andrews. The town's spires pierced the skyline, which was dominated by the bell tower of the cathedral and the tower of St. Rule's Church which was already over a century old and at over a hundred feet high, served as a beacon for pilgrims heading for the shrine of St. Andrew. She crossed herself as she passed the leper hospital of St. Nicholas and cast her mind back to her husband and his suffering. Her back groaned under the strain of the sack stuffed full of coarse worsted which she intended to sell or trade at the market. She shared this task in turn with her neighbours and although she never particularly enjoyed the trek to St. Andrews, she always found herself the happier for being amongst the hustle and bustle of that busy wee town.

"Mornin'," the Redfriars said cheerfully in unison as they stepped out of an inn. "Can we help carry your bag? It looks heavy laden."

"Morning to you, good friars. I have not far to go now and my back is in tune with my load which I foresee to being both lighter and the easier for carrying on my return," replied Christina. People here are so friendly, she thought. Interesting too.

"In that case we will walk with you if allowed," said Callum. "Go you to Skinnergate for leather?"

"Well...aye, but later. First, the market to sell my cloth and then I get food for my village. Bread, kail, wild fruits and the like." She paused. It had been the first time since her husband's death that she had spoken with any man of the Cloth. She felt more comfortable than she had imagined. "Let me think. Two Redfriars in St. Andrews can only be here for two reasons; pilgrimage or to sell your ale and I see no ale so it must be pilgrimage..."

"We come to attend summons at the Cathedral."

"I meant not to pry, good sir. My mind and mouth know not when to open and talk." She was a little embarrassed but need not have been, as neither Callum nor Malcolm of Scotlandwell had taken offence. On the contrary, they enjoyed the conversation for a change as most travellers tended to give them a deferential wide berth. This woman, though, was different. She seemed at ease with them but also, conversely, somehow troubled by them.

"We see Bishop Fraser at his request so we know not why at present," said Callum. "We walk from Cramunde to here and then we walk to where we are bidden. Come you far good wool trader?"

"The Binn Village is my village now, not a distance from Kynkorn nor from Abirdaur."

"I know of it. Small, welcoming but far enough I wager with such a load," replied Malcolm squinting at her. "Your face is kenspeckle...have we met previously?"

"No, I think not..." She blushed, averting his prying eyes.

"And here we leave you. We go this way..." said Callum pointing down a narrow little street piled high with rubbish. "Good bartering today, lady..."

"Christina," she replied. "My name is Christina." She blurted it out before she realised and immediately wondered why she had done so. Was it a plea for help?

"Christina?" Malcolm mumbled under his breath as he tried to place where he knew her from.

Callum linked his arm into Malcolm's, smiling pleasantly to her saying, "Good bye then, Christina. And perhaps we stop at your village next time," and at that the two friars turned into the little street and were gone.

"Please do," she called after them unaware as to whether her offer was heard.

St. Andrews Cathedral was the most imposing, majestic and beautiful structure in the whole of Scotland and as they shuffled down the rubbish strewn, gravel road they could see it growing in front of them looming out of the darkness and reaching up to the heavens. Soon they were waiting in the cloisters to see Bishop Fraser watched by one of the many churchmen buzzing around the scene.

"Gentles! My thanks to you for coming at my request although a turn of events may change our reasons for being here. I shall tell all soon but think that two friars are in need of rest and perhaps wine or ale?"

Bishop Fraser was a kindly-looking elderly man dressed in flowing grey robes tied together with a leather belt from which hung a scabbard. It held his sword.

"Sweet music to us wearies. Ale it is then."

"Ale it is," reaffirmed the Bishop. "Pray follow."

He led them into a small room at the end of the cloisters and sat them down at a table in the centre of the room. Three silver chalices were brought out and filled with beer and soon the three were chatting away idly.

"I am for Stirling today on a matter of extreme urgency," said the Primate after some time and quite out of the blue. "My news is dire. Scotland's King is dead. Found, crushed this very morning at Pettycur Bay, his horse with him, dead." The stunned silence could almost be touched. The room felt cold suddenly as the Bishop uttered those words and as a cloud blocked out the sun for seconds although seeming much longer it took on a gaol-like feel to it. The Redfriars sat awaiting the Bishop's next word. "My plan for you since has changed and it is now one of national importance. You must visit Buildwas Abbey in Salop in England to escort a Bernard de St. Clair back to Scotland. He is a merchant and sea master of Berwick, important to our trade links with Bruges. His ransom has been paid and the Cistercians at Buildwas need recompensing for their hospitality. A menial task it may appear but one that needs must be done for our merchant has ships to reach Norway. His service will now be called on to fetch our Maid, indeed our new Queen, back to the throne. Other ships we have of a surety but St. Clair has a skilled way with the waters and can be trusted to negotiate rough waters better than most."

The two Redfriars sat hanging on every word. Never would they have predicted the outcome of today's meeting. Things have changed, yes, thought Callum, but the size of the change shift is great. The importance of the task was goliath.

33

"You will no doubt miss the funeral. Swift messengers have been sent to inform appropriate Lords not least His Grace Edward, King of England. He resides presently in Gascony and it is essential he hear of the tragic death of his beloved brother-in-law. As I say, the funeral will be at Dunfermline Abbey in two weeks – this you will miss."

"We accept," was all that Callum said.

"Good. You shall be given the monies for the task." He lifted his chalice into the air and ended with, "Your good health!"

CHAPTER SIX

Kynkorn, Fife, 19th March, 1286

The Earl of Fife had been no slouch in making his way to Kynkorn and still the Earl of Buchan had beaten him there. John Comyn, Earl of Buchan had taken control of the situation and was comforting Yolande when MacDuff arrived. The Countess of Buchan, Comyn's wife, was MacDuff's sister and although there was a mutual respect between the two men there was still an air of uneasiness between the two as if there wasn't complete trust, despite the family connection. The two great earls, however, strolled outside to discuss what best to do.

"We must act fast," said Buchan as the two walked over the bright, white sand of Kynkorn beach that the grand house looked over. "Messengers have been sent to tell the news. Bishop Fraser has been told and makes arrangements for a funeral. It is a grim time, our country is without King and we must act swiftly; we move his wife to safety."

Fife noted that Buchan had said 'his wife' and not 'our Queen' when referring to the King's widow; terminology that was, at the least, out of kilter. Strange. Young he may be but MacDuff was acutely aware of the fact that the Comyns may have an interest in who was to be advising a minor who sat on the Scots' throne. Unsettling times, thought Fife. Everyone in the land has an interest in who is to sit on the throne. A few would covet a role as councillor. Careers could be made. Stakes could be claimed. Some may not see a trying time for Scotland but more an opportunity for themselves. MacDuff thought it best to guard his own thoughts and aspirations. Best keep opinions to thine own. Loosed tongues, noosed necks!

"For Scotland's sake we must protect her...at Stirling," Buchan continued.

"Aye, no doubt..."

"Our young captive may explain things for us but the Queen to Stirling must be first. My Lord Earl, the lad is surely one of your vassals so it befits you to speak with him."

"Aye, no doubt…" Fife rubbed his face in the sunshine, gulping in the fresh air in an attempt to clear his system of the fug of alcohol. It seemed to have the desired effect as he burst into life. "Aye you have it. I shall speak with the lad. Thinks you our Queen is well enough to be moved? Her pregnancy…"

"Scotland!" Buchan surprised himself with the abruptness of the interruption. He slowed and put an arm round his companion who was by far the younger of the two. "Scotland must come first; we protect our Queen and Scotland…at Stirling Castle…at once."

"And what of the Maid of Norway? What thought of succession, of an heir?" Fife seemed to be talking to himself, slightly confused.

"For later, my good Earl of Fife…for later. I go now, to Stirling, with God's speed for Scotland and for Queen. Agreed?"

"Agreed."

At that, Buchan left MacDuff standing at the water's edge and headed off back to the Queen's abode. After a few minutes MacDuff followed.

"So…pray tell, young Massan, what see you of our King?" MacDuff leaned in close enough to the boy's face so as to breathe his sickly breath onto him. Massan tried to show no emotion, not least from the foul smell. The room was possibly about fifteen feet square; the walls were in complete blackness so the room's size was difficult to estimate. A small shaft of light pierced the darkness from a high window onto the table at which Massan sat. He had never been in a dungeon or cell before but felt that he was in one now. A rat squeaked as if to remind him where he was and how much trouble he was in. MacDuff's breath had to compete with the smell of the damp room. Wet dogs. That's what it reminded him of.

Massan looked up forlornly and began.

"I travelled on the low road…" Massan recounted his tale again, this time in minute detail to a silent audience made up of MacDuff and what could only be described as four henchmen. Big brutes, Massan had thought on first sight. However, their presence had gradually faded as he recounted his story, standing, as they were in near shadow, completely silent. It was some time before he finished. MacDuff had asked a couple of probing questions but seemed satisfied that the boy was speaking truthfully.

No boar's tooth pendant had been found, MacDuff said, asking one of the henchmen to leave them and head a search party to look for one. Finding it would validate the story although he seemed satisfied already. The animal that had felled the boy was dismissed as bearing no relevance to the evenings events; a disturbed boar perhaps. Events, MacDuff decided, that were a complete accident. He must be sure however, as the King had died in his Earldom and any investigation must prove conclusive. The lad must be held, he thought, until we are sure of the facts. Someone had to be held accountable and this lad was all he had for now.

Massan stared blankly at the figures in the dark recesses of the room and thought of the implications of another search party; for a boar's tooth suspended from a thin piece of deerskin! They may as well be looking for a grain of salt from the Dysart saltpans dropped randomly onto Pettycur beach, a beach that was probably the best part of two miles long. Woe is me…this one could take some time, he thought. His pendant, indeed the proof of his honesty, would be much harder to find than a dead King and horse. He crossed himself at the thought of the dead and felt the hairs on the back of his neck stand at the further realisation that he could be here for some considerable time. He thought of his mother, worrying: his sister missing his tales at bedtime.

He continued staring blankly into the darkness as one of the henchmen took him by an arm to lead him away. A figure in the corner to his right moved slightly. He had not noticed this man before but he moved ever so slightly into light and back quickly as he shuffled his position. Perhaps the light was playing tricks but he could have sworn the man had a large black mark over his left eye.

What no one saw, however, was the man carefully tucking his necklace out of sight. It consisted of thin deerskin, from which swung a boar's tooth carved with a swirling Celtic symbol.

*   *   *

Near the town of Stirling, 19th March, 1286

John Comyn, Earl of Buchan led the party as it wound its way through the countryside headed for Stirling Castle, the seemingly impenetrable stronghold that linked Scotland's Highlands with its Lowlands. The vulnerable, mourning Yolande would be safe there and he had taken it upon himself as High Constable of Scotland to act swiftly and to personally escort the Queen and her attendants.

They were now only a few miles from Stirling Castle but Buchan had noticed that Yolande was flagging and called the group to rest. They halted on the bank of the fledgling River Forth, choosing a spot in a bend that was overlooked by a brae covered in gorse. Men dismounted. Horses were fed and watered. The sun was high in the sky now and was warm enough to have melted all the snow here. Buchan had led Yolande down the bank onto the shingle at the edge of the river where she sat, feet immersed in the cold water. Her eyes were red with emotion.

"My lady…" Buchan sat down beside her. "I know not what to say to mend your heart…" He was genuine despite his large build and fearsome reputation. "You are with child and God willing, carrying our new King. The Lord may taketh away but the Lord can giveth also."

"Aye, perhaps for good reason." She made no attempt to look up, simply content to watch the water sloshing over her feet.

"For good reason, aye, perhaps. Death may come for reasons we know nothing of and only God Himself shall know. I, for one, know one thing that is true, my lady, and that is the life you carry inside you is of great reason: to rule, to judge, to protect, to do for Scotland what she needs. We must…"

"I understand your point good, Buchan. I really do. I know the importance of what is inside of me: my son or daughter. Life will go on. For me, I know not what my head thinks. It cannot be heard for my breaking, sobbing heart. My good Buchan I confess I dare not think of life without my Alexander..." She wept.

"Aye, my lady." Standing, Buchan shouted over to the dozen or so men-at-arms who were stationed by the horses some fifty yards away. "Saddles! We move now. To Stirling."

There was a flurry of activity as the men sorted themselves out and within minutes they were atop their steeds awaiting the Earl of Buchan as he helped Yolande back to her carriage with Isabella and saw to it that the rest of her attendees were helped into the other, smaller carriages.

At the crack of the whip the carriages groaned and creaked into movement and the men-at-arms formed into their ranks at front and back. They started to wind their way alongside the river and soon found themselves intermittently in and out of glorious birch woods. The sun flashed in and out of view rapidly as the trees lined the avenue that the party trotted down. Buchan rode alongside the Queen's carriage, chatting pleasantries with her and making rather a bad job of 'trying to take her mind off things'. Isabella slept as she always did on these types of journeys.

Shortly, the front carriage hit a pothole that made it career from wheel to wheel, causing one of the passengers to squeal. It was Yolande. The wheels settled down with Buchan now holding onto the side curtain looking concerned. Remarkably Isabella was not jolted awake, grunting slightly but still in a fitful sleep.

"Have you comfort, my lady?" he panted as he steadied his horse with one hand. The sun glinted through the trees striking his weather beaten face making him look for all the world like some Roman gladiator or Greek god. He rode alongside, gripping the curtain with a muscular arm and opening it slightly. Inside, the Queen caught fleeting glimpses of him as the carriage rolled past the trees throwing his profile in and out of the sun, flashing them in and out of darkness: Buchan, shadow, Buchan, shadow, Alexander, shadow...

Alexander! Shocked, she checked herself in an instant. The light was playing tricks, surely. She looked again. The sun flashed in and out of the trees. Buchan, shadow, Buchan, shadow, Alexander, shadow...

She grabbed Isabella by the arm causing her to awake with a startle and sit bolt upright blinking.

"My lady...?" said Isabella.

"My lady...?" Buchan sounded more concerned now.

"Aye, fine, I am fine, Sire..." she stuttered throwing a quizzical look to Isabella as if to say: *What is happening?*

It was Alexander! She saw Alexander. She looked again, out of the curtain and into the flashing sunlight.

Buchan sat atop his trotting steed keeping up with the carriage. The trees thinned, the flashing subsided. It was Buchan; swarthy, yes; muscular, yes. It was Buchan for sure.

"Not long now," he said as they turned another corner bringing them out of yet another birch coppice and into view of the mighty Stirling Castle, speed increasing as the horsemen sensed an end to the journey and the possibility of some fine ales and some finer women in the town. The men-at-arms struggled to keep up with the pace.

The path became rocky now on the approach to the bridge and the carriage began to rattle and thunder as it charged along. Buchan kept pace with the carriage but was not privy to the conversation that Yolande was having with Isabella.

"It was Alexander! Moments ago. I saw him…" She looked as if she had seen a ghost, her colour having turned to a pale grey.

"Come now… 'tis Buchan only. You are still in shock…" Isabella moved closer to her sliding a comforting arm round her. "Your eyes, your heart, they play tricks on you, my Queen. Sadness of heart is forcing you to see him where he is not."

"Aye, perhaps you have the right of it," was all she said as she leaned in closer to Isabella's bosom.

Outside, the Earl of Buchan's trumpeter was signalling their arrival to the Castle. The rider's thoughts changed from the task in hand, completed as it nearly was, to those of beer and women. John Comyn, Earl of Buchan and High Constable of Scotland thought too of the night's promises, now oblivious to the two passengers in the carriage he rode alongside.

*   *   *

Dubhshuileach left Kynkorn soon after Buchan and travelled back towards Abirdaur along the low road. He had made a point of stopping every now and then and 'helping' the searchers look for any evidence of foul play. He knew no boar's tooth would be found.

He had left MacDuff at Kynkorn to continue his questioning of the lad, knowing that the boy had told his all the first time round. Buchan had left for Stirling a few hours earlier and Dubhshuileach had made pretence of heading back to Inverkeithing 'retracing the King's route'.

He passed the place where the King's body had been found and headed further inland rounding the busy little hamlet of Kirkton with its market now in full swing, up skirting the half dozen houses at Grange and veering off uphill towards the Binn village.

Presently he was trotting into the main thoroughfare of the little community. He slowed down to peer into the first two timber houses, moving on when it was apparent that no one was around. At the next house he dismounted and rapped on the closed door. Nothing. He walked round to the side of the little building and scanned over the rectangular plot of land at the back. No one. He could see into the next-door neighbour's back plot from here and again it was empty. It seemed the village was a ghost town. At the centre of the village he reached the pottery, another timber and turf construction but twice as big as all the regimented little houses. Lines of pots, drinking vessels and plates both wooden and ceramic, lay outside in neat little rows, leaning up against the wall to the side of the front door. Smoke trickled out of a hole in the roof. Someone home, thought Dubhshuileach.

He approached the door. It was slightly ajar. Stopping, he cocked his head to one side, listening. He could hear a couple of voices. An adult and a child, he realised. A strong smell of wet clay, pungent yet appealing, wafted from inside. It was a smell well-known around Fife where pottery was becoming a bit of a speciality. Why, he had come across Wemyss pottery in the Low Countries once, he remembered. Stepping back, he decided to investigate the rest of the village first. Once again, leading his horse, he slowly moved off to wander along the main street, knocking on doors and checking out the back plots. No sign of life.

As he approached the last house on the left he heard some scuffling from behind the house. Or was it from inside the house? He crept round the side of the house, stepping over the boundary ditch, which he managed in one large stride.

On turning the corner a chicken suddenly flew up awkwardly at him. He aimed a swift kick at it, missing but regaining his balance and composure quickly, eyes scanning the scene, ever alert like a predator stalking prey. The squawking chicken and its mates scuttled off towards the back of the rectangular plot where sat some geese, seemingly oblivious to the disturbance.

The back door was open. He edged up to it, his hand near the hilt of his dirk, again, listening. Leaning forward he reached out and grasped the latch. It felt warm with the winter's sun, which was now working its way round the back of the houses. He stopped for a second, again listening and in one swift movement opened the door and stepped into the darkness of the little mud house. It took a few seconds for his eyes to adjust. No one. Something scurried along the bottom of the wall to his left, then silence. He scanned the room. It appeared that the house was split into two distinct open-plan rooms by a sill beam of oak that lay across a bed of stone. The room he stood in was the sleeping quarters with three beds each made from a base of rushes, hay and heather and covered with sheepskin; one was noticeably smaller than the others. Dubhshuileach had to peer to make the beds out, as the walls here seemed to be double-lined for extra insulation, thus making it darker here than the far end of the property.

He moved forward into the second part of the house, stepping over the floor beam and careful not to stand on a collection of ceramic plates and pots. Was this the right house? He knelt and put his hand into the ashes of the fire, still warm. An hour or so too late he thought, if it is indeed the correct house, and standing, he turned and went back whence he had come.

Outside it was still quiet other than the odd noise from various animals around the village. He looked back over to the pottery and decided to check it out. His bare legs felt a couple of spots of rain and he noticed the wisp of smoke atop the pottery starting to drift as the wind picked up.

He approached the door silently and this time knocked sharply and walked straight in. The two occupants, an old man and a child, seemed startled.

"I beg your pardon, I meant not to startle," he said in a soft lilting tone. "I look to find a villager…"

"Lord above!" the potter said handing the girl a white, gritty-looking jug. "I near jumped out of myself and through yon smoke hole! Shit masel', son. Shit masel' so I did. Dunno the worse o' it the rapping or the bargin'. Near shit masel' so I did!"

"I am sorry. What may a man say? I meant not to startle. I seek only to ask of a lad's mother. I fear he is in danger and needs must find his mother…for…for to tell her," he stumbled.

The old man held on to the jug which was still in the girl's lap. She had her back to Dubhshuileach but did not make a sound and kept her gaze fixed on the old potter.

"The village folk have all gone to markets; Kirkton and St. Andrews mainly. Some shall not return till the morrow," he studied the stranger trying not to stare too much at the black tattoo across the left side of the man's face. "You come far, stranger. From up North no doubt wi' yer warrior's gear…"

Suddenly conscious that he was indeed instantly recognisable, Dubhshuileach seemed to change tack.

"Aye you have the rights o' it, sir. Origins are the North but no longer biding there serving as I am the Earl of Fife. It's on his business that I am here. Know you the lad Massan Gow?"

"Aye that I do," said the old man taking hold of the young girl's hand tightly, "and what kind o' danger may he be in pray tell."

"Danger enough for your Lord to send me tae find his mother. She lives where?"

"Up at the last house but she'll no be there. Away for a few days wi her daughter. Edinburgh I think. Aye, Edinburgh…"

"Edinburgh you say? And does this woman have a name, pray tell old man?" Dubhshuileach took a couple of steps forward and was now towering over the little girl who dare not turn round. What he could not see was the boar's tooth pendant she was wearing, identical to the one that nestled in the bottom of his sporran.

"Aye that she has. Christina is her name."

"Hmm Christina… Edinburgh? Thank you old man," and at that he took out a coin from his sporran and tossed it at the old man bending down slightly as he did so to ruffle Aibhlinn's hair before disappearing outside.

They waited in silence for a few moments until they were sure they were alone.

"You lied…you lied. My mother is in St. Andrews not Edinburgh…"

"Aye lassie and all the better for it. Yon lump o' muscle is on no errand for MacDuff. He acts alone. MacDuff sends men-at-arms to do his searchin' and usually twa or three o' them." He looked up to the smoke filtering out the roof-hole and thumbed his chin, deep in thought. "Lassie…" he continued after some thinking, "you'll come wi me for the nicht. I'll tak ye doon Kirkton to stay wi ma brother. I fancy you'll be safe there. Yon brute gives me the creeps. Come, we go now."

At that the old man scrambled about his house gathering up various belongings, eventually ushering Aibhlinn out the back of the pottery past a small kiln, some large globular cooking pots and over the boundary ditch and into the woods.

*   *   *

Binn Village, Fife, 19th March, 1286

It was dark by the time Christina arrived back at the Binn Village and she was tired from the long day's journeying and trading even though she had managed to get a ride from some travelling performers for the last twelve miles or so. She had had a good day and had even indulged herself by buying some meat from a butcher's stall. She was not able to afford meat very often but this was one of those rare occasions when she could. Perhaps the fact it was lent had something to do with it – the butcher always seemed to be at a bit of a loss during lent as most people bought fish. He seemed only too willing to accept her hard bargaining this time. Choosing exactly what to buy from him with her hard earned coins had proved not so easy. She had approached the stall with vigour after finally deciding to treat the family to some meat but soon found herself shifting uneasily from foot to foot as she eyed the choice on offer: beef, sheep, horse, goat, boar, deer and a plethora of birds. In the end she decided on deer; Massan sometimes brought starlings and seagulls home and they had their own chickens but deer was definitely a luxury for them. She had smiled to herself when handing over her coins as she thought of Aibhlinn's face when she returned with venison.

There was a fine drizzle in the air when she got back to her village and although she could see that candlelight flickered in most of the houses no one seemed to want to venture outside. The village usually fell silent come nightfall so nothing seemed out of the ordinary, except her house, which was in complete darkness. She lifted the latch with apprehension and stepped inside. No sign of life. Even the fire had gone out. She fumbled for one of the cheap tallow candles she had bought at the market and soon had it lit.

"Aibhlinn?" She spoke gently moving as she did to search the front of the house and then the sleeping area. No one.

"Massan...Aibhlinn?" She popped her head out the back door already knowing that she would see no one.

At that, there was a gentle rap on the front door, faint enough for her to have to check herself and listen. Another knock, this time slightly louder.

She moved quickly to the front door.

"Who is there?"

"'Tis I, Christina; David from the pottery. I have news of your children."

"Aibhlinn! Massan! What news!" She threw open the door to see the old man standing in the flickering light.

"Fear not my dear for they are safe," he said in a gentle, reassuring way, reaching out and holding her hands. She guided him into her home and closed the door. "I mean Aibhlinn is safe...with my brother."

"Safe? You talk of safe? Is there danger, man? Where are my children?"

"Sit," said the old man. "I shall explain."

Christina mopped her now sweating brow and sat down on a stool pulling one over for David to use.

"Speak."

David the old potter sat down and told Christina of the day's earlier happenings. He told of the man with the Highland gear and black mark on his face and how he said he was looking for Christina. He told of the man's inference that Massan was in trouble and how the stranger said he represented their vassal lord the Earl of Fife. He also reassured her that her daughter was safe and he apologised if she thought him over-protective; the stranger was mean he was sure, he could *feel* it.

"By the way yer house wisnae padlocked. I came over earlier and found it unlocked," he chastised her.

"Aye you are not wrong but I have little to lose and I keep my cupboards and chest secure," she flashed him a smile. "And thank you...for your concern...and kindliness. Think you we should go to your brother's now?"

"Methinks she will be safe tonight and no doubts already asleep. I take you on the morrow, mid-morning..." he rubbed his eyes. "For now I am tired and no longer can rise at first light. I shall knock for you on the morrow, agreed?"

"Agreed, but what of Massan? We must find him...if...if he is well..." She tried to banish the awful thoughts that were beginning to seep into her brain dripping into her emotions like some sort of water torture.

"Aye, we shall sort out Massan on the morrow also," said David in a very cheery, matter-of-fact way so as to make Christina feel more at ease. It was a simple task tomorrow – pick up Aibhlinn, sort out Massan, avoid the stranger – no problem.

David smiled at Christina, and standing, went to leave.

"On the morrow then," he said, again quite cheerfully.

"Aye, the morrow."

David stepped outside into the drizzle closing the door behind him. He could not remember the last time he felt so uneasy and scared. He would not sleep tonight.

CHAPTER SEVEN

At around the same time that Christina was settling down for the night after her meeting with David, another meeting was taking place about five miles away at Ravenscraig Castle. The Earl of Fife and Dubhshuileach had retired to the solar room where they could enjoy some relative peace. Certainly, the only attendant was Michael the Mute who was always favoured by MacDuff when he wanted to be waited on but needed to be able to speak freely. He could rely on all his staff (obviously not Ewan the scullion after recent events but he need not worry about him anymore) but felt it an added bonus to be able to be attended on by Michael who had not the benefit of speech.

"Gossip was not something Michael the Mute suffered from," MacDuff had sometimes said as a way of reassurance when talking privately. Michael's loss of speech was MacDuff's gain but ironically it did keep Michael in a job and a relatively well-paid one at that.

The solar room at Ravenscraig was one of MacDuff's favourite places and although he tended to move around his lands he always tried to stay here whenever he could; this castle was one of his wife's favourites also, along with Falkland. The room was on the first-floor and offered MacDuff a certain luxury. At the south end of the room was a half-length window with window seats that commanded spectacular views over the surrounding woods and over the River Forth. Many guests sat here in awe, not only because of the view, but also because of the wonderful stained glass that depicted the Crucifixion. The window's interior shutters were richly decorated with colourful heraldic designs. A large fireplace sat on the west wall, its fire throwing out a glorious heat and causing shadows to dance across the far wall from the central table with its ornaments, jugs, candlesticks and the like.

MacDuff sat at a small window to the left of the fireplace looking down, unseen, at the goings-on in the hall. He watched his wife Isabel playing host in his absence and thought of happier times. He had always loved her and she him, but lately he felt she had lost some respect for him what with his liking for the drink. A hazard of his position he had explained: entertaining, socialising, and being entertained. He certainly had no intention of allowing things on his lands to slip any further. He told her only recently that he applied to the King to be allowed to assart part of his estates. Well, actually he had received permission to assart but he actually only wanted to fell some trees in two of his woods – for export. The Low Countries provided a ready market for timber he had discovered, along with the seafood and stone he already sent there. He really must attend to his interests with more purpose he thought, admiring Isabel as she ushered some guests towards a long table bursting with food.

Dubhshuileach sat at the window to the right of the fireplace running his forefinger round the rim of a silver goblet filled with wine, paying no attention to the goings-on below.

"To business, then?"

MacDuff snapped out of his near-trance but continued looking down into the hall. "Aye, but first to other matters. What of this lad's mother? You found her?"

"No, my lord."

"Well see to it. I needs must speak with her to verify her son's character and whereabouts. He tells me he saw someone or something and asks me to fetch his mother. He asks me to speak with her urgently and privately."

"Yes *deagh* lord, although I believe the woman to have fled…" he paused for emphasis, "with guilt no doubt."

"With guilt?" MacDuff finally turned to look at his guest.

"Aye, guilt. The two o' them are in this I'm sure. Stories of fishing trips – at night, pah! I say. Beasts roaming the paths at darkness? Again, pah! Yon lad has feared the King's mount causing death to both. No accident, that boy has killed our King!" Dubhshuileach's voice was firm. "For sure he wants his mother…so she can cover up his deeds. *Drùidheachd!*"

"Just find her…soon," was all that MacDuff said.

Dubhshuileach had chosen his words carefully, timed to perfection. A trump card. The mere speaking of it had sent MacDuff's pulse racing. More importantly his face was now flushed for Dubhshuileach to see and enjoy. He sensed that his guest revelled in making him feel uncomfortable. On this occasion it only took that one word, just as powerful in Gaelic, language being no barrier when it came to *witchcraft*. It would be a card that the Highlander would play again when the time was right.

"Aye, my lord."

*   *   *

At Kynkorn Castle, about four miles to the west of Ravenscraig Castle, Massan was coming to a life-changing decision. He was sitting on the red-painted, tiled floor of a small, sparsely-decorated room, staring intently at one of the narrow window loops. This was obviously an important private room that had had most of its adornments removed so as to serve as a holding room.

His head was a whirr of questions buzzing through his brain like bees in a busy hive. Why do they still hold me? Am I a scapegoat? Who was the man with the black mark on his face? Why do I fear him yet not know him? Do I know him? What happened to King Alexander?

Hours of the same passed making Massan sweat and tremble, pacing up and down like a caged animal. He felt he had to do something. But what? What could he do locked up in this room? Suddenly he decided. He knew what it was he had to do. Answer my questions, he thought. I must answer all my questions…and find my pendant. This boar's tooth can prove me innocent, can it not? Perhaps not. Perhaps it shows that I really did have contact with the King…perhaps it *proves* my guilt. Whichever, it is best in my hands… I have asked to see my mother yet she is not brought here. Why? She would come if told of my plight. Has she not been told? Do they not want her here? Why not? And what of the beast that knocked me flying? Could it have really have been *someone* on a horse? A killer…of the King?

The questions came to him thick and fast making his head hurt.

Mother can help; she will know what to do. I needs must find her…I must escape.

Once Massan finally came to this decision of escape he became focussed, less tired and picked himself up off the floor scanning the dimly lit room, the solitary flickering candle barely enough to reveal the four corners of the room. He peered out of one of the little windows to see the moon peering back through the drizzle. He was on the first-floor. He pulled himself up to try to measure himself against the window to see if he could squeeze through but as suspected the window was far too narrow.

What about the fireplace? The fire was not lit so perhaps he could climb up and out that way. Closer inspection showed only a narrow shaft of pure blackness and certainly not wide enough for him to get into.

The door! He turned to face the room's only door. Surely too easy, he told himself. Perhaps not. He walked over and tried the latch. It lifted slowly. Praise be, it really was lifting! Someone on the other side coughed. He froze, listening. Silence. He put his head up against the wooden door, which was made from V-edged planks slotted into each other, until he felt a draught on his cheek. Shoddy workmanship, he thought. Again he listened, this time holding his breath. Another cough and then footsteps headed off down the corridor leaving only silence. He paused, and now confident that there was no guard, drew in a deep breath and continued to raise the latch, slowly. His heart pounded, his breathing grew heavier. It stopped. The latch stopped, it was stuck. He felt it connect with something on the other side so he added a little force to it, but nothing. It would not budge. He tried it again with more vigour, caring not for the clinking it made. Padlocked! Letting out a huge sigh and sliding down the door he realised he was locked in with no chance of escape. Desperation and depression gripped him making him tremble as he sat on the floor with his head between his knees. All was lost.

Some time passed with the only sound being the occasional bout of whimpering from Massan as he imagined the worst laying in store for him. He was starting to shiver now, this time with chill rather than fear, as the draught from underneath the door combined with the cold, ceramic tiles finally penetrated his short over-tunic and leggings. He needed to pee.

46

He slowly lifted his head up from his knees and began scanning the room for a pisspot. Then, it suddenly came to him as his gaze found the little wooden 'cupboard' in the far corner, just beyond the farthest window loop. He stumbled up to his feet and went over to the little wooden structure opening its door. He could not believe his eyes. He had been in this room sometime and never once considered that there was a latrine in it; he had never seen one like this before, unaccustomed as he was to such grandeur. Now he was standing at the little door looking at a wooden chair sitting to one side of a hole in the floor. The hole in the seat of the chair was considerably smaller than the one in the floor. He gazed at the one in the floor. Big enough, he thought, still staring in disbelief. Aye, it is…big…enough. He peered into the gap and could see clearly that this part of the building was overhanging the small, mainly artificial moat.

"Shit…here goes," he whispered.

He almost squealed with excitement as he lowered himself into the latrine, his legs dangling outside grabbing foothold on a ledge on the outer wall. With great care he eased himself down one of the timber joists hands constantly slipping in the wet conditions. At one stage he knocked a piece of stonework into the moat causing a dull, thudding, splash. He shut his eyes tightly clinging onto the outer wall in utter silence, motionless as if by closing his eyes he himself would be invisible to any searching eyes. After a few moments of silence and realising that he had disturbed no one he continued his slow descent. He picked his way awkwardly round a window, candlelight flickering away inside, then scaled his way down the last few feet of the rugged stonework in the moonlight. Finally he slipped into the waist high water of the moat and slowly made for land.

Wet, cold and bedraggled he decided to make straight for his home at the Binn Village, unbeknownst to him that his family slept soundly a few miles away in Kirkton.

*   *   *

"Yours is a business with which I feel uncomfortable, I say," MacDuff said as Dubhshuileach drained off the last of his wine.

"Aye, no doubt, but one that I am good at and one which can make us all the richer," replied Dubhshuileach. "I am in the business of war, if you like. My services can be bought by whomsoever and all I ask is for the use of your four 'specialists' again, as I like to call them. We are a team I think. They served me well on previous trips and shall do so again, no?"

"The timing is awkward with the situation as it stands…"

"Aye…" interrupted Dubhshuileach, "the timing is not good in some ways, but in others it is. Surely the princely sum of one hundred marks is one to make any timing good? And you know not any of these men so I assume that you would not miss them whether I asked for permission or not?

47

"Aye, 'tis good money…and whom exactly do you have to strong-arm for this…this blood money?" he went straight to the point ignoring Dubhshuileach's cheap jibe about formalities.

"Not your concern, my lord. Suffice to say the deed will be done on foreign lands and will have no impact on lands here. And 'tis hardly blood money although it is money nonetheless and I heard no complaining or concern after my last trip." His tone was more forceful. "Your vow to take part in crusade to the Holy Land does not come cheap, Sirrah!" His tone was more abrupt than he meant. "We are all in this together, my lord. Our purpose – our sole purpose is to serve Our Lord Jesus Christ. We do so with pride and with honour. Our current tasks are but a means to an end – we will see the Holy Land. We will serve."

"You have your men. The very same, but it should be a last request as this type of butchery I will have no more part in…"

"Butchery? Butchery? 'Tis legal payment by one lord to another to help in legal matters on land owned by said lord. I think butchery is too strong a word; there will be no butchery only negotiation by, if necessary, forceful means. Call it what you will, but 'tis no more than aid…armed aid. I like to see our involvement as peacekeeping and peacekeeping is exactly what it is. We should be careful with our views, my lord, lest they be misunderstood," he glanced over at Michael who shuffled with unease and pretended not to be paying any attention. "I am giving you more respect than some may think is necessary considering these men are technically vassals of mine. I do you the honour of respecting your position and would appreciate same in return'" he said sternly. "I will have your men back in Fife shortly. I bid you goodnight."

And at that Dubhshuileach left.

*   *   *

It was a wet and weary lad that sneaked up to the little house, last on the left, in the Binn Village. He tried the front door but it was padlocked. Moving round to the back door he gained entry after unearthing the hidden key.

On entering he realised that no one was home and had not been for some time as no fire had been lit and none of the beds had been disturbed. He toyed with the idea of just lying down and having a long sleep but deep down knew that it would not be too long before he was missed and that this would be one of the first places that they would come looking.

He picked some dry clothes out of a cupboard and changed out of his sodden ones. He decided that his best hiding place would be on the Black Rock, which would be cold but safe, especially when the tide was in and it could not be reached. To that end he grabbed an extra tunic and some leggings, a spare fishing line, a flint, a fleece and a wooden-handled knife.

Just then he heard a twig snap outside, and grabbing the knife, moved up to the back door.

"Massan? Is that you?" the voice whispered. "'Tis I, David…from the pottery.

"Aye, what of it?"

"You are looking for your mother are you not? Well, she is fine, for now," came the reply. "But you skulking around makes me think that you may not be safe…"

"Aye, you may be right, but where is my mother? I needs must see her…"

"She is safe lad, but you are not I fear and may bring danger to her and your sister. You lie low just now, until it is safe and then we all meet up. What have you done young Massan?"

"Nothing. I have done naught and yet the King is dead and no one believes my innocence. My mother will know what to do…" he ranted.

"Calm down, son. For now you hide and in two days' time we meet at the Lammerlaws. There is a cave there at the far end, near to the water. Do you know of it?"

"Of course I know it. The Lammerlaws is but the back of my hand. I knew not it was known by all and sundry however. How many know of it?"

"Methinks only you, my brother and I. I have seen you down there, fishing near the cave. I look away and you are no longer there so I guess you know the cave of the Picts. We meet in two days at sunrise. I bring your mother and sister and we shall have a plan. Now go hide." The old man sounded confident but belied the fact that he had no idea what he was going to do next.

Massan waited until he was sure David had gone and then slipped out the back door. He crossed the back plot taking care not to disturb any of the animals and skipped deftly over the little wattle fence.

Soon he was making his way down the face of The Binn, actually rock-climbing on a couple of occasions, keeping an ear out at all times for any signs of life; search parties could be looking for him already. This route meant that there was little chance of bumping into anyone and he was pleased with himself that he had scoured his entire local environment as a child playing where perhaps he should not have been.

He gave Kirkton a wide birth and headed on down to the beach where he could see that the tide was in, gently lapping the sand. He felt that the Black Rock would be the best hiding place despite David's suggestion of the cave – he could probably see the cave from the Black Rock and could follow them if it was not a trick. He would have to wait until the tide was out to walk out to the Black Rock; once the tide came back in it would be accessible only by boat. He decided to head up the little hill at the west end of the beach which constituted the start of the rough terrain and wooded area that was the Lammerlaws and settled down in a little dip round the side of an outcrop of rocks which gave him a view of the Black Rock. The water was deep here and although still tidal, was about twelve feet deep when the tide was out which meant that he would have to walk back round to the beach to make it out to his sanctuary by foot.

He felt both mentally and physically exhausted, determined to stay alert until he could make his move. All he could hear now was the sound of the ebbing tide splashing against the rocks just below him. It was a sound he was comfortable with; it was soothing.

Soon he was asleep.

CHAPTER EIGHT

Kirkton, Fife, 20th March, 1286

It was a grey morning that greeted Callum and Malcolm as they walked into Kirkton. The wind had picked up; an easterly, which meant that there was a real bite in the air, making them hunch up with their robes pulled in tightly around them. The drizzle had stopped but the place was still damp, the sun unable to fight its way through the myriad clouds hurtling across the sky. There were still patches of snow dotted around but most of it had been turned to slush by the salty air and had vanished as quickly as it had come.

Kirkton was laid out in an L-shape with a total of about thirty homes largely depending on the market that took place there each day. It commanded a beautiful view (on a clear day) over the River Forth, raised as it was about a mile and a half from the water's edge. A little kirk stood between the houses, looming over the goings-on and even indulging in a bit of trade itself; it had the biggest stall, selling religious trinkets by the score. The market grew and shrank from day to day with stallholders coming from St. Andrews, Dunfermline, surrounding villages and hamlets and even Edinburgh. Most of the residents had their own small stalls, which they tended to site in front of their own homes, selling everything from local fish and pottery to foreign wares such as spices and newly discovered fashions like turbans; imports commanded a hefty price, affordable only by a select few. Nevertheless, gentry from larger, wealthier towns in Fife such as Dunfermline, Culross, St. Andrews and Cupar would come to the Kirkton market to check out the latest fads and to flaunt their elaborate carriages and current fashion statements.

Callum and Malcolm had slept well and set off just before sunrise, keeping a steady pace and following the coastal road, which if truth were known, was not the quickest route. They had planned to arrive in Kirkton in the early morning so as to catch the opening of the market and to visit the kirk for prayer. They reached the busy little place as and when planned; Callum sometimes appeared nonchalant when setting out on a trip but he was never far behind his planned arrival such was his preparation. This was the first stop on the long journey to Salop and it had occurred to them a market might be an ideal place to hitch a ride with any browsers or merchants who were going west or south.

Tables were being erected and wares being displayed as they approached, folk nodding reverently no matter how busy they seemed. For such an early time it was a bustling little place with many people heading to and from church where they said prayers for their lost king. The two clerics wandered through the town acknowledging the respects of all the people with a quiet reverence. They stopped on reaching the kirk and set about helping a young lad who was struggling to set up a table on which to set out two sacks of religious trinkets. They spent some time chatting to the lad, pointing out that some of the wares had come from the Holy Land: candle holders, silver lockets and delicately fashioned crucifixes with coloured jewels adorning them amongst the most fascinating.

The two men enjoyed imparting knowledge as they felt it was one of their responsibilities in trying to make the world a better place. Perhaps it was their desire to improve the world and people's lives within it that caused them shortly to accept, almost reluctantly, a second mission to add to the one given to them by Bishop Fraser.

*   *   *

It was morning and Christina had woken up in a cold sweat. She had been fretting about Massan for most of the night and had managed to get very little sleep. Her husband had visited her in her sleep during vivid dreams and nightmares telling her to save Massan and Aibhlinn. He was tall and handsome with no sign of the disease that would slowly eat his flesh away. Her mind had then skipped off into nightmare and she saw Massan hanging from a tree. His eyes bulged from his grey, dead face, his tongue fat and blue sticking out like a lump of rotted meat. His neck was a reddish purple colour where the noose had tightened to choke the last breath out of him, simultaneously snapping his neck like a twig. Blood trickled out from beneath the twine where it had cut into his throat. She could smell shit, an almost overpowering smell of shit. It was getting stronger. She could almost taste it. She nearly vomited. Steadying herself against the trunk of the tree, hand over her nose and mouth, she noticed the ground beneath the swinging body; it was covered in her son's faeces with an ever-increasing swarm of flies buzzing around it. Suddenly, Massan's head lifted, bloody snot dribbling down his nose over his tongue and chin.

"Mother..." he groaned.

She let out a shriek.

"Mo...th...er..." another groan. "Helllpp me!"

The buzzing of the flies was getting louder, the smell of his shit stronger.

She tried to speak, to reassure him. But, she could not. She retched. It was all she could do. She fought the buzzing and the smell, falling onto her knees at the feet of her son. She leaned forward onto all fours, retching, choking with her face inches from the pile of stink on the dirt. The buzzing was reaching a crescendo, the smell unbearable causing her to flop over onto the ground, clawing at the earth, pulling herself away from the noise and smell. She tumbled down a hillock onto cold, damp grass.

The buzzing had stopped, the smell gone. She lay there gasping great gulps of fresh air until she felt strong enough to look back to where she had come from. Kneeling once more, this time in wet grass, she turned to face her son's swinging corpse. It was gone, replaced by the swinging, bloody body of a dead pig just like one of the ones she had seen at St. Andrews market.

She screamed.

The wind rattled the shutters of the little wattle house and she found herself sitting up in bed, sweat lashing down her face and back. She shivered and reached onto the floor for a fleece that had been kindly provided by her host, Drust, who turned out to be his brother David's double.

He sat tending a little fire a few yards away.

"Are you alricht, ma dearie?" He croaked the question out, sounding like the words would be the last he ever spoke.

Nevertheless he looked concerned as he watched Christina blink into consciousness, rubbing her arms furiously as if she was scrubbing herself free of dirt and shit. There was a pause before she realised where she was and what had been said to her.

"Aye…aye…I'm alright sure. Just a dream."

"Some dream. Methinks yon shiverin' and a moanin' have come fae a nightmare likely an' no ony fluffy dream. I was thinkin' o' wakin' ye up such was the state o' ye. Are ye sure yer fine?"

"Aye. Fine…needing some fresh air 'tis all. I'll away for a wee walk," she was grabbing at her overcoat and getting to her feet. "If ye don't mind. I just need to have a think and also prayers should be said for the King's soul. Maybe a prayer for Massan's plight," she nodded over to Aibhlinn who was watching the whole scene intently. "Come Aibhlinn, we're going for a wee walk." Drust was getting to his feet also now as if to make ready to go with them. "Thank you sir," Christina continued, "but we will walk alone today."

"Aye, as you will," he wheezed, looking hurt even though he knew that it was best for the woman and her daughter to be alone for a while.

"See you later," Aibhlinn shouted cheerily as she jumped up, grabbing her overcoat and latching onto her mother's hand. She turned and waved to Drust as they stepped outside closing the door behind them.

They hunched up holding hands tightly as they turned into the wind and headed down towards the little stalls and the kirk.

"Ma, why has that man got a funny voice?"

"Methinks he has spent too many days out at sea in the cold…"

"Does that mean that Massan will get a funny voice too? He spends lots of time on the beach fishing…"

The mention of Massan made Christina's eyes well up again.

"Come. Shall we see if we can get Massan a wee something at the market?"

"Aye," shouted back Aibhlinn, "something nice."

The first stall they got to was laden with different types of rope: long and thin; short but thick; long and thick. Christina paused to scan over the different types but was tugged away by Aibhlinn who had seen bread on the next stall.

"Look ma! Bread! Can we have some?" She pulled her mother right up to the counter and leaned forward to try and smell the loaves but the wind swept away any trace of the normally sweet-smelling bread.

"I also have wheat today…" started the stallholder, "especially brought in to Berwick yesterday."

"And too expensive for the likes of us I'm sure. Do we look like merchants or nobles?" The stallholder took the question as it was meant: rhetorical.

"Bread then?"

"Please ma!" Aibhlinn was getting overexcited. "Please…"

"Alright, alright, just calm down." Christina gripped Aibhlinn's hand a little tighter. "Calm, now. Venison one minute and the next you want bread. You are spoiled you are!"

"Pleease ma!" She held her hands together in front of her as she said it drawing a circle in the mud with her foot; a trick that she knew always seemed to work on adults.

"How can I refuse? Bread we shall have but first we go walking, to freshen up and to think. Bread will come later." She looked at the man behind the counter and continued, "Have you good supplies of bread, sir?"

"Aye that I have, unless it gets overly busy but in this wind I think not. I can put a loaf to one side for you if you wish."

"Aye please do. And make it your smallest one." She nodded thanks and goodbye to him and led Aibhlinn away.

They had not walked far from the baker's stall when they heard someone calling.

"Christina? Christina from Binn Village?"

She looked round warily thinking the worst. Was it the stranger with the marked face coming to get her so she could turn Massan in? Would she know what to say if it was? What if he wanted Aibhlinn as surety? She would not be able to outrun him with Aibhlinn. The thoughts and questions raced through her mind as she turned.

"Christina? It is you," the man continued.

The wind was carrying the words away but she felt that she recognised that voice. She pretended not to hear and started to lead her daughter past the man who was speaking to them. She neatly sidestepped the man and was almost away when he gently took her by the arm.

"Christina," he said again. "It is I, Callum. We met at St. Andrews just past."

Still worried, she turned to see the familiar grey outfit emblazoned with the red cross.

"Ah," she sighed with sheer relief. "We meet again and I for one am the gladder for it." She was not joking.

"And who might this be peeping from behind you?" He bowed down to Aibhlinn's level as he said so and she hid behind her mother.

54

"My daughter good Callum, she is my daughter." Her eyes began to well up as she spoke. "My only daughter…" she sobbed.

"Come Christina. I think you are not one who cries. What can be wrong?" He held her gently.

"My son…" was all she could manage.

"Massan," came a little voice from behind her.

"Come, we speak inside," he nodded towards the kirk door a few yards away. "Malcolm, come… we are finished for now."

At that he led Christina and Aibhlinn into the kirk followed by Malcolm who, sensing all was not well, told the young stallholder to finish putting out the trinkets on his own and not to disturb them in the kirk.

It was dark inside and smelt fusty and damp despite the many locals sitting in solemn prayer. A stream of people wandered in and out saying their own silent devotions to the dearly departed King. Huge candles flickered at the far end of the building, lighting up a mural of the Apostles that was painted in rich colours.

They sat near the entrance at a small table in an alcove that was sometimes used to display wares outside on busy days. Malcolm went off to get some wine and returning with four little goblets he sat down and filled them to the brim.

"Now, your son you say? What is wrong my child?" Callum reached across the table and took Christina's hand. "You can tell me…"

"But I know not…" she started. "The King is dead!"

"Hush my dear…slowly…quietly. We are in the kirk." He spoke softly, reassuring her by taking her hands. "My dear we know of that. Everyone knows of Alexander. God have mercy on his soul," he added, crossing himself. "Your son…is your son dead also?"

"No, no…he…he was questioned, arrested," she whispered. "They think he did something to the King." She sobbed wholeheartedly now for a few moments, the two Redfriars staring at one-another. They said nothing, waiting for Christina to get it out of her system. Aibhlinn was silent, keeping her arms folded out on the table in front of her, head nestling down to avoid eye contact.

Shortly, once Christina had regained her composure and gulped a couple of mouthfuls of wine she began to tell the two churchmen her tale. Massan had gone fishing. He had not returned. A fierce, warrior-type in plaid had come to her village to look for her. She told them of her worry for her family. Why was the King dead? Why was Massan involved? He would not do anything to hurt our beloved King. She mentioned that the stranger had spoken to her friend and neighbour David about being on 'Earl of Fife's business'. She felt that she had told the Redfriars clearly and concisely what her concerns were but in fact she did ramble quite a bit.

"Know you where Massan is?" Callum asked the question quietly hoping that she would reply with a lowered voice. He did not want an innocent to be harmed but equally knew the consequences of conspiring to help outlaws, especially when a charge of regicide may be involved. "Know you where your son is?" Again, he spoke softly.

"No I do not," she replied. "Will you help us?" She looked at Callum and then to Malcolm. "Believe you my son is innocent?"

"Innocence is a word…" started Malcolm only to be interrupted by Callum who was clearly making seniority count in this situation.

"We know not Christina, but you seem to think of him as innocent. *You* believe he is, but he is *your* son."

"Please help me. I know not what to do…please!" She fixed a worried gaze at Prior Callum as she took his hands now, squeezing the ruddy red fingers tightly as she did.

He held her gaze for a while before speaking.

"We needs must talk with him but you may not be safe and we head now for Cramunde and then south. Time is against us."

"Praise be! Thank you," she sobbed.

Callum took a sip from his goblet, placing it back on the table gently. The woman in front of him was clearly distressed but he felt deep down, that she was a good person and that he should at least make an effort to help. "This man who stalks you…he wanted only you?"

"Aye…well, according to David he asked for my whereabouts."

"And what then of little Aibhlinn? She would be wanted too? Along with her brother and mother?" He glanced from the girl to her mother.

"Well, I…" Christina stumbled. She could scarcely believe that she had been so concerned with Massan's plight and that of her own that it had not even occurred to her that her daughter too was in danger. She held her head in her hands, thinking. "Aibhlinn, go you outside and fetch the bread we saw earlier." She handed over a coin and the little girl's eyes lit up.

"Hooray," squealed the little girl as she grabbed the coin and jumped up off her stool. The adults looked in turn at each other round the table when the door slammed shut and Christina continued.

"Think you my child is in danger? My daughter I mean."

Callum stood up now and started to pace slowly round the table as he spoke, his fingers rubbing at his chin. When he spoke his tone was one of complete calm but also one that demanded his audience's complete attention. He was now deadly serious. He seemed oblivious to the others around him.

"As I see it we have little choice and little time. Massan is in peril. He has either killed our King…"

"Sirrah!"

The upturned palm of Callum's hand quelled any further protest from Christina. She fell silent letting him continue.

"I say, he has either killed our King *or* as we believe more likely, he has been framed into being involved *or* he actually was involved in an accidental way. Now, we know not what happened as yet, but we do know he has escaped from his captors – he assumes the cloak of guilt, does he not?"

"Well I suppose," she started.

He continued pacing, turning away from the table as he pondered.

"Furthermore, we have a fearsome Highlander looking for you and Massan whilst claiming to be a representative of Duncan MacDuff, a good man by all accounts. Perhaps it is necessary for us to meet with MacDuff and this henchman along with Massan, you and the Church to put all the cards on the table – to establish truth. As I say, MacDuff is a good man...honest and trustworthy." He sensed Christina's worry and quickly added, "No harm will come whilst the Church is involved." He stopped and turned to face Christina. "Say you that you know not of your son's whereabouts?"

The question caught her unawares.

"Er...at present I know not," she replied rather too brusquely.

"Ah, at present you know not," he wagged a finger at her as he spoke. "Well let us presume that we *did* know his whereabouts and let us say that we could meet with him, think you that we could arrange a meeting with all parties?" He knew he had her where he wanted her. She would have to admit to knowing where Massan was and also agree to bring him to a meeting with his accusers if she was to expect any help from the Redfriars. "Of course any gathering would be arranged by us and would not happen until we returned from South in a month's time. We would also have to guarantee Massan's appearance and also his safety, which would mean that he would have to reside for one month in our care at Cramunde. You can bring him to us within two days from now?"

The door burst open and Aibhlinn charged in running straight up to her mother with a lump of golden bread.

"I got the best one!" She looked proud as she showed it off to everyone around the table. Her mother glanced a quick smile to her and then looked directly at Callum.

"I agree. I will bring Massan to Cramunde within two days. You have my word."

"Excellent! We shall meet with you at Cramunde thirty days from now," then turning to Malcolm he continued. "Come, we make for Cramunde now. Time is precious."

"Good day to you both," said Malcolm as he stood up.

"Good day Christina, Aibhlinn," said Callum as he leant over and drained the last of the claret from his goblet.

"Thank you, thank you both. Good day. Come Aibhlinn."

At that Christina took her daughter's hand, leading her out of the kirk into the wind and heading off in the direction of Drust's home.

*   *   *

Stirling Castle, 20th March, 1286

Yolande sat at the window of her lavish bedroom overlooking the central courtyard of Stirling Castle. She toyed with the white king from the nearby chess set, rolling it around in the palm of her hand and rubbing the head gently as if she was trying to bring it to life. She gazed out at nothing in particular and thought of the times that

Alexander had sat down with her to teach her how to play the game. Initially she had found it frightfully complicated and, frankly, rather boring but Alexander had always been so enthusiastic about teaching her that she had grown to love the game.

The courtyard was now a hive of activity with horses clattering about, men-at-arms patrolling the perimeter, minstrels and jesters cavorting and making merry with locals to-ing and fro-ing with assorted victuals. The noise seemed to get louder and louder, bringing Yolande out of her trance-like state.

She watched the scene with fascination, still constantly turning over the chess piece in her hand. Then she saw him. The chess piece stopped turning. She squinted but could no longer see him. Men-at-arms, now stationed around the courtyard, slowly perused the scene, watching all that was taking place in front of them. She watched as horsemen dismounted and locals scurried about, then she saw him again, this time disappearing behind a cart laden with logs.

"Alexander…?" She said it only very faintly.

She watched intently, standing up slowly as she did so.

The man almost came into view from the other side of the cart but a couple of horsemen pulled up blocking her line of sight. One of the large mounts reared up, spinning round almost out of control and as it did so it followed the path of the man obscuring him from sight until he vanished behind a large group of very animated locals.

"Merde!" Again she spoke softly.

Yolande was standing up on tiptoes now, craning her neck to see the man, her Alexander. He was seemingly calming the group down, pointing and waving in different directions. She could make out his red cloak but not yet his face. She stood up on her little stool, grabbing hold of one of the shutters to steady herself. The man turned and she saw him this time as clear as day. It was her husband, Alexander.

"My love!" She screamed so loud and violently she almost tumbled from the stool. The scene outside stopped abruptly and all the heads turned to look up at her window, but she was no longer there having jumped off the stool, sending it crashing. Tunic hitched up to her knees she charged out of her bedroom door almost knocking over Isabella, who had heard the scream and was heading for the Queen's room.

"Alexander! It is you. I knew you were alive!" She flew down the passageway with Isabella, now recovered, trailing in her wake.

"Stop! Please stop!" But Isabella's shouts fell on deaf ears as Yolande raced down the stairs and out into the courtyard.

"My love!"

She ran across the courtyard, pushing past startled onlookers, with a swarm of assorted bodyguards, attendees and men-at-arms struggling to keep up. The group she headed for were standing agog watching this demented-looking figure heading straight for them.

She could still see the figure in red. It was he, she could see him clearly. He was so handsome.

"Alexander!"

She lunged into the group knocking a small man clean off his feet into a crumpled mess on the straw-covered courtyard. Her arms were flailing as she ploughed through the crowd, her speed having slowed slightly, although still determined to reach Alexander. She was almost there: she could see his overcoat, a glorious red. She could see his broad shoulders. Reaching out she flung herself onto him, her arms wrapping tightly round him.

"Oh, my love…I knew you were alive…I believed!" She was almost ranting now as her entourage finally caught up with her. She smothered him with kisses showering his neck and ear. "My dear…"

"Your Majesty…my lady!" It was Isabella, slightly out of breath but still able to speak with authority. "Clear the area! Now!" She spun round searching out the Queen's bodyguards.

All the various soldiers attending jumped into action under her command and started to jostle people away.

"Move on! Nothing to see!" The shouts went up as the bodyguards leapt into action ushering the bewildered onlookers away.

"Come, my lady… you are dreaming," Isabella spoke softly as Yolande turned to finally notice the commotion around her. She looked quizzically at Isabella and then at the surrounding scene.

"It is my love…he is here."

"Come my dear…with me."

Yolande looked at her, bemused.

"Isabella, it is he!" She faced Isabella, excitement splashed across her face. She still clenched the chess piece as she held onto the surcoat of Alexander. "It is he!"

"Of course it is…"

Yolande's expression changed: first confusion, then anger. She detected a condescending tone. "It…is…my…love," she looked furious, scanning the few people that were left staring at her.

She pulled Alexander's surcoat towards her, causing him to stumble a little. The she turned to look at him again, only this time she found herself clutching on to a complete stranger. He was in red sure enough, but nonetheless, a complete stranger.

"What have you done with him?" Her voice was full of anger now.

At that Buchan arrived to take control.

"Come," he said quietly peeling Yolande's fingers off the merchant's coat one by one, the white king now falling from her grip onto the soft straw. "All is fine. You need some rest." He put a comforting arm round the shaking woman and led her away, across the courtyard, back the way she had come, leaving the crowd to start murmuring about what they had just witnessed.

As they disappeared through a door her head turned searching the floor for the chess piece.

"The King…"

"He is gone," replied Buchan, not realising she spoke of the white piece left amongst the straw.

CHAPTER NINE

The Lammerlaws, 21st March, 1286

Massan may well have been sound asleep when the little group approached the small cave near the waterline but his senses were obviously on full alert, waking him up as soon as they were within earshot. He realised that he had fallen asleep in a hole under some gorse only feet away from the cave that he felt might have been a trap; he had not made any attempt to get to his safe haven at the Black Rock. He must have been tired, he thought. He recognised his mother's voice, excited and trembling. He scrambled up to the mouth of the cave which was partially concealed by the sprawling gorse and as he grew more excited and relieved, watched the party get closer and closer. He dare not rush out to greet them in case they were being followed even though all his emotions pleaded with him to throw caution to the wind and embrace them as he longed to.

Soon David the potter had steered them to the hidden cave and Massan ushered them into his temporary home hugging all his visitors tearfully. The cave had been lit up with joy for a while as Massan, Aibhlinn and their mother, Christina, had their family reunion. Drust and David sat silently to one side allowing the three to enjoy each other's company again before eventually interrupting.

"We should make moves for Cramunde," announced David. "Christina, you should take Aibhlinn to Drust's house. She will be safe there. You should bide there too, for the time being."

"Cramunde? What's of Cramunde?" Massan looked inquisitively at his mother.

"We go to Cramunde for refuge until we resolve this horrible misunderstanding, for that is what it is, is it not? Think you that by escaping you show your innocence?" Her tone changed slightly revealing an undercurrent of anger in her voice. "Think you the Earl of Fife will believe you an innocent man when he finds you escaped?"

"But I am innocent…I—," he started.

"Shoosh laddie! We are fugitives now, all of us. David and Drust are involved now too. We act and we act now. The Redfriars have agreed, thank the Lord, to give refuge to you until we can meet with MacDuff and sort out this sorry mess. They have guaranteed your safety and will guarantee to Fife your attendance at a meeting."

"But Fife's men will have me killed…" His tone was also rising.

"Son, 'tis for the best," chipped in Drust, "we cannae run forever." He paused before adding deliberately, "You will be caught and when you are you will be tried for regicide…and you *will* be found guilty."

"Massan, laddie. What my brother here means to say is that if you volunteer to see Fife you are more the likely to receive understanding. If you run you will be presumed guilty. Why run if innocent?" David sat down next to Massan and put his hand on the boy's shoulder as he spoke.

"But I *am* innocent!"

"Aye, that we know son," his mother sighed.

"If I can find the pendant I gave to our King surely that would help."

"In what way, son."

"Well it would show that I talked truth and that if he wore it round his neck it would be difficult to just slip off…and if it did it should still be there…at the scene."

Drust and David looked at one another before Drust spoke.

"I see not the point. It proves there exists a pendant. It proves not that you killed him and it proves not that you did not."

"Well it belongs to me, given to me by my mother and I want it back."

David was looking bemused now.

"The noose is all but tight around the laddie's neck and all he can think about is a bloody boar's tooth! Can you believe it? The boy has lost his senses…"

Christina threw the two old men a cautionary glance before speaking.

"Son, you shall get your pendant back…sometime. Firstly, we needs must save the neck that it should adorn. What point a necklace with no Massan? You must go to Cramunde, to the House of the Trinitarians. For one month. Prior Callum will return and be your representative at a meeting with the Earl of Fife. We will sort this mess out, I promise."

"Someone else was there." From deep within the cave a drip echoed, and again. Seagulls cackled overhead and waves crashed against the rocks below. Everyone just looked at one another, searching. "I said, someone else was there."

"What do you mean, son?" Drust asked.

"I mean, well…I think there might have been someone else there that night…I was knocked over…by a beast, I thought. But now I think that I was wrong. It was too big…it was a horse…being ridden at speed."

"Shh now, laddie," said Christina. "Think on it later…at Cramunde. First we must get you there. Especially if you were seen…by the…*someone.* Come, we make a move now."

"Your mother and sister will bide wi' me for the month," added Drust.

"And I shall watch your house," said David.

"Aye and we all live happily ever after," Massan sneered.

* * *

"You have the rights of it then, John?"

Prior Callum had stood up as he asked the question of the young lay priest.

"Aye. Well…aye, methinks I have it."

"You are thinking that you have it or you have?" Callum pressed. "Tell me what you have so we can agree that indeed you *do* have it." He seemed to sigh as he continued. "The task is not difficult laddie but it *is* important." He put both hands on the refectory table and leaned forward. "So, tell me."

Malcolm sat motionless opposite John at the long, thin oak table, staring at him, waiting for the right response. The refectory was lit only by a few arched windows sitting atop the seventeen feet high wall on the eastern side with a small round window on the adjacent south wall. It was a cloudy day outside making for a rather sombre atmosphere inside but occasionally the sun managed to peep out and when it did it lit up the room. John sat with his back to the eastern wall which meant that Malcolm could barely make out his facial expressions. He listened intently.

"I journey to Fife to seek audience with MacDuff." He paused, eyes searching the ceiling as if the answer would be up there among the timbers. "I…take Fergus with me so he can learn. I…I speak with Fife to declare our intent – that we have the boy that is involved in the King's death…"

"*May* be involved," interrupted Callum.

"Aye, 'tis what I meant to say. *May* be involved. We know not at present. He is scared and swearing innocence. The lad will have taken an oath on the Holy Book by then, swearing innocence. We say to Fife that Prior Callum will meet with him in one month to resolve the matter. If the boy is incriminated Fife can deal with him, as the lad is one of his vassals, and he can deal with him as he sees fit. If vindicated, the boy is to go free. This is God's will."

"Good. Anything else?"

"Hmm…" Again his eyes lifted to the rafters and the shaft of light streaming through the circular window. He followed the light onto the adjacent wall where it struck an inscription; CUM VENIT JESUS SEQUAX CESSABIT UMBRA. He seemed to go into a trance as he stared intently at it then mumbled to himself, "When Jesus comes the shadow will cease." He seemed to snap out of it then and now seeming full of confidence announced, "We will guarantee to deliver the laddie who shall bide here at Cramunde until said meeting. Fife can chair said meeting with Prior Callum, to be held at a venue of his choosing, and he should bring witness or testament as he so pleases. In the meantime, myself along with Fergus will speak with certain of Fife's vassals given he permits us so to do. There we have it."

"Well done," said Malcolm, breaking into a small round of applause.

"Aye, you have it. But remember we seek not to interfere with our friend the Earl of Fife but only to advise him on a matter of grave importance." He turned his back on the young man as he spoke, ambling over to the wall where John's gaze had been transfixed. He ran his hand slowly over the inscription and turned, continuing, "Young Massan has asked us in good faith for help and he does not wish to offend his feudal lord. He admits his escape was an error but did flee only in fear and not in guilt. Fife should know that the lad recognises his wisdom and wishes to put right this misunderstanding."

"And Fergus is to say nothing?"

"Naught," said Callum. "He should be all eyes and all ears. He is under your wing. You shall show him our diplomacy, our courage and strength, and most of all you shall show him our faith," he continued. "Use that brain of yours, laddie…it is a fine brain. And MacDuff a good man essentially, in a position of power from a young age and with no real guidance he has done well…he tries, I think. See you guide him to do well here too, John. Patience and justice is what we seek."

At that Callum and Malcolm left with Callum turning briefly in the doorway to speak. "See to it, John. And may the Lord be with you."

* * *

The drinking den sat nestled in a little cove halfway up the coast of the East Neuk in Fife. It comprised two little buildings which were buffeted by the strong, cold, easterly winds coming in off the North Sea. Spray from the sea crashing against the rocky shoreline flew up, whirling around looking for all like a constant rain shower. Clouds bustled by, jockeying for centre stage with the ever-feeble sun. The small gorse-splattered cliffs behind the den were just big enough to keep in the salty air and keep out any prying eyes from the main route further inland. The snow had all but gone from here.

The five men had arrived individually over a short period of time, all marching down the steep, sandy path with their heads bowed against the elements. Dubhshuileach, dressed in his familiar ochre-coloured plaid, had been last to arrive, muscling his way past the bushes which tore at him all the way down the narrow little track. He held his hood up, tugging it down over his forehead with a meaty hand, letting it go just as he reached out for the latch of the den. He stepped over a couple of big lumps of wet, brown seaweed and stepped in.

Candles gave the room its only light although there were no customers.

"Through yonder," the innkeeper nodded towards a small door in the corner of the room.

"Aye," replied the big man. He stooped as he opened the door and stepped into the back room.

A long rasping sound greeted him as a strong-looking, squat man with fair hair leaned over to one side on the bench, allowing the fart greater access. As he did so he saluted Dubhshuileach with a jug of wine. The other three men in the room laughed heartily.

"Never the one to let his mouth do the talking when more sense comes from his erse!" Dubhshuileach responded. "Aye, ye'll never sneak up ahind a man wi' an erse as noisy as yon, eh Bash?" He smiled at the group, some of whom had never actually ever seen him smile before. One or two thought he was incapable of so doing.

But this was a different man standing before them. This was a man who was relaxed yet fully focussed. He was on a mission and when he had a purpose he always seemed lighter which often disguised the fact that he was even more dangerous. They all knew they too could relax, but only up to a point. They could laugh with him and even rib him a little. But they all knew that things could only be taken so far. He was still a man to be wary of.

Raassp! Bash let another one rip. "There's yer answer, big man!"

"Sit yersel' doon," a tall man stood up from the bench allowing the Highland man a space to sit. His red hair was ruffled with a parting down one side. The scar which formed the parting had been given to him the year previous whilst on Crusade with the French against Peter of Aragon. He also sported another slash which ran right to left from his brow over his nose and onto his cheek. These scars were the medals by which he showed his bravery. They also meant that he obviously survived which is more than can be said for the opponents that had disfigured him. "Grab a wine and tell us our task," he continued.

"Aye Mool. That I'll do. You are no a man for standin' on ceremony – straight to the point as ever…"

"Well let's call it eagerness – I like ma job!" He burst out laughing along with the other four, all of whom had stopped long after he was still red-faced and coughing uncontrollably. Each one of the men allowed himself a little snigger at Mool who struggled to regain his composure.

When the group had got itself back to silence Dubhshuileach stood up, wine goblet in hand, and addressed them. The tone had now changed.

"I call this meeting of the Hounds of St. Andrew open," he announced. "Do not speak without my permission – stand if you require such. Beege, the flag," he said turning to a weather-beaten, wiry man in his mid-twenties who then rustled about under the table. As he did so the others went about clearing everything off the table so that on finally producing the flag, Beege was able to spread it out so it covered the top entirely.

Dubhshuileach continued, "All hands on the Saltire."

In turn the men, still seated, put their hands onto the old flag in front of them. It had a white, diagonal cross, on a faded blue background and was rather ragged round the edges. Their leader turned to look for somewhere nearby to put his goblet and realising there was nothing within arm's reach let it tumble out of his hand onto the wooden floor. He let it clatter across the floorboards paying no heed to it.

"We do swear," he started, looking up towards the heavens, "by the cross of our Saint Andrew, humble fisherman and first-called of the apostles, evangelist, and he who was martyred for his faith in Greater Scythia, the home of our ancestors, he who is by his very own desire our patron saint of Scotland." He closed his eyes in reverence before adding, "*Andrea Scoti's dux esto compatriotes.*"

The men round the table sat heads bowed in silence as Dubhshuileach continued, now facing upwards as if addressing the heavens. "We do willingly pick up the rod of his faith, we tighten the line between what is his and what is ours doing so with God's blessing and we vow to be the hooks by which we retrieve his bones and capture his enemies which too, are our enemies. We do this for you Andrew, and Our Lord Jesus Christ. Thanks be to thee, O Christ."

"Thanks be to thee, O Christ," the others replied firmly, all standing up quickly as they did so.

"Most wonderful Andrew, brother of Peter, guide us in these our quests. Lead us to drink at your fountain, to eat at your table and to sow the seeds of your faith. Lead us."

"Lead us," the men repeated still standing.

"O beloved and illustrious Andrew let us escort you to this dear place, that which we call home. Amen."

"Amen," they repeated unsmiling.

"Dubhshuileach then turned and scooped up his goblet from the floor. "Wine!" He raised his goblet as he sat down.

"Wine!" the others repeated, all raising their goblets in unison before following the flame-haired man's lead and sitting.

After the wine had been distributed Mool turned to the Highland man who was now sipping at the red liquid, gently sloshing it round his mouth, savouring its full body with his eyes closed.

"So…our task?" Again he stood.

Dubhshuileach swallowed the wine in his mouth in one gulp.

"Sit man, all of you," he gestured that they all sit. "Tasks, Mool, plural. First," answered Dubhshuileach, without opening his eyes, "to travel to Salop, to exterminate a pest, to collect our fee and to return back to this place."

"And what or who is this pest pray tell?"

The question was ignored and Dubhshuileach continued.

"We are nearly set. We have monies enough already I think; courtesy of the young MacDuff, your liege. His wealth is more than he can handle methinks…and a hiding place in the floor is no hiding place at all, is it not, Beege?"

He glanced over to Beege as he spoke, only opening his eyes into slits as he did so. Beege sat silent, grinning and nodding back to him.

"Ah! The man can but only grin. What say you, grinner? Your master would but be all the more wealthy if not for your prying eyes, methinks. No hiding place when you have the eyes of a falcon perhaps?"

"No Sirrah! Mine eyes are guided by the Lord and would not search out that which we need if not so wished by Him."

"Aye, he has the rights of it," he declared, bursting into laughter.

The room crackled with laughter for a short time before Dubhshuileach shattered it.

"The flag, Beege…put it away now."

The flag was then carefully folded up and tucked away from whence it came – a little bag that Beege produced from under the table.

"This pest of whom you speak?" Mool tried again.

"Aye yon bug that needs be squashed. He is known as Gatacre, Cedric de Gatacre, and he wrongs my friend Leonard of Ludlowe with his dealings in wool. Moreover, I have a score to settle since my experience at Yarmouth."

"Wool, you say?" Bash looked puzzled, choosing to ignore the mention of the incident at Yarmouth. They all knew the story and how delicately it sat with Dubhshuileach: he had spoken about it often enough.

"Aye, fuckin' wool. Can ye no hear? Fuckin' wool!"

The outburst came from the fifth man of the group. His head was shaven and he looked like he had just crawled out from under a rock. His bloodshot eyes portrayed a rage that bubbled inside, fighting to get out.

"Your mouth I shall sew shut one day, Skate, when all that comes from it is filth," said Dubhshuileach, "or perhaps your head will fall from your shoulders first."

"Apologies good sir, I forget my place, but Bash here is not one to listen well. Either that or his ears are broken by the noises his arse makes!"

At that Mool burst out into maniacal laughter again.

Ignoring Skate, Bash continued, "Wool? We fight for wool?"

"No, poultice! We fight for our cause and our cause only," the big man said as he poured himself some more wine. "I think a wrong needs righting and I, for one, would lance this boil Gatacre for no monies, but monies we get and enough to secure our passage to recover the bones of our illustrious St. Andrew from Holy Land. You have problems with wool? That which you wear now is wool only cheap and homespun, not quality like that in which Ludlowe deals in. Ludlowe is a rich man through wool and it is best you not forget that."

"Aye," was all Bash could manage, embarrassed at the put down

"Can you make him shut up? Sew *his* mouth perhaps?" Skate was pointing at Mool who, red-faced, had broken into a coughing fit and was gesticulating to everyone that he was fine really.

"I'm…fit," he managed in-between the spluttering.

"We listen to the plan then?" Beege spoke, looking around the table as he did so.

"Aye," Dubhshuileach, who had been smirking at Mool's performance, suddenly went serious. His facial expression changed in an instant as if he had turned a key in a lock; open to closed. He had their full attention again, even Mool suddenly managed to find the effort to get his emotions under control. The room fell silent once again as Dubhshuileach spoke. "First. We have shillings to recover – those that were once MacDuff's. Not as easy as it would be if not for the death of Alexander, he I call betrayer." The last word was spat out. "Fifemen of MacDuff and men of Buchan, comb the coast near said coins. We needs must be careful but these men search day and night. For what I know not – a clue perhaps. A clue to his death? I think there are none. An accident leaves no clue! Do these men not grieve? It is a time of mourning – all should be silent, indoors even…and yet still they search."

"Leave the coins to me," said Bash. "I'll bring them out from under their noses."

"Aye, nae doubt, but let us all hope yer bowels are held in check for that day as I fear you may not be seen but shall be smelt…" It was Skate again. He seemed to enjoy provoking his stocky companion.

Not rising to the bait Bash continued, "Like I say, I shall bring them back. Give me until the morrow nicht."

"Tomorrow night is no good for we leave at noon with money retrieved or not. Make it happen before noon then. Bring them to Rossend Castle."

Bash looked back at Dubhshuileach shrugging his shoulders.

"You have it. By noon it is. To your place."

"We have ourselves another problem; this laddie and his family. I want them found. I have been to their wattle and daub at Binn Village and uncovered nought. They could upset all our plans with their meddling, not least the laddie's big mouth which could swallow us all up with his ranting. I will court Fife, he of little brain and large ego, whilst this family is dealt with. Skate, Mool see to it, the sooner the better. You know what to do – as discussed – and follow it to the letter."

"Aye," the two men acknowledged in unison.

"And let none of them be of concern after the morrow. Understood?"

"Aye!"

"Beege and Bash, we meet at my castle at Rossend at noon for Salop. Meeting over," and at that Dubhshuileach got up and walked out.

CHAPTER TEN

Arab Baths, Runda, capital of Tarakuna district of al-Andalus, Southern Iberian

Peninsula, 6th October, 1275

"So where are you taking me?"

The strapping young lad spoke in his native Scots Gaelic tongue when conversing with his father, although sometimes they were known to speak in Old Scots, English or even French. He had been taught well but had never mastered fully Latin which he was still persevering with.

"*Here*, laddie," said the old man gesturing to the small building in front of them which stood just outside the defensive walls of the *medina* of Runda alongside the confluence of two rivers. He sported a black, swirling Celtic tattoo, Pictish in origin, which encircled his left eye, sweeping out in a knotwork of double interlacing which ended by his left ear. It was quite spectacular and had become quite a talking point locally since he had settled here two years previously. The rest of his face was blotched red with one or two spots turning into full-blown sores which wept with yellow pus; leprosy was as much a talking point, causing fear amongst the locals although the Moors did believe that few strains were actually contagious.

"Here?"

"Aye laddie, the Arab Baths – an experience I guarantee you will never forget..."

"What's...er... a *donkey* doing on the roof?" the young man asked.

His father chuckled which quickly became a spluttering cough.

"That donkey," he said when he had regained his composure, "is the means by which we get the water into the baths – it turns connected wheels which scoop water up from the river onto the open pipe which run into the pools inside." The old man pushed open the small door and slowly carried on up the steps to the main entrance to the baths. Once inside the large hall which served as a reception he handed the attendant a small bag of coins.

"Two hours, remember?" he said, coughing slightly again.

"For sure," the attendant replied tucking the bag away under the counter and ushering an Arab servant boy out to take care of them.

"Come," said the old man to his son as he shuffled over the wooden platform to the far wall which was covered with matting and cushions. "Let us change…"

"Change?" The young man looked rather confused.

"Aye laddie, change. Let me explain. See you, these Moors whom some call – in ignorance mind – barbarians, they are ingenious and also nothing if not clean and these baths are the way it is done. Wonderful! There are three rooms here – one hot, one warm and one cold. We start in the hot room which you will see is both very hot and very damp…"

"Wet *and* hot?"

"Aye son, it is next to a large furnace which pumps hot air underneath the room so that when they throw waters onto the floor it evaporates, creating a humid atmosphere – it is wonderful, that feeling of your lungs being cleansed, your skin soaked." He peeled off his thin shirt revealing a body awash with boils, sores and rashes and folded it neatly placing it on the pile in front of him. He was naked now and paused before turning to take the towel being presented to him by the young attendant who had been allocated to them. Wrapping it round him he continued, "So then we go from hot to warm room and then to cold – well, actually, we can go from whichever rooms we please and whichever order that pleases us."

"And this does what, exactly?" The big lad was now also naked save for his towel, his knife tucked into it behind him, looking at his father intently, eyeing his pock-marked skin up and down. "We can sit under a waterfall in Scotland or jump in a loch; we get clean all the same…"

"No son, we get clean but it is not the same. Come," he gestured stepping out of the reception hall into the corridor off which the three rooms were accessed. It was only now that his son saw the tattoo, in blue, across his back. It covered all of his back and was a phrase written over three lines; across his shoulders said ANDREA SCOTIS, underneath was written DUX ESTO, and over his lower back COMPATRIOTES. Not seeing his son's expression on seeing his back the old man continued, "Here our pores are opened in the hot room and totally refreshed when in the cold room. Let me say – there are two pools of fresh, cold water brought to us by yon donkey on the roof. We have our boy here throw this over us when we have come from the hot making us completely refreshed. There is even soap to use in the warm room whilst we relax. You will see – the baths are somewhere you will miss when back in Scotland." The attendant boy opened the door to the hot room and the three of them entered into the empty room and a haze of heat.

"Sit," the young Arab motioned, pointing through the mist to a bench on the far wall.

"I see what you mean," said the young Scotsman wheezing involuntarily as the heat started to work its way through to his lungs. He sat down on the bench leaning back onto the scorching wall. "Ouch!" He sat bolt upright getting his naked back off the wall.

"Ha, ha," his father laughed, again bursting out into a coughing fit. "The oven is on the other side of that wall," he gasped.

"Thanks for telling me!" The Scots lad then placed the palms of his hands tentatively onto the wall behind him. "Bloody hot!" He bent over, chin cupped in his hands, elbows on knees, now taking huge gulps of moist air into his lungs. His father nodded to the boy standing near him who picked up a wooden pail of water from the corner emptying the contents across the floor. A cloud of stem flew up. "Phew," the Scots lad wheezed.

"Aye laddie. 'Tis good, no?"

"Good, aye," replied his son, head still in his hands, staring at his feet.

The pair of them sat there for a while before moving on into the cold room and finally relaxing on some cushions in the warm room once they had both enjoyed a thorough massage by the young Arab boy who was obviously an expert in that particular art. They chatted for a while about the Arab Baths, both agreeing that the experience was one to savour before the father changed his tone to one that was more serious

"Leave us," he said to the Arab boy and turning to his son once the door closed behind their masseur continued, "it is important we talk. It is time for you to know of your destiny." He coughed a globule of phlegm into his hand and wiped it on his trousered thigh. "You must know all, so you can decide."

His son just stared at him. This was a conversation he had been waiting for for seven years, ever since his father first came home with the inked design on his face – he had asked but had been given short shrift. *You shall be told...when the time is right,* is all his father would say. Now it was time. The wait was over. He sat motionless next to his father stone-faced, all ears...

"Today, son – you are to become Dubhshuileach. I am ill and can do our cause no further good..."

"But father...you are Dubhshuileach. How can *I*—"

"Quiet," the old man spluttered, holding up his hand to silence the lad. He coughed once more, hacking up more phlegm into his mouth. Turning, he spat it out onto the wooden floor – it hit with a splat. "Listen," he said. "By today's end you shall be Dubhshuileach and I shall be dead. I have much to tell and you needs must listen carefully." He paused to listen for any noise. Nothing. It would seem that his payment to the attendant had guaranteed their privacy after all; a rather large payment, but worth it – ordinarily these were busy baths. "Now, what I will tell you will set you off on a path of righteousness, it will enable you to have a life that is purposeful, a life that is pure and one that secures your place at the Lord's garden in Heaven. My son, you have been chosen. You are a leader and from this day forth you shall be known as *Dubhshuileach.*"

"But..."

"Shh! Men are wont to follow a rising sun rather than one that sets. It is time for you, my son, to rise."

The young protégé sat in silence, despite the many questions which whirled through his mind. Why now? What of my older brother Cináed? Why has he not inherited the name 'Dubhshuileach'? What path is it I shall take? So many questions poured through his mind. He had to check himself to concentrate on what his father was saying to him – this was a day he had hoped would come but he had never known why.

"The name 'Dubhshuileach' – 'black-eyed one' – refers to the beating our Holy Saint Andrew endured at his martyrdom. He is our saviour and guide and we owe it to him to bring him home to Scotland. Look, son, look at my back," he stood up to show his back.

"Yes father, but what does it say?"

"'Tis Latin, which you needs must study – it says *Andrew be thou leader of the compatriot Scots*. All the Hounds of Saint Andrew have this marking…"

"Hounds of St. Andrew?"

"Aye laddie, a group dedicated to bringing our Saint Andrew, our patron saint, home. He has been abandoned by the faith but not by us. The Lord Jesus himself selected Andrew as his first disciple," he coughed a little and seemed to be becoming a little agitated as he continued with the story, "but was usurped – outshone – by Peter, duplicitous Peter, who ensured Andrew received little mention in the Gospels. Peter coerced Christ into giving him the keys to the kingdom of Heaven – *he was jealous of Andrew's trusted position as first disciple!*" He screeched the last part, his face now red with anger. "Betrayed! By his own brother! The schism between Rome and the East, the New Rome that was Constantinople was *Saint* Peter's doing…" His voice trailed off into a small wheezing fit but the disgust and venom in it had not been disguised by his ill-health. "Peter helped divide Christianity and now Constantinople is lost to the Lord forever. Andrew brought Christianity to the Byzantines, to the Slavs in Novgorod, to the Russians, the Goths, the Varangians and Skifs and what thanks does he get?" He fell silent staring at the beams of sunlight streaming through the star-shaped holes in the ceiling, his face dripping with sweat which stung the open sores on his face which had been opened further by the heat. He smiled to himself as he thought of Andrew sitting in a sauna in Novgorod – legend had it that Andrew was disgusted by saunas; little wooden huts where the depraved whipped themselves with twigs, lashing themselves until they bled. He was sure, though, that Andrew would have liked the Arab Baths, he would have approved – cleansing, sweet-smelling, pure and indulgent. He snapped out of his musings to continue suddenly, "I will tell you what he got – crucifixion…"

"Aye, on an X-shaped cross, hence the Saltire," the lad said feeling quite pleased with himself.

His father looked at him sternly.

"Listen, I say. I will tell truth, so listen well. Yon cross and our nation's flag comes from the Battle of Athelstaneford in Lothian in the year of our Lord 828; white clouds forming the shape in the blue sky as an omen for Angus and his Picts and

Scots who stood opposed to the Anglians who by far outnumbered them." The listener was nodding in agreement. "Angus saw this omen and fought well crushing his enemy." He again looked up to the shafts of light. "But, make no mistake, laddie; the reality is that our beloved Andrew was not crucified on an X-shaped cross but on an ancient tree: an olive tree, in truth."

"But how do you know this?" His son sat agog.

"It has been handed down amongst the Hounds of Saint Andrew for generations and I now hand it to you…"

"Why me, Father? Why not Cináed?"

"Ah, your brother…he who values himself more than his faith or destiny. He weeps for himself, the worm! Cináed crawled back to Scotland months ago to be with his wife; he has the disease also and rejects the Hounds. He is no longer my son…" He sounded genuinely sad at having 'lost' his son but truly believed that a son not dedicated to Andrew was not a son at all. "This brings me back to here; I have the disease also. I have it sorely and will not last until the year's end so you take over, you fulfil your destiny, and you are to become Dubhshuileach." The old man went on to tell his doting son of all the relics he had taken to Scotland; relics he had gained by intimidation and threat, by monies and favour, by fair means and foul. He talked the lad through all the contacts he would need, those who knew of the Hounds, who did not; those who approved and those who did not. He eventually had to give the attendant more money to secure the premises for another couple of hours such was the length and depth of the conversation. He explained that to give his son the best start he had arranged this meeting in Runda so that they could be joined by three others who would assist the new Dubhshuileach greatly. The first was Mehmet the Mamluk who was to bring with him one of Andrew's kneecaps which he had managed to secrete from the Church of Santa Sophia in that greatest of cities, Constantinople. No deal in terms of compensation had been struck but obviously a relic of such importance would command huge amounts of gold or silver. Mehmet was of noble birth bearing the title of Emir of Marmara and had settled in Sevilla after he had worked for King Alfonso as an ambassador to the East. He also offered his services as someone who could negotiate on behalf of the King's merchants, securing trade routes and building up contacts which enabled the exchange of goods with the region. This he had done well. Alfonso had always hoped to convert Mehmet to Christianity but had never managed to as yet

The second invite had gone to Leonard of Ludlowe, who had long been a friend of the old man, the two men having met on Crusade years before. Ludlowe would be a useful contact in England, being of the aristocracy and owning huge tracts of land in the Welsh Marches and Salop.

The third and final guest was a Redfriar who would escort the relic back to Scotland with the newly inducted Dubhshuileach. Peripatetic monks were used often by the Hounds of Saint Andrew to transport relics back to Scotland: more often than not they were unaware of the treasure they guarded. However, Malcolm the Redfriar was *Andrean Prelate* and *Treasurer* of the Hounds of Saint Andrew and had partaken in many such journeys with enthusiasm and a passion.

The new Dubhshuileach had listened to all that his father had explained to him; he had understood everything and agreed wholeheartedly with his father's plan. It had to be done to the letter; he knew this and accepted his part in it. He would lead the Hounds of Saint Andrew to greater glory than had ever been known. Today was a new beginning for them all. He gave his father a hug and sat down next to him, awaiting the first of their guests.

It was not long until they were joined by Mehmet, who arrived clutching a small wooden box. The old man looked up at the newcomer who was dressed in a fine silk robe over baggy trousers and wore long pointed, red boots which curled up at the toes. His olive-coloured features were tickled by a drooping black moustache, which contrasted sharply with a flashing, white smile.

"Ah, finally you are here. I was beginning to wonder if you had had a lapse of memory," the old man wheezed. "You have it?"

"I have," was all he said, glancing at the young stranger and then back to the old Scot.

"My son," he said by way of explanation. "The others, they are here also?"

"In reception." He ignored the man's son and sat down on the bench on the other side of the old man. "You like to see?" He held the box out in front of him.

"You come alone, as agreed?"

"Yes."

"You are sure you were not followed?"

"Yes, I am sure."

"Good," said the young man standing. He moved to sit beside the Turk caressing his father on the shoulder as he passed him. Mehmet flashed him a quizzical look. "So I can see it," he said staring at the box as he sat down.

"You have money?" Mehmet was straight to the point. He always was, never standing on ceremony and never getting involved personally. He was a fixer; he solved problems for people, whether it was sourcing a relic, hiding a fugitive, arranging an awkward delivery or finding slaves for use in the East. He was happy to use his privileged position to create an even more comfortable life for himself. He would not do this forever; he had decided to do another couple of years and then settle down, after all he had been 'fixing' for nearly thirty-five years now. "You have money?"

"Yes…yes, I have *lots* of money, and gold and silver…"

"Open it," the young Dubhshuileach said, rather impatiently, drawing a look from his father.

"The payment is nearby…let us know your price," the old man said, "but first we must see the relic, for confirmation. I have visited the Church of Santa Sophia and seen the item. I will know if this is same…"

Mehmet smiled and with the box balanced on his lap opened the clasp and lifted the lid. The old man let out a gasp and held his chest.

"Father?"

"It is true…it…is…same," he whispered, mesmerised by the lump of bone in the box. Almost in a trance he muttered to himself, "It is time. You know what you must do…your destiny beckons…"

Mehmet looked at him quizzically not seeing the son pulling out the knife. From the corner of his eye he saw the blade flash as it swished through a beam of light but he did not even manage to turn his head to see what was happening before the *sgian* was plunged viciously into his throat. He fell back against the wall thumping his head against the stone, gasping and thinking *he punched me?* But he quickly realised what the warm sensation in his hands was as he clawed at his throat: blood. He tried to scream, blinking up at the ceiling, light pouring in blinding him as he squirmed against the wall. To his right the old man had got up, presumably not wanting any blood on his clothes.

He blinked again and this time it was dark: very dark. And silent. *Am I dead?* He blinked again and peered into the gloom. A flash of light again and he realised that the young Scotsman was standing in front of him, swaying in and out of the shaft of light, knife in hand, its blade dripping with blood. It was slow, gasping, torture as he struggled to get air to his lungs. He wheezed, gurgling and spitting up foamy blood. He held both his hands up around his throat, the warm, sticky liquid oozing through his fingers and down his bright, silk robe. He blinked again…and spluttered. Sheer panic filled his heart as he blinked up, staring into the young Scotsman's eyes – what he saw was not hatred or fury but sheer contentment; someone who was experiencing a cleansing moment: spiritual. The Christians had a word for it. *What was it? And what am I thinking?* There he was dying, slumped against a wall, covered in his own blood and all he could think about was *that Christian word.* He couldn't breathe, he was faint, eyes blurred over, fighting for air and yet his mind was racing not about pain but searching the depths of his mind, in every nook and cranny for *that word: that Christian word.*

Then, reaching out deliberately towards his assailant with a bloody hand, he remembered and slowly mouthing it he slumped over to one side, eyes glazed, his hand still clenched around his throat, shirt awash with blood: *Baptism!*

The room was silent now as the two remaining men stared at one another.

"Me now," the old man said.

*   *   *

Both men looked up anxiously when the young Dubhshuileach walked into the reception area. He placed a little wooden box on the floor by the door as he came in. Ignoring the two seated men he strolled over to the drinking fountain in the middle of the room and took several large mouthfuls. Once finished he looked up, wiping his mouth with his bare arm.

"Ah, you must be Ludlowe…the pleasure is mine."

Ludlowe eyed him carefully, trying not to stare too impolitely but he could not help but notice the lad's similarity to his father. It was uncanny – as if they had gone back in time and his old Crusading friend was standing in front of him, a young man once more.

"You are your father's son, indeed," he remarked.

"Aye, that I am and in more ways than one. Stand…please." Ludlowe got to his feet and was embraced warmly by the young man. "My father spoke highly of you and your help and loyalty as a friend – for that I thank you and hope I can continue to be a friend."

"Well, you have taken on his role and I see no reason why we cannot continue his good work." They stood at arm's length now watched by the other figure in the corner, the Redfriar. Ludlowe looked into the lad's eyes – they were black and cold, soulless. He shivered involuntarily despite the temperate atmosphere. "He is dead?" Dubhshuileach raised his eyebrows. "And Mehmet?"

"Dead also," Dubhshuileach confirmed.

"The attendant?"

"Aye, dead," said Dubhshuileach.

"Excellent!" Ludlowe rubbed his hands together. "You will need a witness then to all this chaos," he laughed nervously.

"Aye, see to it then," remarked Dubhshuileach and turning to the cleric, "Come, fetch the box and we will away, in haste I think. You have arranged for my tattoo?"

"Yes, my lord," said the monk, bowing deeply.

"Let us go then…and then to Scotland."

At that he left the Baths, trailed by the Redfriar carrying the wooden box.

As he left he briefly thought of his father's words – he had been correct as always: this visit to the Arab Baths *would* be one that would stick in his mind *forever*.

CHAPTER ELEVEN

Cramunde, 22nd March, 1286

Massan sat in the Refectory alone, staring at his empty porridge bowl, head in his hands. Despite the warmth of breakfast inside him he still shivered. How did I get involved in all this, he despaired Why are they picking on me? They must know I couldn't kill the King: that I wouldn't *want* to kill the King Everyone knows it was an accident.

"How are you bearing up, young fella?"

Massan did not look up. He knew it was Alasdair, the Brother who had been given the responsibility of his care. He recognised the slow, lumbering speech; a bit glaikit is how the old potter David would have termed it. He liked Alasdair – he seemed a little dotty, somewhat bewildered at times: Massan felt he could relate to that.

"Oh, alright, I suppose..." he mumbled.

"I suppose?"

"Yeah, well...fine."

"Come now laddie, fear not...the truth will out and you are innocent, you say, so the Lord will show of your innocence. You have naught to fear methinks."

"Think you not? And how, Alasdair? How will the Lord prove my innocence? Everyone thinks I murdered the King!"

"Come, now..."

"And I miss Mother...and Aibhlinn," he sobbed now, prostrate over the table.

Alasdair sat down beside him, putting a comforting arm round him.

"Believe me son, you will be cleared. The nobles are worried, that is all. They know not what to do, their King and liege dead, of a sudden. They panic and finding a young lad at the scene, or as near to the scene as possible, they add up the numbers in confusion and end up thinking you are involved. Nobles and mathematics – not a good combination methinks." Massan lifted his head up slightly, sniffing. "And laddie only the nobles know of you – the heralds have been announcing the King's death as an accident, as we all know it was. The people have been told it was an accident so worry not; we will make the nobles realise their impetuousness. Duncan MacDuff is a good young man, from a wise family – he will see things right…he is confused, that is all. Believe me, Prior Callum will sort things out, you will see. He is adept with numbers, and words for that matter – he will show them their mistake…"

"Promise?" Massan sat up now, wiping his red eyes and drawing his sleeve across his nose to wipe the snot away. "Promise?"

"Aye laddie…I promise."

"So what do we do meantime?" Massan asked, apparently placated. "Will you take me to see my mother and sister?"

"Ah…well…we should stay here – the prior's orders; until his return."

"Please, Alasdair…"

"No son, we must stay here at Cramunde, for safety." Alasdair tried to busy himself by fiddling with a candleholder.

"But, I would be with you – you would look after me…just so I could see my family. I miss them…please Alasdair. You already said I have naught to fear, so what could go wrong?"

"You have lessons to learn; and we must teach you…"

"Please Alasdair, I know where they are hiding. We would not be long, not at all. A quick visit to see my mother and wee sister…please. I could learn as we walked…"

Alasdair squirmed. He was not used to being put under this kind of pressure, especially by such a young lad; such a confident young lad. It could not do any harm, could it, he thought. If the lad knows where they are it would not take long, would it? I could teach him Latin words for his surroundings: the different trees, flora and fauna – Prior Callum said I should be a teacher to him. He would be learning; that would be the purpose and if we happened to see his family at the same time then that would be a bonus. He convinced himself.

"How long will it take?"

Hooked! I've hooked him, thought Massan. The best fisherman in the land does it again. All to do now is land him, he thought. "Not long at all, a day if we set out now. We can be back before sundown…"

"Hmm…" Alasdair toyed with his nose, holding it absentmindedly as he spoke. "You have it." Massan's face beamed. "We will go, but it is a learning trip, you hear. If we stumble across your family then that would be fortuitous." He gave Massan a knowing smile. "Agreed?"

"Agreed," said the young lad, grinning from ear to ear.

"Come; let us go then, to Fife…"

*   *   *

John and Fergus' meeting with the Earl of Fife had been difficult to secure what with MacDuff having just had the King found dead practically on his doorstep. They tracked him down to Ravenscraig Castle and had to wait until being able to speak with him. He was a very busy man and they had needed to be forceful in gaining an audience with him. They found him a pleasant man, reasonable and straightforward with a polite air, granting them the respect that the Church sought and required. His wife had taken a keen interest in the situation advising clemency and MacDuff seemed only too willing to heed her womanly instincts. After all, the lad had mentioned that there might have been someone else there that night. He therefore accepted Prior Callum's proposal, deeming it 'worthy and wise'. He also indicated that he did not entirely believe that the young lad was involved in the King's death and that indeed it could well have been just a tragic accident. Words that would be received well back at Cramunde, they thought.

"Two wines, if you have any of the Gascon nectar," announced John as they stepped up to the bar of the inn. It was on their route home; well, slightly off the beaten track but that was a good thing as they valued their privacy as much as an inn could offer them. They were well ahead of schedule, and so well had the meeting with Fife gone, they could afford to refresh themselves on the long walk back to the Queen's ferry. Taking up the wines they were guided by the innkeeper to an empty table in the far corner near an old door. They sat with their backs to the wall eyeing the rest of the room suspiciously. There were only a few people in all, deep in conversation themselves as if not wishing to be seen.

"Slainte!" They clashed goblets together.

"A surprisingly easy task in the end was it not?" John took a mouthful of the fine wine.

"Aye, I think so," replied Fergus.

"MacDuff seemed not as intent on the boy's guilt as we were led to believe."

"Indeed not. And yet he was still vexed over the humiliation caused him by the boy's escape."

"Aye, but that is good; that can be remedied with ease. The important thing is that he seems relaxed about the boy's involvement. Did you notice the others?"

"The others?" Fergus frowned.

"Aye, the others – sitting in the room off the reception area. Before they closed the door," said John.

"Oh...yes...in the room next to us. I saw them but recognised none."

"Well the tall one with the dark hair was the Chancellor and the one sitting to his left was the High Steward. The others I could not see, but it would seem that Fife has more than a few dignitaries to deal with this day."

"Aye, well we got we wanted and here's to that," said Fergus, raising his glass once more. *"Slainte!* What I would like to know is that if Fife is so placid about the whole 'boy situation' why do we hide him away at Cramunde...?"

"Not so loud..." John looked around not quite knowing what to expect or even why he was asking his colleague to speak quieter although he did appreciate the sensitivity of their quest.

"And why is his family stowed away too?" This time Fergus whispered.

"Pardon? Not too quiet!"

"I said, why is his family in hiding as well as the lad?"

"Search me," said John. "Perhaps a certain paranoia, although I thought I heard Prior Callum talking to the lay priest, Malcolm, about a dangerous fellow looking for the lad. Probably nothing…what was that?" He thought he heard the latch of the door but on turning round saw that it was still firmly shut. "My mind is a wandering – perhaps the wine, what say you? Ha, ha..."

"Aye, 'tis good wine," agreed Fergus. "So what of the laddie then, you think Fife will regard him innocent?"

"Yes I think it so, although he seemed to think that something went on yon night but knew not what."

"So…"

"So methinks the boy stays with us until Fife can meet with Prior Callum and they can all find out the reality of that night." He sipped his wine. A strange sound came from behind the door – not a human noise, more like a banging causing him to turn round again sharply. "Did you hear that?"

"Hear what?" Fergus looked confused.

"That noise – I am sure I heard something from behind that door."

"I heard nought. 'Tis your imagination combined with wine, I'm sure."

"No, I really thought I heard a scuffling noise…"

"No, I heard nought."

At that the innkeeper came over.

"Everything alright, Your Holinesses?" This said with a barely disguised mockery which unbeknownst to the clerics was reserved purely for servants of St. Peter.

"Er…fine, sir, but can I ask…do you keep anything behind this door?"

"What, this door?" He looked quizzically, as if the door had appeared from nowhere and that this was the first time he had noticed it. "Why no – only stores and most probably the odd rat or two. Why? Did you hear them in there scuttling about? I surely needs get my shovel out and set to them again!" He laughed heartily as he turned and went back to the bar, Brother John watching him.

"I might have guessed – rats! Anyway where were we?"

"We were discussing the laddie that we think is now *not* involved in the King's death and why it is essential he stays hidden," said Fergus.

"Aye, we were. This *is* good wine," he swished his goblet round swirling some of the red liquid out onto the table top. "Aye, well his folks are having to stay out of sight too – with the old potter at the Binn Village, I think…or thereabouts."

"No they are at Kirkton with the potter's brother – safe near the Kirk," added Fergus.

"Aye, well they seem to think danger lurks for them also."

"Danger by proxy, eh?" Fergus added rather uncharitably.

"Well, who knows? Better safe than sorry is what I say. I think Prior Callum has the rights of it requesting all to stay out of sights until his return. He will know more about this than us to be sure."

"Yes, you are right I am sure. I am perhaps being rather unkind. Safety first..." He stopped as two ragged characters stumbled over to the table next to them and almost fell over the bench next to them. "We should be off?" He looked at Brother John, glancing back to the two strangers now attempting to line up for an arm wrestle.

"Aye, before someone overhears our idle gossip..."

At that the two Redfriars got up heading for the door.

"Thank you innkeeper," John shouted as he opened the door letting in a howling sea wind. The innkeeper waved in reply hoping that John could not see the far door from whence they had come was now open ever so slightly.

*   *   *

"Would you control that fuckin' animal for fuck's sake!" It was a whisper but one that was said with as much venom as had it been shouted at the top of Mool's voice.

"Shh," replied Skate struggling to control the thrashing animal. "Grab its erse, will you..."

"I knew this was too good to be true," started Mool.

"Just grab it and help me get it tied up again in the corner." Skate had the doe in a firm headlock now and it had given up struggling, its hoofs no longer stamping on the wooden floorboards. "That's it," he said, "ease it over here." Together they dragged the beast across the room and bound its legs, leaving it blinking meekly up at them as they resumed their position at the door.

"Now listen," whispered Mool again, Skate giving him an upturned finger in reply.

The drinking den that the Hounds of St. Andrew used as their base saw many different travellers popping in for a drink, even given its secluded location. In fact, the secluded location meant that those that did seek it out usually had something to hide which meant that when Tam the barman guided the unwitting to the seat by the back door there was a great opportunity for the Hounds of St. Andrews to hear something they shouldn't. Many a merchant traveller had been 'relieved' of his money outside after a few wee drinkies; many a weary pilgrim had revealed some relic source when recounting travels. This time, however, the weary travellers appeared in the shape of two Redfriars heading back to Cramunde after a meeting with the Earl of Fife. The two thugs in the backroom could hardly believe their luck when Tam showed them to the table nearest them.

They were able to listen with the door closed, the little window it featured offering them enough to hear and see through, providing its shutter was open. Today they opted to leave the door slightly open so they could bend down aligning themselves with the seated monks. It was not long before secrets started to be revealed.

"Appears that they know of Dubhshuileach: the reference to 'a stranger'," whispered Mool, his head touching the doorframe.

"Aye, and listen…the boy's at Cramunde," whispered Skate as he leaned into the door his hand on the latch keeping it up and the door cracked open. "With the Trinitarians," he added.

"Aye, well shush just now and let's listen…"

They stood by the door for a while listening intently, having to strain to hear what was being said.

Suddenly Skate's hand slipped on the latch causing it to rattle. One of the Redfriars turned round quickly causing them to back off slightly, holding their breaths. Bash managed to lift the latch back into place, closing the door gently before the monk saw him. They waited a few moments and once they could hear that the clerics had resumed their conversation, quietly opened the door's little wooden window which was used to peep into the bar but designed with mesh so as it was not easy to see back into.

Suddenly the doe behind them scrambled up onto its fore legs having slipped its front bindings. Lurching forward it clattered onto the wooden floorboards and tumbled back onto its knees.

"Fuck!" Mool leaped forward to smother the animal with a grubby overcoat that was hanging next to the door. It jerked forward avoiding his attack, the coat only glancing off its beautiful white fur leaving a dirty brown smudge down the flank of the deer. Mool gathered himself immediately and lunged over the doe again, this time covering its head and wrestling it easily to the ground. "Can't even tie a fuckin' decent knot," he mumbled under his breath as he firmly tied the overcoat round the animal's head. Skate ignored the furore and just stood by the door, listening to the events in the bar.

"Everything alright, Your Holinesses?"

He recognised Tam's voice and sighed in appreciation at the attempt to distract the two clerics from the noise the deer had made. Rats! Nice one, thought Skate, realising that Tam saw and heard more than he ever let on and that he was clearly not as slow on the uptake as he made out either – stupid *looking*, yes but certainly not stupid. Skate smiled to himself as he watched the monks' reactions, ignoring Mool who was on the floor in some sort of tangle with the wriggly deer.

"Come on now…out with it…" he whispered, waiting. Suddenly he shivered and all the hairs on the back of his neck stood on end as the monks revealed the one piece of information that had eluded him up until now: the whereabouts of his prey. He could scarcely believe his luck. Now, time for work, he thought as he watched the two monks leave. Rubbing his hands together he turned to Mool who had finally subdued the doe and said, "Come on then, let us to work. Bring that stupid animal."

*   *   *

Drust's little wattle and daub home in Kirkton was only a stone's throw from the Kirk, which made him feel physically that bit closer to God; he was already close with Him spiritually. He felt he had a special affiliation with the Holy Church; he had almost gone into the priesthood as a young man but ended up only cursing the body that the Lord had given him being as it was feeble; susceptible to every virus around. He spent much of his youth tucked up in bed fighting the latest illness that had befallen him although he bore no jealousy towards his elder brother, David, who had always been fit and virile. David followed in their father's footsteps, taking up pottery, although he always insisted that he would never be as good as his father who had earned his living at that most famous village of Wemyss, the capital of Fife's pottery scene. Those that had known their father and witnessed him at his wheel would not argue: he had been one of the masters of the craft.

His knees popped as he got up from the stool in his main room. Actually, the house only had this room but it was separated from his sleeping quarters by a waist high fence made from lengths of hazel. It all made for rather a squeeze for the four of them as they huddled round the fire in the middle of the room, which rather than throw out any heat, only seemed to be making the air fill with smoke.

"Yon thing is always like this first thing in the morning," he said by way of apology. "More kindling methinks, to get it going…"

"Aye, or…we will…(cough)…all be going – leaving that is," spluttered David.

"Open the shutters to get rid of the smoke," added Aibhlinn. "That is what we do."

"Good idea lassie," said Drust, although in truth he had specifically got up to open the shutters. "Oh dear, hear ma kneecaps popping there? Sounds like there is not so much life in them with noises like that…"

"Away wi' ye man. Yer as fit as any o yon youngsters playing out there," said Christina as she helped Drust tie the shutters back, pointing to a group of children who were kicking back and forth a ball made from a pig's bladder and stuffed with hay.

"Aye, you are right, all the same though I would give anything to be able to do that, even when I was their age I would have given anything," replied Drust with a chuckle in his voice. Christina smiled. She admired the way he could laugh at his own situation; many people would be bitter with such a life of malady. She found it difficult to relate to that type of attitude: she herself struggled, trying not to be bitter over the way her husband had been left to suffer by the Lord, dying in agony, a mere husk of a man. The Lord is all-powerful; He should not have let such a good man die such a horrible death. She had fallen out with the Holy Church. This, Drust knew and he hoped that by lodging in his home for this short period of time he might be able to guide her back into the arms of the Lord. He had never met anyone who had 'lost' their Faith, but he was worried that Christina might be losing hers, yet he knew that only by reaching out to the Lord would she find true happiness for herself and her child. He would help her with that.

"Ah, better already," she said as a cloud of smoke billowed past her. "I must go home this morning to do some work on the spinning-wheel – I still have mouths to feed. Aibhlinn, you can bide here until I return this evening. I will feed the animals for you."

"What if you miss some?" The little girl looked worried.

"I will be extra careful and will watch them to see that they all eat then. Just to be on the safe side," she added.

"And you will be back tonight?"

"Aye sweetheart, before dark. I shall recite a poem for you at bedtime…"

"Hooray! *The Ballad of Sir Patrick Spens*?" It was her favourite and she knew every word, sometimes even correcting her mother at times.

'Aye, and tomorrow we shall visit Massan if David or Drust will escort us," she checked the men's reactions.

"Well of course," said David. "I shall come with you to the Binn Village; I have some pots to throw I am sure. We can return together."

"Aibhlinn and I can go for a wee walk then, if my knees hold out. Perhaps we could do a spot of fishing," said Drust.

"No we cannot, that is Massan's job," squealed Aibhlinn.

"Aibhlinn!" Christina looked annoyed.

"No, she has the rights of it; indeed it is the young man's role. Perhaps we can go to the beach to collect seaweed," Drust said, looking to Aibhlinn for approval.

"Yes, that would be nice," she conceded.

The adults smiled at one another.

"See and behave yourself with Drust then lassie. I'll hear no bad reports about you when I return," said Christina and to Drust, "Dinnae be takin' any lip from her, she can be a cheeky wee bisum when she puts her mind to it."

"Right you are," replied Drust.

"Come then," said David, reaching for his overcoat, "I'll be wanting this today methinks."

Christina leaned over and gave her daughter a kiss on the top of her head and blowing into the girl's golden locks gave her a little squeeze also. At that she gathered up her things and she and David set off for home.

*   *   *

The two Redfriars had been shown out of the castle grounds at Ravenscraig before Duncan MacDuff, the Earl of Fife returned to the Quiet Room where his other meeting had been taking place. The interruption of the monks had been a welcome one for him and under usual circumstances he would not have allowed it being that his other meeting was dealing with matters of State. On this occasion he took the chance to escape for a while to allow himself to gather his thoughts and to seek guidance from his wife, whose opinions he valued. She had also expressed an interest in the young lad who had escaped from his custody, judging him a 'frightened wee rabbit being chased by slavering hounds'. Lady Marjory would never know how accurate that description was.

The couple remained seated in the Solar Room staring at the door at the far end which led to the meeting. Fife looked worried. He knew he was impulsive and apt to make decisions without thinking through all the implications, which was why he valued his wife's opinion: she was his opposite. He felt that they complimented each other as she was very much the type of person to weigh up all the odds using all the available facts to come to a rational judgment; she had a logical brain, enabling her to see things far more clearly than he, and she was adept at removing emotions from influencing her decisions. He loved her more than she would ever know; he loved everything about her. He loved her beauty; he loved her personality, shy in company, vivacious when they were alone; he adored her sense of humour, how she could see the amusement in most things. Of course, she could be serious too, deadly serious, and he valued her opinion more than any other person he knew. He missed her when she was not there, craving her even more than when she was. He wanted to make her happy, but although he desired her love and tried to please her when they made love, he felt that the infrequency of their lovemaking was more down to his sexual inadequacies than any lack of wanting to please her. He sometimes felt he loved her too much. Why else would he be panting on his back, satisfied, while she craved him still to be in her arms?

"My love," she started, clasping his hands in hers, "fear not. You needs must only go with what is within your heart..."

"But..."

"Sshh, my love...I can see the fear in you and it is a fear of someone who only wants to do the right thing. A fear that responsibility brings to a young man, but you are man enough; man enough to let your heart help you make the right decision. Our Lord and Saviour will guide that tender heart of yours, fear not."

"Aye, you are right as always, but our King is dead and his body lay cold on my land, possibly slain if this lad has the rights of it. He made mention of seeing some person or some *thing* that night. I could never forgive myself..."

"Fret not," she reassured, lifting his hand up to her mouth and kissing it tenderly.

"I could never forgive myself," he continued, and then in a whisper, "if the Hounds are involved. My father's 'gift' to me – patronage of such a rabble...and that man! I wonder if my loyalties are not misplaced sometimes although he has protected my family in the past. What am I to do?" He turned to her in desperation.

"Well, you deal with the first thing first and as such you attend your meeting thinking only of what must be decided therein. This man Dubhshuileach, Rossend or whatever his name, you can muse over later."

"We only decide on funeral arrangements and when we meet for *Parlement*. It should not be overlong to decide such," he wiped his forehead. "I go now and shall see you anon, my love. Will you arrange for food to be brought in and for something especial to be prepared for this evening?"

"I will, my lord," said his wife, curtseying as she did so.

MacDuff kissed her passionately and straightening himself up, rejuvenated, marched into the Quiet Room to resume the meeting with his peers.

CHAPTER TWELVE

"It must be here somewhere…" Beege scrambled down through the bushes onto the main Kynkorn to Kirkton track which wound its way through beech woodland set in the coastal hillside. "You know not where it is?" All he got from Bash in reply, who was now scratching his head, was one big, long, rasping fart. "Is that all you can do? Know you where it is, fart-master?"

Bash looked up and down the path.

"Here, I thought…here," he pointed to a thicket and waded his way into it discovering no cave. "It is hidden by a clump of bushes like this," he shouted clawing his way back out to join Beege on the track. He checked both ways trying to get his bearings but the path was well enclosed by trees and undergrowth allowing him no clear view of where they were. "Come…west I am thinking…this way." He headed off in the direction of Kirkton with Pettycur Beach down below him to the left. They followed the track until they came to a small clearing which felt familiar. To their right the scrub gave way to a sheer cliff which shot upwards twenty feet, which they realised was where their ancestors had lit beacons to guide ships along the Firth of Forth. This particular beacon spot was situated atop this crag by the side of the steep path which headed up and towards the Binn Village forking off right and back down to Kynkorn along the way; the path known as the High Road. They checked their track once more for any signs of MacDuff or Buchan's men and saw none. The patrols had thinned out now and it seemed that some of them were merely making pretence at searching for clues to the King's death, believing that the whole affair was accidental. Nothing out of the ordinary had been found at the scene originally so why did the authorities expect to find something now? It was all a waste of time, they said privately. Regardless of the soldiers' current languid attitude, the two Hounds of Saint Andrew would not become complacent given their sponsor and they agreed to look up and down the track once more just to be on the safe side.

"Clear," said Beege turning and heading to the bushes on the other side of the clearing from the cliff where Dubhshuileach's hidden cave was. "How in the Lord's name did he find this in the dark?" he asked of Bash whilst squeezing through the gorse with his arms above his head. His thick woollen leggings protected his legs but he could not help but wonder how Dubhshuileach had managed to get through in his bare legs and in the dark!

"Beats me," replied Bash, "but if there is ever a man to defy rational thinking it will be that man…"

"Aye yer right there," said Beege as he disappeared into the cave.

"I'll be waiting here then?"

"Aye," came the reply from within.

Bash wandered back to the pathway and surveyed the approaches strolling down to the first bend in both directions. He saw three men scouring the shoreline in the distance but no-one anywhere near to disturb them. He sauntered back to the clearing.

"You found it, falcon eyes?" No reply. He waited, listening with bated breath, hearing nothing. "You still in there?" This time he scraped a little way into the gorse. Still he heard nothing. He cupped his hands round his mouth and shouted. "Beege, you in there?"

"Aye, be quiet. I cannae find it. Oh, got it!"

There was a faint chink as he picked the bag up and seconds later he reappeared once more holding his arms up over the bushes, his right hand clutching a shiny red bag with gold stitching round its edges.

"Well done, falcon eyes. Your Hounds' name should be 'Falcon' not Beege with the eyesight you have…"

"No, my friend, Beege is all I need as a name; names are not important although I believe yours is well earned," said Beege.

"You were given it why?"

"That I cannot say as you well know, *Bash*," he emphasised his colleague's nickname dramatically. "Our names are not important: what is important is this bag of coins which we must now take to Rossend." He eyed the grey sky. "We needs must hurry to be there afore noon." At that he brushed past Bash and headed off towards the path leading west towards Kirkton and Rossend, which lay less than two miles beyond.

The two men had a quick look round as they left the glade but not even the falcon eyes of Beege noticed the two figures atop the crag looking down on them in amazement.

*   *   *

Massan and Alasdair left the House of the Trinitarians straight after breakfast with Alasdair excusing them by telling the other Brothers that they were on a nature walk. Massan had shown some interest in the hives that the Redfriars kept for bees and Alasdair was able to use this curiosity as a means by which they could leave without attracting any suspicion. They agreed to be back by nightfall which meant that they would have to travel fast if they were to travel the twenty-odd miles to the Binn Village. They made good time catching the boatman at the Queen's ferry, just before he slipped anchor. The crossing was uneventful with the boatman ignoring them once accepting payment. Once over the river, Alasdair hired a horse from the nearest inn which doubled as a staging post for fresh horses.

"I did not know monks rode horses…"

"Not as a rule, but in exceptional cases it has been known. Think you can sit up in front of me, young man?" asked Alasdair.

"Of course, I can ride a horse on my own," replied Massan, "I learned when I was young. This last comment made Alasdair smile: you are still young, he thought.

The two of them then made light work of the journey through Abirdaur via the coastal route, skirting round Rossend and Kirkton and up the trail towards The Binn, Massan pointing out things of interest on the way whilst Alasdair tried to steer the conversation to the Latin names of the various species of tree they passed. Massan struggled with the Latin names but surprised his tutor with his knowledge of the local names, recognising Hazel, Birch, Rowan and Yew easily.

"Rowans protect us from witches and fairies," he announced at one stage.

"Aye," replied Alasdair guiding their horse up the steep, twisting loan to a break in the woods. "*Sorbus aucuparia.*"

"And Yews are bad…they represent death, do they not?"

"Well, it has been said, yet they are taken more to be symbols of immortality. We shall rest here a while," said Alasdair pulling up the horse, "to give this fellow a chance to catch its breath." He patted its sweaty neck and dismounted. "*Sorbus aucuparia,*" he said again this time tying it to one. "Here, let me help you down."

Massan ignored the outstretched hand, jumping down clumsily, "I can manage," he said. "What have you in the satchel?"

"Our lunch," replied Alasdair, "crab and oatmeal. You like crab?"

"Aye! Crab is one of my favourites but we hardly ever catch any."

"Aye, well perhaps it is time we showed you the secret. There are special ways to catch them: it depends on where you look for them. Where do you fish?"

"Come, I'll show you. We should be able to see from here," said Massan heading for the edge of the cliff. "It's called the Black Rock."

"Ah! Perhaps it is the place we know as the Burnt Island."

"Beege, you in there?"

Man and boy stopped in their tracks.

"Hear you that?" asked Alasdair. Massan nodded slowly. "Listen…" Alasdair put his finger over his mouth to indicate silence. "Come," he whispered, crouching down as he approached the edge of the cliff, Massan now behind him flat on his belly. The two of them peered over to see a man standing in some bushes down to their left, seemingly talking to the rock face. They watched the scruffy, fair-haired man in silence and looked at one another in amazement as a second man appeared from the rocks.

"A cave!" whispered Massan excitedly.

The second man was brown of skin, wiry with muscular arms and he held aloft a scarlet bag which glinted gold as it swayed above his head. They looked on, speechless as the two men below covered their disturbance to the bushes checking the path both ways before heading off down towards Kirkton.

"What think you?" Massan asked, sitting up cross-legged.

"I think they are not Fife's men and they are up to no good. Why else do they seem so cautious?"

"Aye, and methinks it is but only a mile or so from where the King was murdered…"

"Murdered?"

"Well, died…but I am sure someone else was there that night. It cannae be just a boar that tumbled me – it was over big for a boar."

"That is as may be laddie, but what is this pair of ruffians up to?" Alasdair looked puzzled, "And what was in yon bag?"

"Evidence? Treasure?" offered Massan.

"Could be…"

After a quick bite to eat they decided to head on up to the Binn Village which they agreed they should make sometime in the afternoon. They saw no-one else on the remaining part of the journey and after a while they pulled up outside the village and walked down to Massan's home only to discover that it was empty.

"Are you looking for your mother?" It was one of the elders of the village who had seen them ride up the little thoroughfare that dissected the houses. He was balding with rotten teeth, making Massan hold his breath whenever he spoke. "She is with David, the potter's brother: in Kirkton I think."

"We are grateful," said the monk, giving Massan a look meaning that they should have known that. "Know you where he lives?"

"No," was the stern reply. "Are you not biding with your mother?" the man asked Massan.

"Yes…well, no," was all the lad could manage, now annoyed with himself for bringing them here and not Kirkton. He should have known; should have remembered.

"He is with us for the moment…to learn. He is being given an education."

"Is that so?" said the elder, pausing. Then he turned and hobbled away.

"Kirkton now?" asked Massan.

"Alas, we have not the time for another such journey…"

"But, it is on the way…"

"Massan, listen to me, we have not the time now; it is a lost cause today. We must head back to catch the Queen's ferry. We must return another day once we know where your mother and sister bide. I have decided and will hear no argument. Now come…"

*   *   *

Christina and David headed up out of Kirkton at a brisk pace.

"Hold up woman, I'm no' as young as I look," panted David as he struggled to keep up with the pace.

"Apologies…I was far away then. I just cannae help thinking over what Massan said the other day. About there being someone else there I mean."

"Aye. It does sound a wee bit strange and judging by the size of the thing that knocked him o'er it could well have been a horse and rider. Maybe it was the King himself…"

"Aye that thought had occurred to me…I just know the laddie himself couldnae have done it. It's just stupid to think he would. Why would he?" She stopped herself before she went off on a rant but she felt helpless again.

"Well Prior Callum will return soon and we shall meet with our Lord Earl of Fife. Methinks sense will prevail once men of such wisdom set their minds to it…so worry not."

The two of them walked the rest of the way, the best part of three miles, in silence. Christina worried about all sorts of things over which she had no control: her son's plight, her husband's death, the King's death, the stranger who had been looking for them, and even her spinning work which paid for their food. She was troubled. She needed to get some work done but found it difficult to know where and when to start. She decided that the best policy would be to transfer her things down to Drust's home so she could work *and* keep an eye on Aibhlinn. Anyway, it was probably not a good idea to be seen around home before their meeting with the prior and MacDuff, especially if the stranger were to come calling again.

They reached the village well before noon and stopped at the head of the village exchanging pleasantries before heading into their respective homes. Before long Christina set about gathering up all her tools and equipment and setting them down outside: distaff, pins, a trussel of wool, and even a spindle which she never used as she was only ever involved at the preparation stage. Little did she know that she had been watched from the moment she and David had arrived at the village. Of course they had seen various neighbours and exchanged pleasantries on the way through, and of course some people had peeked out of their front doors or through their shutters, but Massan's mother and the old potter had been observed by eyes that had been glued to the approaches to the village; eyes that had been on vigil watching for this very moment, the moment she revealed to them which one of these little wattle and daub houses was that of her and her family. These were most certainly not nosy neighbours.

She crossed over to the pottery and rapped on the door.

"David?"

"Aye, come in hen," he said.

She entered. David had his tunic sleeves rolled up and already had wet, muddy hands. He waited to hear what she had to say, hands dripping onto the hay-covered floor, which quite frankly Christina thought should have been changed a few weeks ago.

"Erm…I…er…"

"Come now lassie, out with it. You have something to say; well just say it."

"I was thinking…about Aibhlinn and Massan…and my spinning…and…"

"And thought it might be for the best that we move your things down to Kirkton and spend more time there and less time here…until we meet with MacDuff."

Christina was dumbfounded; how on earth had he known that? She stood wide-eyed, searching for something to say but what was there to say?

"Would you mind?"

"Of course not," he smiled. "I did actually see you putting yer spinning things outside yer front door," he said. "I am not a reader of minds as you may have thought."

"I did wonder," she said as she turned to leave. She stopped and turned back to face him. "Only, I do feel worried being here what with that man looking for us – you understand?

"Of course I do. Now shall we head?"

"Thanks," she said and turning once again she left.

The two of them got themselves organised; Christina fed her geese and chickens, pouring an excess of the feed over the back plot so as they would last at least a few days on their own. I will check on them in a couple of days, she thought. She was confident they would last over a week, they were not stupid after all, but she had never mentioned that to Aibhlinn as it would demean the importance of her daughter's job. David dried his hands off and grabbed a few belongings then swept up the smelly hay, tipping it out into the main street. He had noticed Christina's reaction when she had come in earlier and realised that he should do something about the smell from his floor.

They were heading back down through the village and out down the loan towards the coast once again at around noon. One of the elders, a little man with bad teeth, waved to them as they left the village and all the time two pairs of eyes watched their every move.

*   *   *

Skate had taken up position at the bottom of the village, sitting amongst the forest of Scots Pine which dominated the scene. He wore leggings which hinted at the colour of the bark of the trees: a sort of blue-green. His thick overcoat covering a knee-length tunic was a dim reddish-orange, splattered with grass and mud stains. A long hood with a fringe down to his elbows covered his shaven head. Next to him lay a wicked-looking, broad-bladed sword with a distinctly rounded tip. A bag was thrown over his shoulder; it moved as something wriggled inside it. He was the first to see them. He watched as they appeared up the track and crossed the loan, heading to the first of the village's wee houses. A crooked smile crept across his face as it sunk in that here was their quarry.

The scar-faced Mool also sat just within the tree line, his red hair blowing in the breeze, but he was further up the hill, almost three hundred yards away from Skate. His thick legs were bare despite the cold as were his muscular arms, one tattooed up the inside with the mark of the Hounds of St. Andrew: *Andrew be thou leader of the compatriot Scots* – in Latin. He could see the two figures stop and chat in the middle of the road and then duck into their homes. Just what he wanted: he now knew where her home was. Excellent!

Sitting next to Mool was not only his Jedart axe, a kind of polearm with a sharp, curved blade with a vicious hook but also, the white deer, motionless, its legs and feet well and truly trussed up. He ran a chubby, dirty finger over his facial scar: drawing it down the length from the top right of his brow over the bridge of his nose and onto his left cheek. He held his finger there for a while, watching the scene and when Christina walked over to the pottery and rapped on the door he traced the scar's line back up again.

He twisted his torso and fumbled to reach his sporran which had slipped so far round his side it was almost behind him. Pulling out some long, iron pins he started to count them. Not long now, he thought, losing count and having to start again. His eyes narrowed as he concentrated, his face twisting into an evil grimace. Ten. Now they will see my real skills come to the fore, he thought. It may be that at my weakest I am a match for ten men; it may be that hundreds have fallen to my blade, but my true strength will now out: warrior I am and always will be, he thought, but witch-pricker is the role that sends the blood pumping through my veins like no other. And it's witch-pricker that I must be soon.

The two Hounds of St. Andrew sat in amongst the trees carrying out their surveillance until Christina and David finally grabbed all their belongings and headed off towards Kirkton. Skate watched until they disappeared and got up and walked over to Mool who had started counting his pins again. He sat down beside him.

"Shall we go down then?" he asked.

"No, we wait a little…nine, ten!" He tucked the pins back in his sporran. "They may return so we sit awhile."

"Aye, so be it…"

Skate played with the tip of his sword as they sat, tapping it gently on the wriggling bag on his knee. Mool just sat toying with the iron pins, staring down at the village and checking every movement.

Shortly, two more figures appeared; this time they came from the left, coming down the hill; it was a Holy Man and a boy pulling a horse by its reins.

*   *   *

Darkness had fallen and a fine drizzle had begun by the time the two Hounds of Saint Andrew left their cover, scurrying down to the sleepy village through the undergrowth, dragging with them the white deer which was stubbornly resisting. They had waited until the curfew bell had been rung, watching the shutters close over windows house by house, and waiting for all the fires to be put out. They slipped into the back plot of Christina's home unseen, making sure they disturbed none of the birds and set about picking the simple lock which fastened the door.

Once inside they set about their task with gusto. Skate reached inside his bag and pulled out a black-looking toad which he held tightly in one hand as he unlatched the doors to a little wall-mounted basket made of strips of hazel.

"Easy does it," he said as he plopped the toad in, shutting the doors quickly to block its escape. Next, he took two wooden crucifixes out of the bag and placed them on the floor. "You fuckin' done yet?"

"No," answered Mool. "I could do with a hand."

Skate held the animal while Mool tied up its legs double-checking the knots to ensure no repeat of its earlier escape attempt.

"Heave…"

The two men lifted the jerking beast up onto a hook in the main rafter which was normally used for hanging up fish and game. It held firm.

"Ha," Skate laughed. "Let's just fuckin' leave it."

"No, idiot. Pass me my Jedart…"

"Let me do it!"

"I told you – this part is important. Not for brainless thugs like you," said Mool, snatching the Jedart from Skate as he spoke.

"Why, you…"

"Shh Skate," he held a finger over his lips, "I jest, 'tis a joke, but this *is* important and needs be done with a careful hand. 'Tis my area of expertise, one of them anyways," he chuckled, "and with respect our orders are to be followed by the letter." Skate scowled. "Stand back," he motioned with his arm, trying to move Skate but realised quickly Skate was not going to give way. "As you wish," he said turning and plunging the blade and hook deep into the deer's soft underbelly ripping it upwards to its throat with the hook in one mighty two-handed thrust. A sudden shriek of pain went up followed by silence as the animal hung dead swaying gently from side to side gravity slowly helping push its innards down and out. Skate leaned in further to inspect the damage, his face splattered with the animal's blood. "A perfect, straight line. Top to toe, you might say," said Mool, admiring his own handiwork, "Now step back lest you want wet feet." This time Skate moved back as Mool drew his dirk and stuck it in just below the thigh. Using both hands he drew it methodically across until it met the original slash allowing the animal's internal organs to finally spill out. He hacked at them allowing them to slop out onto the floor and felt the still warm blood gush over his hands. He then methodically repeated the process drawing a line across from the other side.

Skate watched in awe, mesmerised by the sadistic butchery. He wiped his eyes and gently ran his fingers over the bristles on his head as if pulling himself out of his trance. "No wriggling now is it, the wee shite?"

"Just give me the bag," said Mool, "and finish off what you are doing." Skate handed him the bag and picked the crucifixes up. "Not an obvious place mind," he said watching Skate move towards the front door. "In with the toad for one and on the back door for the other," he added as started to stitch up the animal's wounds up, "and remember, upside down." Inverted, he thought, just like your brain.

Before long the two men were finished. Laughing and joking they set off towards Rossend Castle, content that the day had gone well, Skate reliving the deer's final moments every step of the way.

CHAPTER THIRTEEN

Stokesay Manor House, Salop, England, 28th March, 1286

The three Hounds of Saint Andrew had made it down to the middle of the Welsh Marches in less than seven days due to the insistence of Dubhshuileach that they travel with haste, covering a minimum of fifty miles each gruelling day. Bash and Beege had met him at Rossend, handing over the bag of coins which he squirreled away. They left immediately.

They travelled in the shadow of the Long Mynd, a long escarpment which drew them south until they met the River Onny which they then followed for about three miles. Here they took the old roman road, the main Shrewesburie-Ludlowe route bringing them to the west of the manor house, which they could make out in the distance adjacent to a large pond. Tenants ploughed the fields to the north-west which the men skirted and soon the impressive west range of the complex came fully into view resplendent in sunshine, its whitewashed walls gleaming. Pigs foraged in the nearby woods, squealing and grunting a welcoming chorus. They followed the moat round past the north tower and presented themselves to the stone gatehouse which was built from local stone and topped, like the rest of the buildings, with sandstone slate from the nearby ridge of Wenlock Edge. The whole place reflected a man with taste; a man with an eye for the best in modern design.

"Friends from Scotland to meet with Leonard de Ludlowe," shouted Dubhshuileach in response to the gatekeeper who challenged them from a first floor window.

"Not much of a castle is it?" said Beege eyeing the place which seemed far too 'pretty' for his liking. "Wouldn't take long to take this place I'd wager, storming or besieging."

"Aye, Ludlowe does have a taste for elegance, but it is strong enough for these parts with the Welsh submitting to Longshanks barely two years ago," said Dubhshuileach, "and I tell you that it is a peace that Ludlowe welcomes as he is ever the hunter: the hunting grounds here are excellent. I helped him celebrate getting his royal charter of free warren about five years ago and that first ever day of hunting here was as good as I have seen anywhere."

The drawbridge started to creak and chains chinked as it started lowering, revealing a small passage with a large wooden gate at the end. The wicket gate within opened and a young man popped out.

"Enter," he said. "My Lord Ludlowe welcomes you heartily and asks that you accompany me to his private quarters in the north tower. Follow me."

They followed the gatekeeper, Bash taking particular interest in the mechanisms behind the drawbridge as he walked past. The splendid courtyard, enclosed by an imposing curtain wall about thirty feet tall was strewn with builders' materials which were being used to complete the south tower. Currently the weak link in the complex, the south tower, had been demolished and was now being rebuilt with plans to crenellate, if Ludlowe received the requisite permission from his King.

They passed the stables, a buttery, and the kitchens, from where a pig squealed in agony as the butcher set to work.

Entering the large hall they followed the gatekeeper up a flight of stairs, the treads of which were made from solid tree trunks, with a rope banister looping up and round to the door, leading into the north tower. This room was full of barrels of cider and wine, the pungent aroma escorting them up the next timber staircase and leaving them as they closed the door having entered Ludlowe's incredible second floor reception room. The guests, Bash and Beege in particular, were visibly impressed almost not noticing Leonard de Ludlowe sitting amongst plush, velvet cushions toying and untwisting his moustache whilst warming himself in front of a large stone fireplace, its wood and plaster hood directing the smoke up and out the chimney. Class, thought Dubhshuileach, no smoke filling this room.

"My good friend, you look well, as ever," the tattooed man greeted his host heartily as he stood up, the two embracing each other in a warm hug. "My associates..." Ludlowe nodded to the others.

"Welcome to the three of you. Sit! Sit! Wine? Cider? What to drink, friends?"

"Three ciders it must be," answered Dubhshuileach.

The gatekeeper nodded to his master and vanished, returning with a servant a few moments later with four jugs of cloudy cider.

"Looks awful," Bash breathed to Beege who, looking at his jug, indicated his agreement with raised eyebrows.

"Your journey was uneventful?"

"Aye," nodded Dubhshuileach. "We travelled with speed...to do your bidding, you understand?"

"Yes, I appreciated your help against this turd of a man. He...he truly infuriates me..."

"Aye, that we know. Remember Yarmouth?" Dubhshuileach took a glug from his jug. "Oh, this is nice," he said glancing at his colleagues who now having supped theirs agreed.

"Yes, how could one forget? But Yarmouth is not the half of it: this man, I believe, is now arranging for shipments to be swapped, his inferior wool for mine. The cheek of it! The liberty!"

"And you want us to sort him out?"

"*I want* that he stops, immediately! No roughing up you understand? I am not a thug. I am a man of honour, a gentleman. But enough is enough! It is time to come to an arrangement...one that is to the benefit of all parties..."

"Hmm..."

"One that means we can both trade and both maximise our profits...I would like you to propose an alliance..."

"An alliance?" Dubhshuileach looked confused. "An alliance?"

"Yes. To benefit us both," said Ludlowe as if that explained everything.

"This turd, as you say, this turd has been stuck to the sole of your shoe for sometime. This turd is in your hair, in your affairs, bespoiling your trade, besmirching the very name of Leonard de Ludlowe...and you want me to 'propose an alliance'..."

"It must be done, man. I have neither time nor patience, nor for that matter the inclination to go to war with this man. He is an irritant. And besides he holds the keys to Yarmouth and perhaps I too could benefit from his holding of such keys."

Bash and Beege looked slightly confused by all this but watched as the expression on Dubhshuileach's face changed.

"Sirrah!" he said rather too loudly. "This is a man who, by his very actions, needs cutting down in size. He is not a man we...you should be negotiating with. He should be stamped on! Your attitude has been softened by wealth: I find a very different Ludlowe from the one I met first in Runda."

Ludlowe flushed whilst trying to ignore the last comment. "Yes, yes, I agree, he needs to be stamped on, but this is easier. Besides, he has items which you may find interesting..."

"Items?"

Ludlowe stood up and wandered to one of the three, unstained, feature windows which allowed a breathtaking view out over the nearby Church of St. John the Baptist with its little graveyard creeping up to the moat, and across the floodplain to the surrounding woods. He gazed out for a moment, seemingly oblivious to his guests.

"It is beautiful, is it not?" he said staring out of the glass.

"Aye, it is. You said items..."

"And so peaceful," Ludlowe added.

"Leonard, you mentioned items, what items?"

"Ah! Yes," he snapped out of his daze, "the very small matter of wood," he said.

"Wood?"

"Yes, a very particular kind of wood...olive wood..."

"You jest!" Dubhshuileach was on his feet in a flash.

"That I do not; it is truth. Gatacre still has the relic stolen in Yarmouth."

"The little..."

"But," interrupted Ludlowe, "he knoweth not what he has. And yet he keeps it locked away."

"Where?" asked Bash, barely able to contain his excitement. "Where?"

"Where is it hidden?" asked Beege, joining in.

Dubhshuileach now stood at the window watching the vicar flailing about, seemingly swiping at the air above and around him like a man possessed. "Why is yon vicar waving his arms about like a madman?" He turned to face Ludlowe. "You said items: plural."

"Yes. He is is said to have the nails that were used at His death."

"Saint Andrew's death? His crucifixion? He has the nails from then?"

"Yes," said Ludlowe.

"And he is aware that they are as such? But, he knows not what the wood is?"

"He is one of those who believes that Andrew was crucified on an X-shaped cross. He is not privy to the truth," added Ludlowe, "and our friend in the churchyard is no doubt swiping at his honeybees. He is not a very accomplished beekeeper, as you can see…"

"So, how do we get the relics? Are they to be part of the negotiations…for the alliance?" chipped in Bash who, remarkably, had kept his flatulence under control since arriving at Stokesay.

"Yes, you can negotiate them into the deal if you can, offering him one-tenth of all profits from my trade which passes through Yarmouth, providing we can come to some arrangement concerning the taxing of same trade. Your payment shall be ready on your return."

"And where can I find this Gatacre?" asked Dubhshuileach, sitting down once more and studying the red clay tiles adorning the walls.

"Why he lives at Gatacre Hall. But, you may find him via the Church of All Saints at Claverley which is nearby: he even has an underground passage leading to the church. It is said that is where he keeps all his relics, shared with the church."

"Claverley?"

"Yes, 'tis around twenty-five miles to our north-east; there is an old track which follows the Wenlock Edge, through Hope Dale and up to Much Wenlock where you can hire a guide to take you the rest of the way." Dubhshuileach leaned forward in his seat. "No, wait," continued Ludlowe, "I will provide a man to guide you to Claverley, 'tis the least I can do."

Suddenly they all seemed to notice the smell of roast pork drifting in through one of the open windows.

"Let us eat!" announced Ludlowe.

"Aye," said Dubhshuileach, "and then we go to Claverley…"

*   *   *

Less than twenty miles to the north of Stokesay, as Leonard de Ludlowe met with his guests from Scotland, Prior Callum, Brother Malcolm and Bernard de St. Clair were recounting tales of their travels in fantastic detail. The Cistercian Abbey of Buildwas, sprawling over twenty-two acres of land, sat on the south bank of the River Severn. The whole complex was an off-white colour having been treated with lime wash. Some of the buildings were joined by masonry painted deep red, a colour the Scots had noticed a lot in this area. They were sitting in the parlour, one of the only rooms where talking was permitted, the Cistercians having taken vows of silence, having a very loud conversation where Bernard retold his tale of being shipwrecked, captured by Moors and finally ransomed by their hosts. The reason the conversation was so loud was because the Abbey's silence was being broken rather dramatically by a shipment of thirty oaks being delivered, the shouts of men and noise from the horse and oxen being used to drag each one down from the river, echoing around the walls of the buildings. This delivery supplemented the timber gained by assarting, or land clearance, so despite its aim of self-sufficiency the Abbey still had to maintain its contact with the outside world.

"And that is how I ended up here," finished Bernard. "I have had many a Scots noble on board my ships which gives me great honour and pride, so to be requested for this mission of national importance esteems me."

"Your name is one that is known over Scotland as being one who knows the waters of Scandinavia better than most. The delicacy of our predicament means that only the best will do," said Callum, "and hence, your hosts have been recompensed and we make haste for St. Andrews and my Lord Bishop."

"Your Holiness, what of the scriptorium and the library? We must indulge ourselves whilst in the presence of such a fine library at the very least," asked Malcolm, giving away the fact that he could read which was against the principles of being a lay brother. Malcolm was, however, a special case being that he had originally entered the priesthood, learning to write as he progressed. He had found the life difficult at first as a young man, and when asked to don the robes of a fighting man had done so on the condition he was able to 'demote' himself to lay brother. This only served to make him all the more studious in theology and the psychology of man.

"The library is especial?" asked Bernard. "I have been here two weeks and have seen nothing of it."

"It is one of the very best, I can say with surety. Over one thousand books, I wager, many of which were written here in the scriptorium: theology, spirituality, great travels, language and writings of the monastic fathers, the subjects themselves are wide and varied. Abbot Joseph has whetted our appetite by mentioning some of the titles here."

"When do we leave for Scotland if your instructions are to make haste?"

"I do not envisage spending long here. Perhaps you would indulge me by allowing us to spend the night here, thus allowing Malcolm and me to study the wonderful array of books."

"Good Prior, it would be remiss of me not to insist on it," said Bernard.

"Many thanks," said Malcolm, thinking of the literary treasure trove awaiting them; the Abbot had mentioned the book by Hugh de Fouilloy, *The Cloister,* which Malcolm particularly wanted to read, being a classical depiction of claustral life.

"Indeed, we are grateful," said Callum, standing up. "Shall we walk?" he opened the old wooden door and stepped out into the sunshine bathing the cloister, which was alive with activity. This square garth with its flowers and herbs was surrounded by tiled walkways, again a deep red, which managed to cut their way across, slicing the beds into smaller squares. Apple and pear trees dotted the edges near the covered walkway which surrounded the area. Monks walked up and down in silence, criss-crossing over the garth and in and out the arches in silent meditation. Beds were tended. Books were read. Callum could not help thinking that considering the austere Cistercians needed solitude, to be away from the general population, they were by no means 'alone' out here. It was a veritable hive of activity.

The three men walked past the chapter house, which was next to the parlour, and knocked on the door of the book room. An old monk answered, pointing to a sign in Latin which directed visitors to the office of the librarian to obtain the necessary pass to the scriptorium. They bowed reverently, turning to seek out the librarian's office. After pausing they decided to wander up to the Abbot's lodgings, a little to the east, thinking that office bearers may have their rooms nearby. Once there they found a queue of people outside the Abbot's house: seemingly the foreman from the timber delivery, two men with a cart full of fleeces, a monk holding several exchequer tallies, the notches in one of the sticks large indeed indicating large amounts payable, a gang of local villagers, and a man with a falcon on his arm.

"Yon's a braw bird," mentioned Bernard to the falcon man.

"Yes, I believe it to be lost," he said.

"Begging your pardon, but pray tell, are you Scots also?" asked one of the men with the fleeces.

"Aye, that we are, and what of it?" answered Malcolm, the red cross on his robe bright in the sunlight

"We have just come from your compatriots, over at Stokesay."

"Over at Stokesay?" Callum looked confused.

"Yes, sir. Three of them, from your parts, I am sure of it…welcomed as such at the gatehouse."

"Redfriars?" asked Callum.

"No sir, mercenaries, perhaps. They were well-armed. One was strong-looking, fair hair, quite stocky." Malcolm and Callum shook their heads. It was no-one they knew. "The second man was dirty-looking, with a shaved head, neck like a bull. Strong as an ox by the looks of him, too." Could be any one of one hundred men, if he is a warrior-type, thought Callum. "The other man, the leader I think, had the devil in him. A strange man: evil-looking. Perhaps it was the red hair. Oh yes, and he has a black pattern around his left eye…" Suddenly, Callum and Malcolm looked at one another as the rest of the man's sentence faded away.

"Thank you sir, but Scots they may be but with us they are not." They looked to the monk now. "Know you the librarian's office?"

"Above the Day Room," he said, pointing back towards the cloisters.

"Thank you," all three nodded, heading back whence they had come.

*　　　*　　　*

"A small token of our appreciation," said the big Highlander resplendent in his ochre plaid as he pushed a coin into the guide's hand. "You say All Saints Church is atop this rise?"

"Yes sir, up on your right hand near to the top," said the wizened old guide as he tugged at the reins of the donkey, urging it to move; a sudden dig in its ribs with his heel spurred it into life. "You do not want my services for the return?" he reiterated.

"No, we said already. Enough," snarled Beege, searching through his shoulder bag for the old Saltire which he imagined for a moment he had lost: it was something that he was apt to do and he never once found it missing which is just as well because he knew not what Dubhshuileach might do under those circumstances, and he never wanted to find out.

"Away wi' ye, old man," Bash said ungratefully only to be flashed a look by his superior. "And safe journey," he added, looking over to the big man rather than the little man on the donkey who was jabbing his heals furiously into the animal's flank as he disappeared round a bend in the trail.

They walked up through the sleepy little village of Claverley and found the old church midway up, set back off the main track on a mound to their right. It was dark now and they could see lights dancing across the stained glass windows. The three men entered to find the church ablaze with candles: giant pillars of tallow surrounding giant pillars of stone. The tallow pillars lit up the nave revealing an ornate orange-coloured wooden roof crowning a spectacular frieze which straddled both the north and south nave walls, attended to by a man on a scaffold who had still not noticed the visitors staring at his work.

"What you painting?" shouted Bash, wincing as the sound of his voice was thrown back at him by the church's acoustics. The man stopped.

"I am refining, not painting," he said. "If only I were such an artist as to paint such a vivid scene. It is as if the 'Legend of the True Cross' is being acted out here in Claverley such is the clarity and vision," he said, gazing around him at the walls taking in the depiction of Constantine, Roland, Heraclius and Charlemagne as if for the very first time. "The Knights of the Cross…," he said as if faraway, reliving in his mind's-eye the adventures that these heroes of his would have encountered. "The Cross…lost at the Battle of the Horns of Hattin," he said, wiping a tear from his eye.

"Aye, well many thanks for the history lesson," snapped Dubhshuileach, "but we were more interested in finding our way to the Lord Gatacre's estate. Know you how to get there?"

The man now eyed them ever the more suspiciously, especially the Scot in the plaid who visibly bore arms: sword *and* meat-cleaver, he thought, not recognising the weapons attached to the man's belt for what they were – a long dirk and a falchion. He was no warrior, however, so it was a good enough guess. The others look none so mean either, he thought.

"Gatacre?" he asked, trying desperately to look like he had never heard the name before.

"Aye, Gatacre. He is lord here, is he not?" said Dubhshuileach, picking his way through the pews until he looked up at the man from the foot of the scaffold. He leaned on the wood frame causing it to rock slightly.

"Oh Lord Gatacre!" said the man in revelation, clasping onto the side of the scaffold. "Yes, he can be found three miles from here: to the north-east..."

"He asked that we remain incognito and that we should arrive by his *secret place* – 'tis how he put it. Know you of this *secret place*?"

The man relaxed as Dubhshuileach ambled up the nave towards the magnificent east window arching almost twenty feet high over the Sanctuary and Altar checking every nook and cranny on the way; he also realised that these men were, indeed, friends of his lord knowing as they did of the hidden passage which ran from here to Gatacre's estate. He knew of it as church elder and surmised that he was one of only a dozen people to know of its existence; if these people knew of it they were to be trusted, he reasoned.

"'Tis near the west window," he said scrambling down, "I will show thee." He jumped the last few feet and herded the strangers back up the aisle. "Here," he said, pointing at a grey slab in the floor. "Use this," he said grabbing a long metal bar and levering it under the lip of the stone. Bash and Beege decided to help as the man's face turned purple putting their weight into it as they muscled him out of the way, popping the slab up without too much effort. Herculean strength, the man thought, these two men are incredibly strong. Bash looked it, being brutish-looking, but the thinner man, sinewy, was obviously a powerhouse also: it normally took one man to work the lever into position and four to lift the slab up. He stood with his hands on his hips, puffing gently.

"Come, show us the way," Dubhshuileach put his arm round the man's shoulder guiding him down the steps to the crypt using a candle to light a wall torch as he did so. Bash ran back to the church door running a wooden beam through its four metal hoops thus barring it from the inside. He joined the others in the crypt.

"This way," said, the local holding aloft another torch. He lit more of these tallow-soaked torches as they moved out into the darkness of the passage. Rats squeaked and scurried away as the flames took hold finally bursting into life and illuminating the tunnel. The Scots followed the leader, the local with his torch forging ahead until they reached a wooden door. It was bolted from the other side. He listened with his ear pressed against the cold timber. "I hear something," he said. Dubhshuileach nodded; Bash and Beege following suit, perhaps a little over-enthusiastically. He passed his torch to Beege and rapped loudly on the door. "My Lord Gatacre, your guests have arrived," he shouted.

"Who goes there?" came the faint reply from the other side.

"'Tis I, my lord. Theodore of Claverley. Open Sire!"

"Who goes there?" Again a faint cry from behind the thick door.

"My lord 'tis I, Theodore of Claverley," he bellowed into the wood.

"Theodore? Is that you?" Gatacre sounded faint but he too must have been bellowing.

"Yes, My lord!"

100

A scraping sound came from within as bolts were eased and padlocked catches released culminating in a loud crack as the old hinges jolted into life. Dubhshuileach, who had been demanding silence from his colleagues with a finger over his lips, now peered over Theodore's shoulder. He caught Beege's eye and issued his next order by slicing a finger across his throat indicating with his eyes his prey in front of him. The door finally opened further and Dubhshuileach leapt into action; he burst through and in one sweeping movement grabbed Gatacre by the throat almost lifting him clean off his feet pinning him up against a cold wall. Bash was behind his leader in a flash brandishing a dirk in case of any resistance; there was none. Beege followed immediately with blood splattered across his beige surcoat and across his cheek. He wiped his face with the back of his hand still gripping his braig in readiness, its blade dripping with blood. There had been no scream from his victim: his jugular slashed he had slumped to the floor in a heap.

"Sirrah! By the grace of God," started Gatacre who fell silent on recognition of the monster that man-handled him; flames contorted the big man's face into a demonic expression which turned Gatacre pale. He wretched, dribbling bile down his chin onto the huge hand that was now squeezing the breath out of him.

"Ah! 'Tis the ignoble thief of Yarmouth!" said Dubhshuileach, releasing his grip and allowing his quarry to slump onto his knees in front of him. "I have been ever swimming to catch hold of your tail since that fateful night, and lo! Here we meet again."

"How did you get in...who are you?" Gatacre wept as he watched Bash and Beege patrolling the empty passage.

"Your nemesis, perhaps? But never mind...'tis you in whom we are interested. I believe you still have that which belongs to me," he said calmly, "from Yarmouth...remember?"

Petrified, Gatacre nodded his head.

"Over yonder," he indicated, "under the table...in the chest," he wheezed, his neck still burning red from his foe's grip. "It is unlocked," he said as Dubhshuileach dragged the chest out. He flipped the lid. "See, 'tis still there...the...wood," was all he could say. "A significant find, yes?" he said.

"Aye, significant," said Dubhshuileach as he rolled the relic round in his hands, eyes closed, "and yet you know not what you have here, I think."

"Well..." stumbled Gatacre as Dubhshuileach squatted down in front of him.

"Know you!" he spat. "Know you, what you have here?" he said, shaking the relic above his head. He waited for a response. "No," he resumed quietly, "I think not. What we have here?" he addressed his two comrades. "Is a magpie who knoweth not what he hoards, coveting others' possessions." He turned to face Gatacre once more. "Well the worm has turned, my friend and I am here coveting possessions of yours..."

"They are yours! Tell me of what you search and I shall gladly turn them over to you..."

"Ah! The arrogance has vanished; that air of superiority gone; gone as have the soldiers behind to whom he barked his orders."

"I acted on behalf of His Majesty, King Edward," he started.

"Ah! Longshanks! Another coveter of others' possessions – only the scale is larger. Unfortunately our very own King Alexander, although able to stand up to Edward in respect of that which was his, was not prepared to stand up for that which was mine! Hence, your legalised robbery for which now you must pay."

"Speak of your wants and they shall be yours," he gasped, "and yours," he offered to Bash and Beege.

"Ah! My wants…well I shall tell you, Sirrah! This Cross of St. Andrew…" he held out the olive branch.

"Cross?"

"Aye, this ancient piece of wood upon which Christ's own favourite, Andrew, was crucified must rest in Scotland where it belongs; and you have the nails also, I believe, although admittedly knowingly this time." Gatacre nodded slowly. "And where we might find these nails?" Gatacre pointed to a second, smaller chest which was tucked into a hole in the wall which the first chest had concealed. Bash forced it open revealing six rusty old nails. He wrapped them gently in a cloth and bound them with twine tucking them into his bag along with two small bags of coins. "Your adversary, Ludlowe, is the man you should curse as he is the same who summonsed us to negotiate with you."

Gatacre sat against the wall rocking back and forth, holding his knees with hands clasped. He sobbed gently. "Negotiate?" he snivelled.

"Aye," Dubhshuileach laughed, "he asked us to come to terms with you…to offer one-tenth of his earnings from Yarmouth and that he would increase his trade through that port." Gatacre looked confused as he rocked on the floor. "He wanted no 'roughing' considering such as ungentlemanly…"

"Praise be to God…"

"Ah! My Lord Gatacre you celebrate prematurely," Gatacre was wide-eyed now, staring at the kilted beast now towering over him, "you see, I am not interested in Ludlowe's feud with you. I am here to right a wrong; to claim that which is mine, to offer up your soul to Our Illustrious Andrew for the follies committed by the usurping Peter, He whom you call Saint. And this shall be done here below the house of Peter by way of pledge by the Hounds of Saint Andrew to wreak vengeance on those who sin against Him." Gatacre was wailing now so Dubhshuileach kneeled down and lifted the wretch's chin up. "Shh!" he whispered, pulling out the boar's tooth pendant from his sporran. He rolled it all up into his fist and stuffed it into the mouth of the sinner.

The three Scots stood over the sobbing figure stripping to the waist. The red-haired Highlander, muscles rippling, turned on his prey to display his tattooed back; the stocky Bash revealed the same words across his chest; and the wiry but powerful Beege, turning his back on their victim, revealed the same tattooed Latin phrase.

Gatacre attempted to flee scrambling to his feet like a newborn deer: uneasy, unsure and with no great conviction. Bash grabbed him easily and pinned him back with one arm against the wall, his rotten breath puffing into Gatacre's face, whilst holding his forearm across his throat. Dubhshuileach calmly drew his large dirk from its sheath and set it down on the table. He held his hand out as Beege rummaged in his bag pulling out a different six nails which he placed in the outstretched palm in front of him, "Scottish iron," he said by way of explanation. Gatacre whimpered. A hammer appeared next. Beege and Bash swapped places, Bash taking up the hammer in one hand, nails in the other.

"Close your eyes Sire! And think of Saint Andrew!" announced Dubhshuileach helping spread Gatacre into a wriggling X-shape, spread-eagled against the limestone wall.

"Dastard!" Gatacre spat defiantly in his face before the first iron nail pierced his left palm pinning him to the soft stone causing him to writhe and scream in agony. Bash took another swing and the nail plunged deeper, more securely into the wall; its head sat flush with Gatacre's soft palm: a palm that had seen no heavy work, thought Bash as he gathered up a second nail. He worked his way round the man, turning to his feet which they stripped bare, ignoring the initial screams which vanished as unconsciousness took over. Finally he rammed a fifth nail into the exposed underside of the left elbow forcing out a sickening crunch as the iron penetrated the gristle and bone which had formed the elbow. He repeated this macabre exercise on the right arm to leave a rag doll of a man firmly secured in six places to the wall. Blood poured from the wounds running crimson down the whitewashed walls.

"Well-named that man. Him that *bashes* in nails," Dubhshuileach laughed causing the other two to roar in appreciation. "Let us gather our belongings and head for home," he said once the laughter died down, and turning to the now moaning figure on the wall, "Sore is it not?" At that he thrust his dirk so hard into the man's heart that, like the nails, it too found purchase in the limestone behind.

CHAPTER FOURTEEN

Dunfermline Abbey, Fife, 29th March, 1286

Dunfermline Abbey and Palace combined to be one of the largest and most impressive complexes in the whole of Scotland and had been chosen by Malcolm III as his burial place back in the days when Dunfermline was recognised as the capital of Scotland. His wife, Queen Margaret, had also been buried here in 1093 near the high altar until both their remains were moved to a special chapel at the east end of the choir in 1250 after Margaret's canonisation as a saint. Alexander's first wife, Queen Margaret, had also been buried here in when she died in 1274. She was followed soon after by their sons, David and Alexander. Now the nation's beloved King Alexander III, King of Scots was to join them all in their grand resting place.

The newly finished Pends Gate, to the west of the abbey precinct, provided mourners with the main entrance to an area covering over twenty-three acres, all of which was surrounded by a stone wall some three-quarters of a mile long. Accents from all over Scotland could be heard in the crush at the gate and voices from afar were recognisable amongst the nobles already inside the Abbey itself: French, Latin, Germanic, Scandinavian, and English to name but a few. Here was to be buried a truly loved and revered king.

A watery sun shone on the crowds of commoners immediately outside the Abbey who stood silent listening to the chanting from within. Most wore garments of russet and ecru which were the normal colours for those in mourning. The super-rich, however, had taken to using clothes dyed black, an expense afforded only by them which meant that the congregation inside was attired mainly in black lending to the sombre occasion. Some wore their armorial surcoats which ensured that flashes of colour were dotted around the assemblage. Huge candles lit up the beautiful interior which resonated with the monks' chanting. The thronging mass awaited the funeral procession, which was due to arrive imminently via the Pends Gate and up to the nave's grand processional entrance which was flanked by two imposing towers. The huge doorway was framed by five arches and shafts which peaked just below three arched windows, displaying the Holy Trinity within its beautiful stained glasswork. The window glittered and twinkled from the flickering candlelight from inside the nave which itself was three stages high, culminating in a vividly-coloured painted ceiling which showed Scotland's rich heritage and Celtic past. Large, painted columns hoisted up the two layers of arches which supported the vast ceiling leading up to the main altar where most of the ceremony would take place.

Soon, the noise was tumultuous with trumpets and drums announcing the arrival outside of the funeral cortège. Alasdair lifted his grey hood up over his head out of respect and nudged Massan, who was chatting with a lad next to him, into silence. Heads were bowed as the procession filed past. First were the Bishops of St. Andrews, and Glasgow, followed by the horse-drawn hearse, and then the country's magnates: Buchan the Justiciar and Constable supporting Yolande, James the Steward, John Comyn, Lord of Badenoch, MacDuff, Earl of Fife to name but a few. The procession inched past at a snail's pace giving Massan a sore neck as he continued to bow. He fidgeted, trying to keep up his respectful bow, but also trying to sneak a peek at the Earl of Fife; the man that had his destiny in his hands. Alasdair, on the other hand, tried to nudge his way in front of the boy backing them both away from the front of the on-lookers, hoping to ensure that no-one in the procession saw them. I should never have allowed myself to be talked into coming here, he thought as he steered Massan gently backwards through the wailing crowd.

"Please Alasdair; I feel it is only right that I should pay my respects. It is the least I can do considering I am or was the main suspect…" Massan had said. How could he refuse? So they had left Cramunde, sneaking out through the orchard, Alasdair telling only Fergus of their purpose. He had felt worried all day about leaving the house, but reassured himself that the lad needed to pay his respects and that is what the Lord would have wanted.

He was confident that no-one had particularly noticed them as he kept a watchful eye out for any potential kidnappers and, deciding it was time for the two of them to make a move, he gently took Massan's arm and led him away from the mourners and out the gate. Massan said nothing, realising that he had been lucky to get to the funeral in the first place. They travelled back down to the Queen's ferry along peaceful sylvan trails, talking only to identify the flora and fauna on the way.

The ferry crossing was uneventful despite a seal swimming alongside, occasionally diving below the boat and popping up the other side. The ferryman had seen her before, naming her Maggie. She turned tail as they entered shallow waters, disappearing back into the depths of the icy water, no doubt heading for all her noisy friends on nearby Inchcolm Island.

As man and boy stepped into the mud that landlubber Alasdair had ironically referred to as the sanctuary of 'dry land' they spotted a grey-clad figure rushing down towards them. The red cross became apparent as he neared them; Fergus even made an awkward attempt at running which was impossible given the robes. Something was not right.

"Massan, go see if there is any broth to be had in yon bothy. I can feel the chill bite." He spoke firmly and Massan got the message leaving him to greet Fergus alone.

"Brother! Brother!" Fergus shouted, face crimson. "Terrible news!"

"Calm down Fergus, you are flushed," Alasdair put an arm round the monk who seemed at the point of collapse and now completely breathless. After a few moments he managed to regain his composure. He checked to make sure that they could not be overheard ensuring backs were to the bothy in which sat Massan chatting to the ferryman who was stoking the fire.

"It concerns Massan's mother," he said.

"Yes?"

"Well, I know not a good way of telling…"

"Speak only. Say what has to be said, Fergus."

"She has been taken…to Rossend Castle, we think."

"Taken. Why?"

"She has been accused of witchcraft, seemingly accurately by all accounts."

"What accounts?" Alasdair checked over his shoulder to make sure Massan was still with the ferryman. "What rumours?" he said.

"No rumours I am sure. Facts. News comes from the Binn Village. One of the eldermen, name of Guthrie, made a search of her house; it contained evidence of witchcraft. Indisputable evidence. They then marched down to Kirkton and dragged her from her hideout, taking her to Rossend."

"Why Rossend? That is the Pict's place…"

"Aye, it was his men that took her…"

"What is this 'indisputable evidence' of which you speak?"

Fergus was ashen-faced as he spoke. "A sacrifice; to the Devil: a white deer…"

"Death?"

"Aye, 'tis true; inside the house they found the old Celtic symbol of death hanging from the rafters. Its belly had been ripped asunder. Surely this is the reason for our monarch's demise. He was bewitched by this woman. The whole village believes it so."

"And what of her daughter?"

"She is with an elder by the name of Drust of Kirkton. His brother bides with him also; recuperating from the beating he took trying to protect her. He was no match for Rossend's men…"

Fergus searched Alasdair's face for answers; for some sort of reassurance. There was none. Alasdair, too, was worried. His furrowed brow portrayed a man in anguish. Eventually he looked up and into his colleague's eyes.

"Indeed you were right, dear Fergus; this *is* terrible news. We needs must say nothing to the lad; his world is falling apart and again he is in grave danger. Let us take him back to Cramunde and decide from there what next to do. If only Prior Callum were back; he would know what to do…"

*   *   *

"I beg of your pardon, Prior Callum, but I must protest. To go to Stokesay now would just put us at least a day behind when we must be pressing onwards to St. Andrews…"

"A fine attitude Malcolm, but one dispensed with at the behest of a fine library. Perhaps yesterday was the day we should have been pressing on? Besides, I am intrigued as to what Rossend is doing here, so far away from home," replied Callum as stoic as ever.

"I think this man cannot be Rossend, Your Holiness, as yon monk would surely have mentioned the plaid he wears," said Malcolm.

"Unless he is in disguise?"

"And," continued Malcolm, "perhaps this 'pattern' was mud…"

"Come now, Malcolm. You are far too worried about this journey of ours, and I admire your concern, however a trip to Stokesay will not take us entirely out of our way," he lied, it being in the opposite direction from their goal, "and I for one would like to feast my eyes on such a grand place. I hear Leonard de Ludlowe has a keen eye when it comes to furnishings. It will be interesting to see how lavish and absurd a man can be when he has too much wealth."

"As you will, Your Holiness," conceded Malcolm.

It was noon when the two monks, the seaman and their guide arrived bedraggled at the walls of Stokesay manor house. A light rain swept down from the hills shrouding the valley in a wet veil. The visitors kept their hoods up as they approached the gatehouse, ready to identify themselves when asked.

"Two Redfriars and friend, come to see Leonard de Ludlowe!" Malcolm shouted up to the seemingly deserted outpost. No answer. He shouted again: still no reply. The three men waited in the rain as their guide sloped off. "'Tis no good," said Malcolm, "There is no-one to receive us."

"Oh, but there is! Listen…" said Bernard, and they could hear murmuring coming from the gatehouse.

"Name yourselves!" came the cry.

"I am Prior Callum de Cramunde of that ilk and I come with Brother Malcolm of Scotlandwell, both newly down to Buildwas Abbey to receive our friend, here, Bernard de St. Clair, noted ship's master at the behest of Bishop Fraser of St. Andrews and Scotland."

"More Scots!"

"Let them in!" It was Ludlowe, viewing the proceedings from the solar room above the great hall. And so the three men were allowed in and escorted courteously to the great hall. A servant took their wringing overcoats and placed them near the grand fireplace to dry out. They were shown to a long table on the dais at the far end of the hall as food and drink was brought in for them.

"My Lord de Ludlowe shall join you shortly gentlemen, so meantime, please eat and drink," said the servant smiling and bowing as he left.

Prior Callum pointed the impressive cruck roof the timbers of which stretched up from halfway up the wall to the top of the roof twenty-five feet above them. Two long tables ran down the sides of the hall away from them; one finished near the foot of the wooden stairs used by the three Hounds so very recently, the other near the entrance. The three men admired the grand room, warm with its brightly coloured wall hangings, its glassy arched windows, and its glowing fire near them, the smoke drawing up to a small hole in the roof sitting in-between two filled in trusses.

"Duncan MacDuff could learn from this man," he said gazing upwards. Bernard looked confused and realising this Prior Callum continued, "See how the surrounding panels invite the smoke upwards filtering it up and out through the hole." Bernard nodded. "Well our Earl of Fife has no such mechanism which means that when he entertains his guests sit with eyes sore with smoke. We have no such problem here, have we?"

"No, well observed. I have noticed the smoke at Fife's castle at Abirdaur, but not at his other places," said Bernard rather politely, but not wanting the Earl of Fife whom he had worked for to be unfairly accused. "Perhaps mine eyes are more accustomed to smoke than those of the Trinitarians."

"Aye, perhaps," said Callum with Malcolm nodding agreement. "I may also do him a disservice as it has been some time since I visited Fife anywhere but Abirdaur," he added. "I shall commend to him the use of similar trusses in drawing the smoke out of the great hall at Abirdaur when we next speak which will not be over long."

"French..." the flamboyant man standing in the doorway shouted fiddling with his moustache as he did so. He had watched them a while from a spy hole in his solar room which peered down onto the hall from a position above and behind them on the dais. Striding up the hall towards them his posture gave him an aloofness that Callum had not noticed in Scottish nobility. "I find the French have a particular skill with building works. I use the French whenever I can for that very reason. My Master mason is French; Master carpenter, French also; glazier, French," he declared, sniffing a little bag of herbs tied to his wrist. "What next? A French chef in my kitchen!" he laughed, snorting a little. "But listen to me – I talk over much. You did not come here for a lecture on the benefits of French workmanship. Delighted to meet you," he said bowing gracefully before Callum whilst taking his hand and gently kissing it.

"I am Callum de Cramunde of that ilk," he said standing up. The other two did the same.

"Malcolm of Scotlandwell, my lord," said Malcolm with an inclination of his head.

"And I am Bernard de St. Clair, a humble merchant based in the town of Earlsferry in Fife."

"Good, good," said Ludlowe sitting down at the dais. "Sit, sit!" he insisted. "More food," he waved a hand towards the servants nearby who whisked some empty plates away, returning a few moments later with hands full of plates: cold pork, roast pigeon, roast dove, nuts, and trout from the nearby pond.

"You spoil us!" Callum said.

"I do what I do for any valued guest, but beg of you to tell me what it is I can do for you? I believe such a visit, unannounced, is one with a purpose? No?"

"You are right, of course," said Callum nibbling at a succulent chicken leg and wiping his mouth with a sleeve. "Your reputation as a man of class goes before you – we have heard such a great deal of your wonderful place here at Stokesay – and we wished to be able to view it for ourselves."

"I thank you for these kind words and beg you to make this home of mine yours also…"

"That will not be necessary as we must return to Scotland immediately," said Malcolm watching his host subconsciously pull out his moustache then let it spring back into place. He found the man's fixation with his moustache fascinating, completely unaware that he himself was fixing the man with a stare.

"I beg your pardon, my lord, but I have dire news from Claverley," said the messenger approaching the dais and snapping Malcolm out of his trance, to the relief of Prior Callum. "It seems the Scotsmen have—" he started.

"Yes! What news have you," said Ludlowe jumping to his feet, putting his arm around the messenger and guiding him away from the guests who sat watching the two men have quite an animated discussion despite their best efforts to stand out of earshot. The messenger tucked something into Ludlowe's hand as Bernard strained to listen, catching the odd word here and there: dead, church, mouth, and crucified featured more than once.

"Can we be of help?" asked Prior Callum once Ludlowe rejoined them at the table ashen-faced.

"Yes, perhaps," replied Ludlowe, "but first we should retire to my private quarters in the north tower. Come, please follow." He led them up the stairs and into the room where he had sat scheming with the Hounds of St. Andrews. He flounced down onto his favourite velvet cushions begging his guests to do the same. "Wine?" The three men said yes. "French," he said matter-of-factly. "I have been used, I feel," he continued. "Used by one of your fellow countrymen, but admittedly I have given them all the opportunity in the world to do so. I have been naïve, so naïve," he said, shaking his head in regret.

"As I said, if we can be of help…"

"No, I think not," he stared at the floor. "Although, I may need absolution for a crime that I feel has been committed in my name – because of my own selfishness and stupidity."

"This crime," said Callum, "Does it involve the death of someone?"

"It does." He was toying with his moustache once more.

"Could you leave us?" Callum asked Bernard and Malcolm. "Perhaps our host's staff can show you around?"

"Yes of course," said Ludlowe, indicating to a servant to see to it and asking him that he and the prior be left alone. When they were he continued. "I can ask for absolution at the Church of St. John, but would prefer if my involvement in this heinous crime was not known locally."

"And did you order this death?"

"No, but I fear that I caused it by involving persons who should have never been approached. I knew not what I dealt with." Again he stared at his feet.

"And in your hand, what is this? Evidence?"

"Oh yes," said Ludlowe realising that he did indeed hold something in his hand. He sat forward facing Callum opening his hand to reveal a thin piece of twine. No, not twine, it was deerskin, thought Callum. Attached was a boar's tooth. "Know you what this Celtic pattern means?" asked Ludlowe of Callum who was sitting astonished, mouth open.

*   *   *

It had been a few days since the assault by the two brutes and David felt no better: he still coughed up blood and still suffered pain throughout his midriff. He gently peeled off the makeshift bandage, torn from an old nightshirt, and stopped: the bruising was particularly tender. He remembered being called in as a young man by the first Dubhshuileach, his landlord, to help with a boar hunt and managing to get himself isolated from the hunters with only two beating brushes. He had inadvertently worked a sturdy young boar into a corner, causing it to charge him. The solid mass of muscle that was the boar had been far too fast and swift of foot for him to avoid and he had taken a hefty thump and tumble. His side had ached for weeks after that incident, and he had really only been glanced by the beast in its attempt to escape. He remembered the thunder-clap noise of its hooves as it neared him, the thick, wiry hair raking him as he was sideswiped, grazing him badly and the thick trunk of the old oak tree as he was launched headlong into it, knocking him spark out. It had been some time before he was discovered prostrate on the mossy floor. This is worse, he thought, reliving the whole experience over again in his mind.

Drust had got up from the fire to answer the door. He had opened it and two men burst in knocking him out of the way. The first man, red-haired with a scar across his face, leapt across the room pinning Christina down onto the floor face-down. He had held her wrists behind her back, tying them roughly with twine calling her witch as he did so. Aibhlinn had screamed, frozen to the spot. The second raider, a dirty-looking thug with a shaven head had then calmly walked over to David, who was remonstrating with the first man, and smacked a powerful blow into the old man's kidneys. He hit the floor with a splat not unlike the clay thrown onto his pottery wheel and was unable to move the whole time the men were there.

"Spawn of the Devil!" Mool had shouted as they noticed Aibhlinn who promptly unfroze, shooting out the back door like a startled hare darting round the shaven one's grasping paws. "Grab her!" She had run out the door, skirting round the side of the house, not once looking behind her, and she had not stopped until she was in the sanctuary of the nearby kirk where she had been instructed to go in an emergency. She had cowered amongst the pews stifling her sobs in case her pursuers dared enter Holy Church to get her. She shook uncontrollably with fear, but need not have as the Hounds had given up as soon as she got out into the open.

"We have you now, witch!" spat Skate into Christina's face.

"We have seen your witch's lair, and now you will face justice, witch," said Mool, lifting Christina to her feet. She was winded and unable to protest as much as she wanted due to this fact and because she had had a clump of earth stuffed into her mouth. She choked unable to spit the whole thing out. Bits of dirt sprayed into Mool's face as he manhandled her to the door and the figure waiting there.

"You are found, witch. We have witnessed your depravity: the sacrifice of a white deer, the sign of death, innards removed, no doubt for subversive magic, the sign of the Anti-Christ stitched into it," Guthrie, the elder almost heaved again, as he had on first entering Christina's home. "The toad, your familiar, brought to you by the Devil Himself of a certainty, black with hatred, hidden from sight; and the upturned crucifixes," he crossed himself, "taunting Our Lord Jesus Christ, inviting Satan in to be suckled at your bosom – the very bosom suckled at by your children. Children who have been damned by your evil-doing…"

Christina shook and tried to speak, but was held fast by Mool who dragged her outside, her protests silenced by the sod of turf in her mouth. A crowd had gathered to watch many of whom had come down from the Binn Village; David could hear their mumblings although still unable to stand he could not see them.

He remembered the tears swelling up in his eyes. They were not shed for him but shed out of shame for his fellow man and for Christina's plight. How could fellow human beings act as such? How could Guthrie be taken in by these lies, these fabrications? And how would Christina cope? And Aibhlinn, the sweet little girl; what was to become of her?

"Follow us at your peril," threatened Skate as he pushed past Drust on the way out. The expression on Drust's face showed he had no intention of doing so. And then they were left alone; Drust standing by the doorway and him lying in agony on the floor. The two men were in a sorry state and now had a child to find.

"Think you Aibhlinn hides in the Holy Church?" said Drust with a worried look on his face.

*   *   *

"Rumour has it that Rossend's men are planning to 'swim' the lad's mother to prove her guilt," said Lady Marjory solemnly. "And if such a tale has made its way in one day to here, Dunfermline Abbey, think on how far around the rest of Fife it has spread."

"Aye, 'tis same as I have heard," MacDuff replied, "I must do something, but presently I know not what."

"Aye my dear, 'tis a difficult situation," she mused sitting down on the bed, running her hands across the linen sheets. "Even I know that 'swimming' witches is illegal," she added.

MacDuff was staring out the glass window which afforded a spectacular view of Pittencrieff Glen sprawling away to the south-west with its lush green meadows dissected by the winding Tower Burn. He tapped the glass with a finger.

"Wonderful stuff this," he said as if the Guesthouse's glass was the first he had ever clapped eyes on.

"Think you we should be discussing the witchery on your lands?" It was a rather brutal way of bringing him back to the subject in hand but it worked.

"Aye, er…" he stumbled.

"Let us think on what we know; facts only," she said, gently taking him by the arm and drawing him down beside her on the bed. "We know that this woman…Christina, is it?"

"Christina, aye."

"This Christina has lived at the Binn Village for some time. She has caused no problems before, has she not?"

"No I believe not…"

"She has had villagers in her house before? Recently?"

"I know not. Why do you ask?"

"Because if she were a witch she would not want people to see her den – witchery is not hidden easily. And if she is a witch she would not leave her den unattended, surely? And she was found in Kirkton was she not?"

"Aye, I see. You have the rights of it! There is something amiss…" MacDuff became animated. Marjory put her hand on his knee to regain his attention.

"Furthermore, my love, did you not say that she had sought help from the Redfriars? And did you not agree her safety until a month passed?"

"Again you are right, in part. She did indeed seek help from the Trinitarians, but for her son, the young scamp that escaped from Ravenscraig. She did so because she believed in his innocence. She insisted he was innocent. Would one of Satan's own seek refuge from the Holy Church? I think not." She nodded her agreement as he continued. "However, I did agree with Prior Callum that the Redfriars should look after the boy, not his mother, until his return from England."

"Can Rossend do as he likes in this, your land of Fife? Surely you have overlordship?"

"Aye, but that is where it is complicated…he has regality. Technically Dubhshuileach can dispense justice on his own lands, and we are talking about his lands," he glanced at her to gauge reaction. "Even though they are in my Fife," he added.

"Complicated yes, but not insurmountable. Again, let us look at the facts. This Highlander is given rights on Rossend Castle and the surrounding lands, yes?"

"Aye," said MacDuff.

"These rights were given to him by whom?"

"By his father who received Rossend from mine," he said looking exasperated. Lady Marjory dug deeper.

"And he has inherited regality also, has he not?"

"Aye, that he has."

"From whom?" she pressed.

"His father before him?" he said, unsure of her line of questioning.

112

"Duncan, think," she said wanting him to come up with the answer himself. One can lead a horse to water, but one cannot force it to drink, she had often thought. She pressed on. "Regality. Who gave Rossend regality?"

The earl sat on the bed beside his wife, searching deep into her eyes for the answer that he suspected she already knew. She fixed him with a stare, full of concentration, as if somehow she could transfer her thoughts across to him.

"Aha! The King," he said at last. "God rest his soul. King Alexander is who ultimately presented Rossend with regality." He got it! He felt good, although very quickly his face changed from elation to confusion once more as he tried to analyse the ramifications of this; he could not think why this was important. Why is this important? He racked his brain until it throbbed, gazing upwards searching the ornate ceiling for clues.

"And…" his wife encouraged as she felt his angst.

"And Dubhshuileach still has jurisdiction in this case," he said forlornly admitting defeat.

"Aye my love, to a point you are right, but with no regal presence now in Scotland, surely that very regality issued to Dubhshuileach's father has died along with our King or at the very least it is in abeyance."

"Yes!" he jumped up and grabbed her, kissing her hard on the lips. "Again, you have it!"

"And," she continued, "if Dubhshuileach is not here at present, you as Earl of Fife have overriding judicature, regardless of regality."

"Yes!" He grabbed his overcoat and threw it on. "I must to Rossend Castle go and put a stop to all this. If she is a witch then they needs must prove it so to me!" He swung open the bedchamber's door and turning before he left said, "I love you!"

She allowed herself a wry smile as the door slammed shut.

CHAPTER FIFTEEN

"She will be safe here. My brother and I are too old to be able to guarantee safety – David, as I speak, lies in pain still suffering from the attack by those two thugs."

Alasdair the monk, facing yet another dilemma, looked from him to the little girl holding his hand and could see the sadness in her face. One so young should not have to deal with problems such as these, he thought: her brother in hiding; her mother taken from her; her guardians assaulted; none of these loved ones were guaranteed to ever see her again. Only he could make it so by taking her in and reuniting her with Massan.

"She may stay here awhile," he concluded.

"Bless you," replied Drust. "Go on Aibhlinn, in you go. Your brother is waiting..."

"Will you live here with us, Uncle Drust?"

It was the first time she had referred to him as 'uncle'. He fought a tear back.

"No my love, I needs must attend to *my* brother in much the same way you must yours."

"Maybe Brother Alasdair will let your brother stay here too," she said fluttering her big eyelashes up towards Alasdair. Her innocence was almost palpable and Alasdair was sorry to have to say, "David needs to rest at home; Drust is best served attending him there. Worry not, young Aibhlinn, your friends will be in our prayers and will no doubt visit soon." He glanced at Drust as he took Aibhlinn's hand. "Come, Massan will be thrilled to see you."

The little girl shook herself free for a moment to give Drust a loving hug, squeezing him tightly. He had a tear in his eye as she turned and left with the Redfriar but he knew that she was better off here at Cramunde. They could provide the security he and his brother could not, he thought. Those thugs would never dare to snatch her and Massan from the Holy Church. Or would they? He tore himself away from that horrific thought and headed back towards the Queen's ferry.

"Massan!" She flew at him, tearing away once more from the Redfriar holding her hand, and bursting into sobs as she clutched him tightly.

"Come now, sis. Yer squashin' the life oot o' me!" He struggled to break free from her, but realising she was more distressed than happy at seeing him changed his tack and comforted her in his arms. "Whatever is the matter?" he asked, trying to lift her chin up so as to see her face. Alasdair watched them, his face slightly flushed. Massan studied the monk's face and realised that something was awry. "Alasdair?" The monk looked away, unable to hold the boy's gaze. "Alasdair, what has happened? Where is my mother?" He peeled his sobbing little sister off him and raised his voice. "Tell me!" he pleaded, staring at Alasdair who could still not bring himself to face the boy. Massan turned to his sister.

"They took her!" sobbed Aibhlinn.

"Who took her?"

"The nasty men!"

"Alasdair?" Massan looked forlorn.

"He that is known as Dubhshuileach has taken your mother," explained the monk, "to Rossend Castle."

"Who is this man, Dubhshuileach? I know not the name…"

"She is charged with witchcraft," added Alasdair solemnly at once silencing the room as the words sunk in. Time seemed to stop for the two children as the muffled sound of monkish chanting whispered in through the door shrouding them as they clutched each other, Massan attempting to shield his sister from their desperation.

"She is not a witch!" screamed Aibhlinn tearing away from him and plonking down onto the floor, her arms folded as if that was the end of the matter.

"I give up," Massan eventually declared softly. "'Tis no use…my family is doomed unless I admit fault for our king's death…"

"And were you at fault, laddie?" asked Alasdair taking a seat on the floor alongside them. "Do you have reason to give up? The King is dead, yes; your mother is held, yes; but does fault lie with you for any of these things?" He leaned down further so as he could look into the lad's tear-filled eyes. "I think not! My Brothers here think not. Prior Callum, who has guaranteed your safety and vouched for you with your lord the Earl of Fife, thinks not. So why admit to something that is not of your making? The Lord knoweth the truth as assuredly do you. So, wisdom and truth be the best policy, not lies and deceit which is what you propose. No blame is being laid at your feet for these mishaps. Strength of character only is required from you; for the sake of your mother *and* your sister, and it is needed now. Worry not, for Prior Callum shall return soon and will attend to your family's predicament under the watchful eye of Our Lord, in whose home you now rest."

Massan smiled. He hoped Alasdair was right.

*　　　*　　　*

Duncan MacDuff, the enthusiaic young Earl of Fife had rushed to Rossend Castle which sat on a promontory about a couple of miles from Kirkton, but not without making the necessary preparations. He had not been so rash as to charge there alone: first he had sent messengers out to request assistance at Rossend Castle from his vassals.

So it was that MacDuff came to be astride his horse outside the main gate to Rossend Castle with about fifty men-at-arms. The rendezvous place had been set as the small church at Kirkton from where they had marched down the one side of the little valley and up the other to Rossend.

"Open the gates Sirrah," commanded the earl, "in the name of Duncan MacDuff, Earl of this County of Fife I demand audience with Dubhshuileach, resident within."

"He is not in residence, my lord," came the answer, "but abroad in England."

"You have a woman, held captive within and I *demand* to see her and those that have taken her." The tone of his voice ensured that seconds later the familiar grating sound of a portcullis opening was heard. Fife's men stood ready behind him, weapons to hand; awaiting orders.

"Enter, my lord," said the man on the other side of the portcullis, stepping forward as it cleared his head. It was Mool. "How can we be of assistance, my lord?" he said holding onto his plaid at the shoulder which was flapping in the wind.

"I have declared my request already, Sirrah! A woman you have here, I believe, under accusation of witch."

"Aye, you have the rights of it," Mool said approaching the mounted earl. His red hair blew in the breeze allowing the earl to get a good view of the scar on the top of his head. "And forgive me my lord, but of what interest is this witch to you?"

"She lives on my land," he started.

"Begging your forgiveness, my lord, but the Binn Village is a fiefdom of Dubhshuileach of Rossend is it not? The right of regality sees to that, does it not?" Fife's horse shied as if Mool had plunged one of his witch-pricker pins into its side. He reassured it calmly using the time to think. Mool was conducting himself with great aplomb having listened to his lord well; he was well-versed; he knew what to say; he waited for an answer. He was not prepared for the one he got when eventually it came.

"In the absence of your master I believe I am lord of these lands and maintain jurisdiction over such. As for regality, I do declare that any such regality needs further ratification by a new monarch, which in this case would be Her Majesty Margaret, Maid of Norway who will shortly be crowned Queen of Scots. You are aware Sirrah, that the crown of Scotland will be placed on this infant monarch's head by these very hands," he held up his hands in a prayer-type pose, "as the Earls of Fife before me have always done placing the crown on the heads of our royalty." Mool shifted on his feet rather uneasily, but otherwise maintained his defiant stance. "Think you that regality is a shelter in which wrongdoers can hide forever? Think you that the wind of change that brings us a new monarch cannot become the gale that destroys this very same shelter which seemed so secure in past days?"

"Sir, I mean no disrespect," started Mool with a light, cheery air. "You are of course correct in all you say, and I thank you for pointing out my error. However, we *do* have a witch in custody and we had every intention on waiting for our master to return before demonstrating her guilt. I fully understand your concern, my lord, and therefore would be pleased and honoured if you would be witness to the proving of such." He ended with a respectful bow.

"I...I..." started MacDuff rather taken aback, "I would be delighted," he said, dismounting as he did so in the hope that he could disguise the concern on his face. Following Mool into the small courtyard MacDuff could sense that he was dealing with a slippery character; someone who had obviously been around Dubhshuileach a long time. Why do I not trust this man? He is a friend of Dubhshuileach who is a friend of mine, he thought, but maybe that is it. I doubt him *because* he is connected to Dubhshuileach. "I hear you intend 'swimming' the woman?"

"Not so, my lord: trial by water was banned by Popish command over seventy years ago and it is not for us to go against the Holy Church. I, on the other hand, am a witch-pricker who needs no such methods. *Drùidheachd* leaves its mark, you might say, as I shall demonstrate."

"Its mark?" said MacDuff who sensed that this man was just getting into his stride, his comfort zone. Mool seemed to be enjoying the conversation and had become quite animated.

"Come, follow...she is in the bottle-neck dungeon. We can wait while she is brought up to us." He opened the main door to the castle and asked a servant to have Skate retrieve the witch. "Come," he said, hurrying off down the corridor and into a small, well lit room. MacDuff motioned to the majority of his men to wait outside the main door; the rest were to wait in the corridor. "Wine?" said Mool as he took a seat by a large, arched window. Glass, wall coverings, and gaiety were not features here in this sparsely decorated building which had a damp reek about it, making MacDuff wonder how miserable the bottle-neck dungeon would be. A shutter banged gently and rhythmically against the stone as the breeze rushed in, trying in vain to dry out each murky nook and cranny.

"No wine," said MacDuff looking up as the shutter banged once more. On doing so he noticed a small red bag on the window seat just below the rogue shutter. Where have I seen that before? he thought, struggling to place it, then realising he was being watched continued, "I see no reason to celebrate." Mool ignored the comment pouring himself a large gobletful.

Shortly, a dull, muffled sound came from the passage as Skate manhandled the bound and gagged prisoner, dragging her semi-conscious and semi-naked towards her waiting interrogators. The door burst open and she was thrown violently to the floor. Mool checked Duncan's reaction as the quivering wreck of a woman hit the floor, and was disappointed to see that he showed no emotion.

"Shall we?" said Mool placing his Jedart on the table and pulling out his favourite iron pins from his sporran. MacDuff nodded.

Christina moaned as Skate dragged her up to her feet by her arms which were secured at the wrists. He hoisted her arms up, hooking the twine over a metal spike protruding from the wall, leaving her dangling on the very tips of her black and blue toes. She hung there almost lifeless, her beauty drained from her; her skin no longer soft but dirty, rough-looking with bruises and dried blood. Skate stood next to her grinning, eying her naked breasts reliving how not long before he had tasted them;

salty, but smooth, tender but firm. He had suckled like a newborn babe, running his rough tongue down her, his rancid breath oozing out from behind grey teeth, his body odour unbearable. She had tried to will herself into a state of catalepsy but had been unable to do so which meant that her guilt was all the more magnified as the brute assaulted her womanhood, first with his tongue and then with his dirty, stubby fingers and later his equally stubby manhood. MacDuff noticed a trickle of blood running down her thighs.

"Allow me to demonstrate – your arm, my lord," said Mool.

"There is no need. I know exactly the methods of a witch-pricker although know not the reasons, but what of this mark that you mention?" replied MacDuff, examining the woman from where he sat opposite Mool at the window.

"The methods and the reasons are as you would imagine, connected," he whispered, careful that Christina should not be able to hear them. "I seek the Devil's Mark. A witch becomes possessed by Him when they enter into their pact, and when He leaves the host body He leaves a mark: a mark insensitive to pain. It is this mark that I intend to find and find it I will."

"How do you know where to look?" MacDuff was intrigued.

"Experience. But this witch's guilt is all over her face," he said pointing an accusatory finger at Christina whose bloody and bruised face could be said to display the guilt of others.

"Do it then," said MacDuff, "show me."

The witch-pricker stood up and approached his wretched specimen pausing only to hold her head up. She opened her eyes, which Mool stared into, twisting his head askew as if probing into her depths. He then slowly stuck one of his iron pins into her soft left cheek causing her to squeal in agony. Blood ran down her face as she wriggled on the hook groaning once more from behind her gag.

"See, she can feel the pin," said Mool, "now come closer my lord and watch this." He slowly waved another pin in front of Christina, far enough away as not to hit the one still dangling from her cheek. "See, the Devil's Mark," he said. MacDuff nodded. "Two of them," said Mool pointing the two moles out with the tip of the iron instrument before carefully piercing one with it. Christina was frozen in fear waiting for the rush of pain, which did not come. No pain. Her eyes were wide as he pulled both pins out inserting one into the other mole on her right cheek. Again, she felt nothing. "Witch! Of that there is no doubt," announced Mool, "and the punishment for being so is death. She shall be burnt alive..." he started.

"Not too fast, my friend," said MacDuff putting a hand on Mool's shoulder. Skate watched in silence, confused. "As she is guilty and was found on my land I shall decide her fate..."

"But Sire, the punishment for witches is always death," Mool said.

"Aye, that is as may be. But, I insist that Prior Callum examines her also."

"You do not trust my examination? You witnessed it with thine own eyes...she is a witch!"

"Aye, agreed. But she may be redeemed by the Holy Church and I will have her taken to my Ravenscraig and held until the return of Prior Callum. We wait until then."

"But…"

"I have decided! Cut her down!"

Mool was furious. Fighting the desire to snatch up his Jedart and finish off the conversation in his own inimitable way, he just clenched his fists by his sides. Probably not a good idea to kill the Earl of Fife in broad daylight, he thought. As it was he and Skate just stood staring at one another, not quite sure what had gone wrong with their plan, but already fearing the reaction of their master on his return.

*   *   *

"But why are you leaving?" Isabella gasped as she slumped back onto the bed beside her Queen. Tears welled up as she sought an answer. She could not believe that after all Yolande had been through she was intending on heading back to France. Surely now was the time for Her Majesty to contemplate, to get over her loss, to recuperate with her subjects. "Your Majesty….I….." She wiped her eyes with the bed-covering without even thinking of the poor etiquette of using the Queen's bedclothes thus. Yolande let it go. "Your Majesty, you have just buried your beloved and are of a surety upset. 'Tis no time to be making a decision such as this…"

"Sweet Isabella, you mean well I am sure," said Yolande sitting down beside her favourite attendant. "However, you are not privy to all the facts which I have thought long and hard over to come to my conclusion," she sighed. "I feared I was mad; after my visions of Alexander at Stirling I feared for my sanity, but I realise now that my broken heart was responsible; my bleeding heart was the cause of my confusion: it pined for my love. It was my heart that was playing tricks on me, not my brain. I am no more a mad woman than you, my sweet. I am no use here; a hindrance to the powers-that-be is all I will become. That I understand and accept. It is time for Scotland and I to part ways; for us both to move on."

"But, your baby…"

Yolande sighed once more and turned to look Isabella straight in the face, pausing, unsure how to continue. How could she tell this most loyal of servants the truth? How had she managed to keep from her the truth, to not confide in the one person she trusted over any other? She could feel her own guilt at having acted thus. However, she knew that the truth will break her hear also. She deserves to know she decided.

"There is no baby," she said, "I am not with child."

"But…"

"It is true. I have undergone a thorough examination by the King's physicians who do declare that I am not with child. Thankfully they declare me sane also," she smiled weakly, "There is to be no monarch come from my loins." She took Isabella's hands tenderly in her own trembling fingers to reassure her.

"But, when? When did this tragic news come to light?"

"No matter when; it is fact and that is all that matters," she whispered trying to disguise her sadness. "I have struggled with my conscience, wanting to tell you, but I needed to be sure, and needed time to compose my thoughts. I can only ask your forgiveness," she said. Isabella took her in her arms and the two of them sobbed a little, she more than her queen who was coming to terms with all the implications this brought.

"I forgive you." Isabella uttered the words that Yolande had desperately wanted to hear: that genuine conformation that she was valued, not as Queen, but as a fallible human being, a friend, who could make mistakes like anyone else. In three words Isabella had made Yolande take the first step on the long road to recovery. Perhaps, thought Yolande, I will survive; I will rebuild my life. It was the first time she had felt that she might have a future without Alexander.

"'Tis why I leave," she broke away from Isabella's embrace. "And I do so with the full consent and blessing of the country's nobles who have agreed that Margaret, Maid of Norway be returned to the throne of Scotland. It is how it should be."

"And you go back to France?"

"*Oui*," she nodded, "back to my father the Count de Dreux's lands west of Paris. Fret not. I shall be fine with time, that great healer. But what of you my dear, I worry also about you and what will become of you with a young Queen to look after. I will miss you…unless…no, 'tis a selfish idea!" she chastised herself.

"What idea?"

"'Tis nothing," she said getting up and wandering to the wall to study the crusader scene emblazoned across its full length. Isabella could not see her close her eyes as if dreaming of happier times to come. "Forgive me Isabella, but I have asked that you be allowed to accompany me if you so wish," she announced. "I should be delighted if you were to accept and agree to come with me to France, but will understand if you wish to remain in this your native Scotland." She gave Isabella a wide smile which lit up her face banishing for a moment all the sadness that had been borne there recently. Isabella was speechless. "Of course I require no answer immediately, however I am to leave in two weeks so would require an answer before then," she continued.

"I will need no two weeks, Majesty," said Isabella, "I will serve you if that is your wish. I can think of no-one I should wish to serve more than Your Majesty," she said curtseying deeply as she did so and kissing the back of her queen's hand.

"Arise, my Isabella and think on what you have decided. I will no longer be your Queen and you will be in a foreign country. Know you France?"

"No, Majesty, I know the language but not the country, but I would gladly go to such a place being as it is the country of your birth. Do not protest as my mind is made up."

"So be it!" said Yolande. "We are both for my father's lands at Dreux! Let us celebrate with some wine," she insisted, ringing a little bell to alert the attendants outside to her forthcoming request.

CHAPTER SIXTEEN

Rossend Castle, Fife, 8th April, 1286

The journey back to Scotland had taken them longer than expected, but with Dubhshuileach insisting on spending some of their spoils they had indulged in some serious drinking on the way home as reward for a job well done. They arrived back at Rossend Castle in good spirits, but that was soon to change.

The punch to the stomach came as swiftly as it was unexpected for Skate who had spent most of the time since Dubhshuileach's return with his head bowed in submission. Bash and Beege stood silent, safe in the knowledge that they had performed their tasks to the letter and with undoubted success. The verbal assault spewing forth onto both Mool and Skate had led to both of them imagining that they were going to escape physical abuse as their leader tended to bite rather than bark. Now they truly were worried. Dubhshuileach was not a man to upset: he had been known to slit a man's throat for the most trifling of offences. This was serious, thought Mool, and in the light of the crumpled mass on the floor he decided to try to reason with his master, realising that he had more chance of doing so than the brainless wreck on the floor.

"He has agreed that she is a witch," he reasoned, "so it is inevitable that she will be condemned to death..."

"Inevitable? Inevitable? What is inevitable about it, pray tell?" Mool decided against any further protest at this juncture as Dubhshuileach struggled to contain his rage. "And you tell me that MacDuff has the woman at Ravenscraig and that he wants the Holy Church to decide her fate? Well it *should* be inevitable, but my instructions were for you to reveal her as a witch and then to execute her before anyone could interfere!" The veins stood out on his neck as if about to burst with the bile and wrath that consumed him. "Why was this not done? Why has MacDuff been allowed to interfere?" he shouted.

"Er, Skate," he started.

"Skate what?" snapped Dubhshuileach.

"Er, nothing," said Mool deciding against speaking of Skate's demand to have time alone with the woman as this could reflect as badly on himself for allowing it as it would on Skate for indulging himself.

"Nothing? Are you sure? Do you have something to say?"

"No, my lord, only that we wish to atone for our mistake and ask how we can go about doing so," he said glancing at Skate who had stopped writhing on the floor.

"Aye, my lord, we wish to atone," agreed Skate, content to leave the thinking to Mool.

"Aye, and atone you will, but now I need time to think; time to regroup and plan our next move," he turned his back on the men. "What to do next?" he asked himself.

"Kill the boy?" asked Skate from the floor, causing the others to cringe. Dubhshuileach stopped, frozen, an uneasy silence falling over the room.

"Kill the boy?" said Dubhshuileach, breaking the unbearable silence to the relief of almost everyone there. "Is that the best you can do? 'Kill the boy'," he mocked. "You were unable to kill the woman, you fuck! And you dare suggest that we saunter into the House of the Trinitarians and in front of all and sundry announce 'begging your forgiveness good monks, but we are come to slit the throat of the little boy you have agreed to protect until his trial so we will be on our way now.' *Do you believe that that is what we should do?*" he screamed. Skate averted his eyes meekly. "This boy has become an ogre – a mockery to our ineptitude! How did he become so? This lad who has done nothing, seen nothing? He has us in the palm of his hands and we fear him and yet we know not why." The Highlander was pacing the room now, scratching his head and rubbing his face furiously, nervously. "Any other ideas?" he addressed the others, searching for any hint of a response. "Good," he concluded, "then leave me," he said dismissing them. Bash pulled Skate up onto his feet roughly ushering him out into the corridor to safety.

"Idiot," he whispered as Skate hurried away.

"Mool, you can stay," said Dubhshuileach grabbing the redhead's arm as he went to leave. They sat down at a table. "What of the girl?"

"She ran, my lord. I know not where…"

"Well she must be hiding with someone; she is too young to manage for over a week on her own." He paused. "Hmm…tell Skate to visit Kirkton and the Binn Village to look for her. Discreetly mind. We do not need to arouse any more suspicion from our Earl of Fife. In fact, you should do it, not that lumbering oaf. Use your witch-pricker credentials as a ruse to 'look' for other miscreants. Meantime, I needs must meet with Fife to smooth things over and to pay him his one hundred marks, as promised."

"His one hundred marks?"

"Aye, our Duncan MacDuff may be a young man, but do not underestimate him. The payment buys his silence," he explained, "wrapped up as a payment in lieu of his vassals' feudal duties. This he accepts without question as it is what has gone on before. His father was a good man, one of us; this Fife does not seem fully committed to the cause of the Hounds of Saint Andrew, hence there is much he does not know."

"Nevertheless one hundred marks is considerable," said Mool.

"Aye, but MacDuff is a rich man and likes imbibing overmuch which means that I am able to 'acquire' the monies to pay him from the very same man to whom the payment goes." Dubhshuileach gave Mool a knowing smile as he thought of the bag of coins stolen from under the floor at Abirdaur Castle.

"MacDuff pays himself!" Mool declared.

"Aye, 'tis one way it can be said."

"Think you that we can get Fife fully on board with the Hounds?"

"No, I think not. He seems too unsure," mused Dubhshuileach with a furrowed brow, "methinks he is not so stupid as I perhaps thought. He has the woman; he has the boy, in effect: he has 'check'. I must escape this 'check' and deliver 'checkmate' to the Hounds. I shall visit Fife to insist on an immediate and public execution of the boy's mother, Skate shall deliver the wee lassie who shall 'disappear', leaving only the boy to be dealt with, and I have a special plan for him," he grinned at Mool who smiled back nervously.

*   *   *

"Think you I should have the woman taken to Cramunde?" asked Duncan MacDuff as he and his wife strolled through the woods surrounding his castle at Ravenscraig, the sun shafting between the trees as they went. They enjoyed walks together finding that the peace and quiet gave them both time to think, time to talk and more importantly the time to listen to one another. These walks saw them agree many strategies, and today would be no different. "I mean, she has barely spoken this last week."

"No, my dear, I think it right of you to keep her here until Prior Callum's return. He has already agreed to come see you about the boy on his return, has he not?" replied Marjory, ducking under a branch as they came across a particularly unkempt spot in their path. MacDuff took her hand, guiding her through a maze of rabbit holes, taking care not to be clawed by one of the many overhanging branches whilst nodding his agreement. They won through in a few careful moments.

"Aye. He shall be back soon, when I will request that he oversees the woman's execution," MacDuff mentioned matter-of-factly. Marjory looked at him in horror.

"Execution?"

"Aye, my dear. The woman is a witch, of that there is no doubt. I saw it proved in front of my very own eyes: she feels no pain in those marks on her face. Devil's Marks they are. I saw it!"

"But I have spoken to her and she is willing to repent saying that she is not a witch, but fears that the Lord has abandoned her. She seems very confused…"

"You have spoken with her?" MacDuff looked disappointed, "I asked that no-one see her save for the servant delivering her food…"

"But she is a woman," explained Marjory, "with womanly needs. She does not seem a witch that will turn on anyone. Otherwise, would she not have cursed us in some way for holding her? Would she not have dealt a blow to those that sought to hurt her and her family?"

"She has been stripped of the tools by which she is able to make her spells. You have seen her, she has nothing. She has no clothes in which to hide her tools of witchcraft; she no longer has the means by which she can practice her dark arts. Dubhshuileach's men have at least done something right by keeping her thus," he said stopping Marjory dead in her tracks. "Whatever is the matter?" he said, watching the colour drain from his wife's face. Her rosy cheeks seemed to disappear in front of him giving way to a pallor he had never before seen in her. She looked like she would be sick. He pulled her to him as her legs gave way, wrapping his arms around her and gently supporting her whilst lowering her down to sit on an old fallen tree trunk. They sat in silence for a few moments rocking slowly together until the colour began to return to Marjory's face.

"You know not what has happened to your witch," she said forlornly. He looked perplexed. "Or do you?" she added searching his eyes for some sort of truth. Surely his eyes would betray him if he was hiding something? She saw only bewilderment.

"What are you saying?" he replied rather puzzled. "What has happened?"

"I wonder if you already know," she replied curtly.

"Know what? What am I supposed to know?" he pleaded seeming to her more genuine in his protestations this time. "Tell me my love..."

"You say that Dubhshuileach's men have done well in keeping her naked and battered," she started.

"Aye, of course. She is a proven witch and who knows what devilment she may be able to get up to if not kept in check," he reasoned. "They have ensured that she has no weaponry..."

"Oh, Duncan," she interrupted, "how can you talk of the woman being stripped of her weaponry? 'Tis not all she has been stripped of I fear," she sighed.

"What are you saying?" He looked concerned now; a deep furrow ploughed across his brow.

"I am saying dear husband, that along with her clothes you woman has been shorn of her dignity by brutes that have been unable to contain their urges, witch or no witch. Her demeanour, her bloodied and bruised thighs, her silent suffering: all are signs a woman can see; as clearly as you can see the stars at night."

MacDuff was wide-eyed. "They defiled her?" he gasped incredulously.

"Aye my love, that they have. 'Tis indeed even possible this violation was taking place as you stood outside Rossend Castle, but do not chastise yourself for a woman can see a woman's hurting more easily than a man. 'Tis the defilers we needs must chastise; for justice alone shall deal with our witch not the savages who seek only to satisfy their loins. Think you that men such as these would pluck the flower of some witch who seemingly is one with Old Nick? And has the Devil's Mark to prove it? It makes no sense to me..."

124

"Aye, you have the rights of it," MacDuff was agreeing, slowly shaking his head in disgust at what he was hearing, "and it makes no sense to me either," he said. "How could I not see? How could I be so stupid? She told you of this...this...molestation?"

"She did, and I believe her – as I say she has bruised thighs, bloodied legs – it is just awful," she sobbed a little. "Do not blame yourself, my love – you deserve no blame. You are a good man, but a man all the same. But, the woman...I believe her Duncan, but the witch-pricker proves her a witch," she shrugged her shoulders. "I know not what it all means, but what I do know is that woman has been viciously attacked by those very men you met..."

"My lord!" The shout came from towards the castle and was followed by another. "My lord!" This time a little nearer before a young man came into view, his face flushed with running. He was one of MacDuff's household. "My lord, begging your forgiveness but you have a visitor." Man and wife were intrigued. A visitor? One that is important enough to cause them to be disturbed on their walk.

"Go on," said MacDuff.

"He says his name is Dubhshuileach."

*　　*　　*

Massan toyed playfully with his sister as they took a break from their studies, which served more to take their minds off the fate of their mother as endeavouring to import any real knowledge into them. Clearly, for the moment, it had worked. They were joined by a Fife merchant, Walter de Balwearie, who had stopped to rest on his way home. He sat beside them playing the triple-pipes, mesmerising them initially with the delightful tunes, until Aibhlinn had lost interest and started thumping her brother playfully. Alasdair sat chatting with David the potter and Drust who had not taken long to come over from Fife to visit. Drust finally relented after suffering a constant barrage of requests from David to be allowed, and assisted, to travel to Cramunde. David's willpower and pride stopped him from mentioning his pains during the journey, preferring to suffer in silence all the way, although Drust, fully aware of this insisted they stop frequently using his age and frailties as excuse. David secretly thanked him for it. He coughed a little, finding it difficult to breathe, but had been so determined to come to Cramunde on hearing of the taking of Christina to Rossend Castle that he was not going to allow a little bloody cough spoil things.

"They say she has the Devil's Mark and it was proven at Rossend," he said careful to keep his voice low enough so as not to be heard by the boy and girl. He hoped the music being played near them would help drown out their conversation.

"Indeed," said Alasdair thoughtfully, "and of that there can be no argument."

"Aye," nodded Drust.

"Aye," said David, clutching his stomach.

"A witch she may be, but not one who is beyond redemption," offered Drust. "She may have slipped into witchery in the very near past by denouncing the Lord, but surely it is only He that can rescue her from the precipice of Hell. What say you, Brother Alasdair?"

"I know not, my friend. Only the Lord knoweth."

"Drust believes…that she no longer has any faith," strained David, "and I confess…I think he may…have the rights of it," he stumbled, hacking up a nasty lump of crimson phlegm and spitting it into his shaking hand, the splat of which served as an effective exclamation mark.

"Surely with death as punishment she is sent to join Old Nick's flaming hordes? Better to forgive, to love, and to nurture this misguided patient; nursing her back to the bosom of Christ," Drust reasoned.

"It could be…" started Alasdair, stopping as the door creaked open revealing a familiar stooped figure. "Prior Callum! Welcome back!" He scuttled over to proffer his sincere thanks to the Lord for ensuring the safe passage of the prior and Brother Malcolm who stood behind the little man's shoulder.

"Prior!" Massan exclaimed rushing over to join Alasdair in the welcome.

"Many thanks indeed," started Callum, the whole room now hanging on his every word. "We have come far, and Bernard de St. Clair is being tended to as we speak. But, my thoughts are with you now, Massan," and on noticing Aibhlinn adding, "and you, Aibhlinn What news?"

They all knew at that moment that the prior had not been updated immediately on his return. "You are not privy to recent events?" asked Drust forgetting himself for a moment.

"I will leave you," said Walter, "it looks as though you have much to discuss." At that he left.

"No," said Callum turning back to Drust, "although it seems by the glum-looking faces before me that I have missed much, and I fear that the news you have for me is not the brightest news. Not for a long time have I seen such expressions on so many. Come, let us sit Malcolm, and become better informed." He pulled up a chair at the room's only table joining Drust. David stayed where he now sat: on the floor with Aibhlinn hoping that they would not overhear the conversation about to take place over at the table. He wiped a trickle of blood from his lips with the back of his hand and set about trying to distract Aibhlinn by asking her what her favourite animals were. Massan joined the rest of the men at the table after encouragement from Prior Callum. "Sit lad, 'tis your fate we discuss no doubt so you should join us."

A few moments' awkward silence passed, no-one quite knowing where to start. Finally, it was Drust who started pouring out the details of Christina's alleged witchery, and he did so to a silent listener, Callum preferring to just gently nod or shake his head in reaction. Malcolm remained motionless.

"These are indeed strange goings on," Callum mused. "We too have been involved in strange goings-on," he added, putting his hands on the table. He held something.

"Alasdair and I saw some strange goings on too," gushed Massan before realising he may have just got Alasdair into trouble.

"Oh you did, did you? And where were you and Alasdair?" enquired the little prior.

"Near the footpath – near where the King was found," continued Massan, reckoning that the truth had to be told regardless of who got in trouble from it. Well, that is what Brother Alasdair had told him only yesterday, was it not?

"Go on," said Prior Callum.

"We saw two men enter a cave and come out with a bag of coins."

"You saw these coins?" asked Malcolm.

"No," said Alasdair.

"But you could hear them clinking," said Massan. "And it was a silk bag, by the looks of it, so no bagful of oatmeal," he added for effect.

"They looked to be acting suspiciously," agreed Alasdair.

"It sounds so," said the prior.

"What have you in your hand?" asked Massan suddenly, noticing a thin piece of deerskin peeking out from the prior's clenched fist. "Can it be…?"

"That is for you to tell *me*," said Callum revealing the boar's tooth pendant to all.

"'Tis mine!" Massan was thrilled. "Where did you find it?" He ran over to Aibhlinn and with a little persuasion gently removed the pendant from around her neck. "See," he declared laying it on the table alongside the one in Callum's hand. "'Tis my boar's tooth, found at last!"

"You took the boy out?" asked the Prior of Alasdair, ignoring Massan's excitement.

"Yes Prior, he was…" he paused, "very persuasive."

"As persuasive as you were weak, it seems. I deemed it prudent to keep the lad here."

"Yes Prior."

"Then you knew your actions went against my wishes which were for the boy's own safety?"

"Yes Prior," admitted Alasdair.

"Then the boy's care shall be entrusted with Malcolm here who is able to carry out instructions with greater success."

"As you wish, Prior."

"But, it was my fault we went," added Massan, "and we did see some strange goings-on."

"Aye son, but Alasdair should not have risked your safety. He knows that, and it is punishment enough, I think, that he is no longer your guardian. He seems to have taken to you. Malcolm will see to your care in the meantime." Massan looked as if he would appeal. "It is my decision," added Callum. Massan fell silent.

"May I be excused?" It was Malcolm who spoke. "I need time to prepare if we intend to complete our task on the morrow. Bernard rests now and we need rest also your Holiness, notwithstanding the preparations I must make beforehand."

"You are excused, Malcolm. We leave for St. Andrews first thing on the morrow," said Callum, watching him leave and turning to those left at the table. "It seems we have all been witnessing strange goings-on," he said thoughtfully.

"Uncle David!" screamed Aibhlinn, shattering the pensive mood, staring at the old man slumped in front of her and causing those at the table to leap up and rush over to her. Massan knocked his stool over as he shot upright causing it to clatter across the floor behind him. Alasdair made it to David first, lifting his head gently off the cold, stone floor. He knew immediately. David was as lifeless and cold as the floor on which he lay. Blood trickled from his mouth, the only outward sign that anything had happened. Unbeknownst to all in the room the goings-on within David's body were a total contrast to his current, serene expression; his stomach was filled with blood, his spleen badly ruptured from the punch he had taken two days previously; he had literally drowned in his own blood.

* * *

Dubhshuileach sat once more in the solar room of Ravenscraig Castle, awaiting the Earl of Fife. Michael the mute had shown him there and then left leaving the big Highlander with his own thoughts. He felt uneasy despite the contempt in which he held MacDuff. He thought of how he had come to be here, how he would explain things. He wondered about that fateful night when he had found King Alexander dangling, powerless, from the root of a gorse bush.

"In God's name! Help! I fear I cannot hold much longer and my arm is broken," the King had shouted. Dubhshuileach could barely believe his eyes as he peered down the precipice at the desperate man clutching onto life by the slenderest of nature's lifelines. He could see the earth bulging out from under the snow as the roots of the little bush struggled to maintain their firm grip. The King held on with one hand, the other hanging loosely by his side. He could barely see the figure above him, assuming he was one of his guides. "Hurry!" he shouted, "reach down and grab my hand," he gasped.

Dubhshuileach came to his senses. "And what shall I achieve by acting thus?" he shouted back.

"Save me, you idiot!" shouted the King.

"Ah, I am idiot! 'Tis strange, my good king, as it is not I who hangs from the roots of a small bush staring death in the face and you deem me idiot."

"I command you..."

"To what, Your Majesty? What do you command? You *command* me to interfere? This from a king who believes it better not to interfere," he shouted through the wind which seemed to snatch the words from his mouth.

"You say what?" The King could barely hear what was being shouted to him but was quickly beginning to realise that it was not friendly.

"You want that I interfere?" Dubhshuileach shouted, louder this time. "You that could not bring himself to 'interfere' when I needed help?"

"I know not of what you speak. Perhaps we can discuss..."

"The time for discussion is over I think. We are ten years too late!"

The root gave way a little, spilling earth and grit into the King's face. He spat out some dirt, blinking, now consumed with fear. This man was not here to save him he realised. He gripped the feeble shrub, desperately trying to pull himself up. It shifted once more. "Please I beg of you, I know not of what you speak."

"Perhaps," agreed Dubhshuileach, "but allow me to remind you."

"I can hold on no longer!" the King shouted anxiously.

"Remember you Yarmouth? And the ship you allowed to be ransacked by Edward's men?"

"I am afraid…"

"Over ten years ago. Much has happened since, save for me forgetting. I am not one to forget such a betrayal." He paused watching the King straining for purchase if not for recollection. "It is the reason I choose to act as you did then," he shouted.

"What…?"

"I choose to do nothing, just as you chose to do nothing all those years ago," he yelled as he watched the King's expression suddenly change. Was it recognition? Or was it simply the fright of the gorse finally giving up on its attempt to stay rooted to solid earth? It slowly peeled away, detaching itself from *terra firma* leaving the King to a swipe in vain at the immediate lifelines clinging to the sheer slope. Dubhshuileach sat on his haunches watching with morbid fascination the expression of horror on the King's face as he disappeared into the abyss, a rag doll crashing and tumbling over rocks on his way to a grim death. He was dead long before he hit the bottom, his skull taking the full force of his momentum on a jutting boulder, shattering it like a dropped egg and splattering the surrounding rocks with shards of bone, chunks of brain and a shower of blood and hair.

"Dubhshuileach?" Fife asked for the second time, jerking him out of his daydream. "You seem pensive. Are you troubled?" asked MacDuff.

"No, my lord," he looked up, "I was figuring on your payment."

"Ah, my dues," he said. "Perhaps we can discuss these a little later as we have other, more pressing matters to discuss I think." He pulled up a chair and sat opposite the Highlander, picking up the bishop from the chessboard in front of them. He waved it gently before them. "You have no doubt spoken with your comrades? About my intervention?" Dubhshuileach nodded, content for the moment to let the earl lead the conversation. "Ecclesiastic guidance is what is called for here I think," he emphasised his position with a gentle wave of the chess piece once more. He seemed to be talking to the little wooden figure rather than the intimidating figure sitting across from him. "Prior Callum, what say you?" he asked the figurine, pausing as if expecting a reply. "Your men have served you well in one sense Rossend, and at the same time have not. That the woman is a witch there is no doubt – I have seen proof of such with mine own eyes. Your witch-pricker was precise in his disclosing her thus. I therefore believe of her guilt." Dubhshuileach let slip the faintest of smiles, almost undetectable, but perceived all the same by MacDuff who was being careful to study every reaction, whilst remaining outwardly casual. "However," he continued, "I am confused by the abuse meted out by your men when a simple pinprick suffices in proving guilt." Dubhshuileach had not seen her of course and had certainly not been informed of any abuse.

"Abuse you say?"

"Aye."

"Surely any injuries were sustained during the witch's capture. She would have resisted leaving my men no option to take her by force. Scrapes and scratches, bruising and the like are inevitable," he reasoned.

"Agreed," said MacDuff parrying the answer and returning with his final, fatal challenge, delivered with a slow calculation, "so you know not...like I...why this woman, nay this witch...would be assaulted by those who had only interest in the fruits of her loins?"

Dubhshuileach opened his mouth but nothing came out. He searched the young earl's face hoping that what he was saying was some kind of trick, an evil deceit. He felt trapped. He tried to speak but knew not what to say. His mind raced beneath the calm, silent exterior like the furious paddling of a mallard below its graceful upper body on a placid loch. He felt trapped, yes; but he also felt humiliated and betrayed. Why had his men not told him? Why had they let him meet MacDuff ill-advised and ill-prepared? He hated feeling vulnerable; he hated not knowing all the facts; it made him feel exposed. He would have felt no better had he lifted his kilt up and allowed the earl to take his bollocks in one hand whilst crashing a fist into them with the other. Now he felt angry and betrayed: and woe betides anyone who betrayed him, as the King could testify if he were alive today.

"My lord, I can assure you I know nothing of this rape," he finally offered softly. "I needs must investigate immediately. My instructions were for my men to follow up a suspicion that the woman practised *drùidheachd* and to confine her until my return when we would expose her as a witch." He managed to talk with composure despite his inner rage, which impressed MacDuff. Perhaps Rossend was not the ogre that MacDuff was beginning to think he was.

"That is as may be, but nevertheless she has been treated thus..."

"And I shall deal with it," interrupted Dubhshuileach rather abruptly, "but first I would like to discuss your opinions on regality."

"Ah, yes. It seems clear to me that any regality held by you must be ratified by the new monarch, and as we currently have no monarch the decision needs must be taken by the appropriate overlord..."

"I must protest!"

"Have you a better solution?"

"I...presumed..."

"Good!" said MacDuff. "Then that settles it! As you would, under any other circumstances, be a vassal of mine I deem that regality be suspended pending the inauguration of our new monarch. I think I will have the backing of my fellow earls in this judgment along with the blessings of Bishop Fraser."

"But..."

"Would you have me contact these dignitaries for confirmation of such?"

"That will not be necessary," said Dubhshuileach meekly, realising that his lack of noble blood had finally caught up with him. MacDuff was in a position of power, given his earldom and status, he was not; it was that simple. "I think it best for all concerned that I am not pushed into a corner, my lord," he stood up. "Begging your pardon, but I must attend to the brutes who wronged your witch."

"Perhaps I can ease your burden somewhat by having the woman provide a description of the wrongdoers," he said getting up and ordering one of the guards on the door to retrieve an answer. The two men waited in an awkward silence until his return at which point, supplied with the details of her attacker, Dubhshuileach left. He had completely forgotten to reintroduce the subject of payment due to the earl such was his desire to get away from Ravenscraig.

*   *   *

Walter de Balwearie left Cramunde not long after Callum's return, but not before a secret meeting took place. He rushed to the Queen's ferry carrying him over to Fife where he hired a horse to take him all the quicker to Rossend Castle. He now sat in a second-floor apartment slightly breathless trying to regain his composure. He was not used to such hard riding but much depended on him now and he was not one to let a cause down. It had been a long day, however, and he was tired.

"You say Dubhshuileach is not at home?" he asked again, having already been informed that was the case at the front gate. He insisted he be allowed entry as he brought very important tidings from over the water. Mool decided to allow him access.

"Aye," answered Bash, drawing a look from Mool who felt he was in charge.

"Leave us Bash, if you will. Find Beege and Skate and prepare the horses," ordered Mool.

"Skate has gone," replied Bash, "so I will have our three horses prepared; for a long journey?"

"I know not as yet," said Mool looking at the man hoping he would give them an indication shortly perhaps. "Once finished take yourself to Kirkton and the Binn Village and on my behalf, as witch-pricker, recover the little girl."

"Aye." The door banged shut as he left, leaving Mool with the visitor.

"Well?"

"It seems," started Walter having composed himself, "that our master is exposed, rather. Prior Callum has returned from England and must now meet with MacDuff. Unfortunately he has with him information which undermines the Hounds of Saint Andrew."

"What information?"

"Firstly, he has a boar's tooth identical to the one lost by the boy at the scene of the King's death."

"And, what of it?"

"This boar's tooth can only be the one the boy claims to have given to the King as it has the Celtic design he described. It is also the twin of the one his sister has."

"So?" asked Mool impatiently.

"So, it corroborates his story that it was in the possession of the King," he paused for effect, "and know you where they found it? In the mouth of one slain Cedric de Gatacre, Sheriff of Claverley in Salop."

"And the prior knows this?" Mool was stony-faced.

"Aye, and they know that Dubhshuileach was at Stokesay. I fear we must suspend our activities within the Hounds of Saint Andrew until this all dies down. What say you?"

"I think it best that we inform Dubhshuileach who is the one who shall make such a decision if he deems it necessary."

"'Tis not all. He also knows of the bag of money taken from the cave."

"Linking our master to the theft of it?" added Mool.

"Possibly," surmised Walter.

"We must speak with Dubhshuileach at once then. Your quickness in coming here is appreciated. It is best you return now to avoid suspicion. Have one of the men give you a fresh horse to see you back."

At that the two men stood and shook hands, and then Walter left.

*   *   *

Dubhshuileach left Ravenscraig Castle, but instead of heading back towards Rossend seven miles away to the west, he turned east following the coastal route, the Firth of Forth off to his right, ducking and diving in and out of sight as he raced towards the East Neuk. Taking his anger and frustration out on his steed he jabbed his heels into its flanks, gripping its mane tighter than ever and riding it hard straight to the cliff top above the drinking den. He left the animal foaming at the mouth, hiding it in a thicket, and unseen save for a cloud of steam rising up out of the scrub into the chill air. He knew his horse would not move from there, such was its obedience; it never occurred to him that it would not have been able to wander off in its present exhausted state even if it wanted to. His pulse lowered now as he picked his way down the broken path, taking care that he was not being watched, his plaid pulled up over his head. Kicking the ubiquitous seaweed out of the way with his open-toed boots he entered the den, dirk and falchion swinging from the belt around his waist.

"Evening, my lord," said Tam jumping up from a table he was lounging at.

"Is Skate in?"

"Aye, through the back…"

"Drunk?"

"Aye, could be…"

"Gie's a wine," said the big man towering over Tam before taking a seat for himself at the table Tam had been sitting at. He clattered his falchion onto the table top, the fine, steel blade scarring the wood as he did so.

"There," said Tam offering him a large goblet of wine.

"Take a seat," said Dubhshuileach. Tam sat down nervously. "I am going to teach you a valuable lesson today," he said. Tam looked worried. "Och dinnae fash yersel'," he said taking a sip of wine, "there is no need for *you* to concern yersel'," he continued, "but it *is* important that you learn from this lesson, so as we understand each other. Tam nodded. "You see, I was given a mission as leader of the Hounds of Saint Andrew, and of course *you* know my mission – indeed it is the same as yours – but, it seems that others have let their focus slip. And that is not good. It seems that certain people are not as dedicated as us, or as loyal; they are not prepared to make the same sacrifices as us; they are not as aware as us." Tam suddenly became aware of the empty room, he stared at the front door handle for a moment willing it to move, hoping against all odds that someone would walk through. The fire nearby just cackled and spat at him; it seemed to be laughing at his awkwardness; it roared at his feeling of unease. He leaned over and threw another log on. "I am not one who embraces failure, Tam," continued Dubhshuileach. "We need to be careful in everything we do."

"Yes sire," said Tam, "I always take care to…"

"Never mind," interrupted Dubhshuileach, "I know you are vigilant Tam, and loyal," he paused for a moment and studied Tam's body language. He studied Tam's blushing face, the nervous eyes flitting backwards and forwards from his master's face to the weapon on the table. "You are loyal, Tam?"

"Yes sire. Loyal to the cause – of course. And to you, my lord."

"Aye, that you are." He sipped his wine nodding in appreciation as he sloshed it around in his mouth.

"Wine!" The mumbled, drunken shout came from the back room causing Tam to freeze with indecision. Should he jump up and serve the man and cause his master offence? Or should he listen to his master, thus causing Skate offence? It was the lesser of two evils; it felt like he was in a no-win situation.

"Give him some of our wine," said Dubhshuileach freeing Tam from his turmoil.

"Aye," said Tam jumping up. He took the flagon of wine and went through into the back room to refill Skate's goblet. He returned empty-handed. "He was quite insistent," he said by way of explanation.

"No matter," said the other man calmly, inviting Tam to join him at the table once more. "Sit," he said. The two men sat in silence whilst Dubhshuileach drained his goblet of wine, seemingly savouring every mouthful. "French wine is good, is it not?" he said eventually, placing the empty goblet down . "Très bien!" he said getting up from the table. "Now Tam, remember today's lesson; it is one you as one of the Hounds should think on." He picked up his falchion using the tip to scratch the side of his head. "How is your family?"

"Er, fine," said Tam.

"Good," he nodded. "Good."

"Can I get you anything else, my lord?"

"No, I must go to Rossend," he said ambling over to the door at the back of the room. Tam watched as he lifted the latch carefully and disappeared. He wiped a bead of sweat from his forehead and took up position behind the counter feeling a little less tense now.

Once in the back room Dubhshuileach stopped, closing the door behind him. Skate was sprawled across the table; the table that they had all stood round not long ago, swearing allegiance to the flag and to Saint Andrew.

"You are a liability," Dubhshuileach announced, causing Skate to lift his head up as if trying to focus on who was addressing him. "And a monster," he added. "And I have something for you: a message from the woman you defiled..."

Skate tried desperately to focus his eyes on the man who spoke. He knew it was Dubhshuileach but could not see him clearly. Once more he slumped face-down onto the table groaning slightly. The 'message' being delivered by Dubhshuileach came in the shape of the falchion he held. The crack as it shafted Skate's skull in two was loud enough to make Tam outside wince. He dare not imagine what the noise was but had a rough idea as he watched Dubhshuileach come out from the room wiping the blood and tissue from the blade.

"Learn well," he said as he opened the door allowing the wind to rush in, causing Tam to shiver once more.

CHAPTER SEVENTEEN

Abirdaur Castle, Fife, 9th April, 1286

The porter on gatehouse duty swung open the portal to allow the little party of monks in. They arrived with an escort who had been sent to Cramunde by MacDuff to ensure that their journey was a smooth one. It seemed that the whole country was still in a state of shock from the King's death and the kingdom of Fife seemed to be more unstable than most areas. Perhaps the Hounds of Saint Andrew were to blame? MacDuff did not believe that the group was entirely to blame for the strange goings-on, but he had more of an uneasy feeling about them than ever before. They certainly seemed to be involved in something. Perhaps that was why he had sent an escort to collect Prior Callum and Massan. Aibhlinn had been left in the care of the Trinitarians for the moment, her mother still a silent victim at Ravenscraig.

Once the guests had been fed Callum and Massan were shown to a private room above the great hall. It was small but comfortable with a fire blazing on one side of the room. A chimney drew the smoke out. Dubhshuileach would have been impressed had he ever seen this room. The walls were adorned with wall-hangings, the like of which Callum had only seen in Bedouin tents. MacDuff showed them in and then made himself at home, lying across some large cushions. Prior Callum pulled up a stool. Massan joined MacDuff on the cushions.

"So, what news have you?" said MacDuff. "I hear that Bernard de St. Clair is on his way to St. Andrews as we speak – Bishop Fraser will be pleased. Our little Maid of Norway must be brought back with great care and Bernard is the man to do so I think."

"Yes," nodded Callum.

"Your guidance in this tricky situation is most welcome, good prior," said Fife, glancing at the boy and feeling rather awkward about his presence now. He continued without looking at Massan again. "The woman has been proved a witch – I bore witness to that fact." Massan said nothing having been briefed in no uncertain

135

terms by Callum that if he were to speak when not spoken to he would be told to leave.

"Is that so?" said Callum, unaware that Massan hung on his every word.

"Aye, but she was assaulted by one of her accusers – she is recovering – and it concerns me; there seems to be something amiss and I know not what."

"Is that so?" Callum appeared deep in thought.

"Witchery has a death penalty attached to it," Fife continued, not noticing Massan's eyes widen, "so sayeth the Holy Church, but my intuition says this case is different. Why would I not want to see a witch hanged? It is how things should be…it is right and proper…and yet, I feel uneasy."

"Perhaps you do not believe, deep inside you, that she is a witch?" said the prior leaning forward, hands clasped as if in constant prayer.

"But, I saw the witch pricker, I saw that she *is* a witch!"

"And yet you do not believe her to be one. So my lord, what would you have me do with this witch? And her offspring?" he glanced at Massan who shuffled on his cushion uneasily unable to hold the old monk's gaze. "I have sought guidance in the Lord and have had my prayers answered. My mind is made up, but I would hear your solution first if I may." MacDuff wished his wife was here to support him despite the fact that the two of them had had a long talk about the current situation. He still felt confused, however. "Perhaps you need time to think," said the prior, "so I will tell you of my news."

"Aye."

Massan smiled; this was the bit he had been waiting for. He thought the prior would never get to it; too much talk of his mother and the lies about witchcraft. He watched as Prior Callum opened the little bag attached to his sword belt and pulled out the boar's tooth pendant. He watched Fife's expression change now from confusion to something akin to comprehension. A dawning.

"The boy's pendant!"

"Yes," said Callum, "identical to the one little Aibhlinn has round her neck."

"But where…?"

"Found in the mouth of a dead Englishman: a sheriff no less."

"What?"

"Found in the mouth of one Cedric de Gatacre of Salop, slain by your associate with the tattooed face," he handed MacDuff the boar's tooth. "I believe he is the slayer – he seems involved "

"Dubhshuilleach? But how could he come to have the pendant? He spent the night here, in the great hall – with me…"

"You were with him all night?"

"Well, yes…"

"He slipped out!" shouted Massan, unable to contain himself any longer. "He slipped out whilst you were asleep, and it was he who knocked me off my feet! It was a horse, not a boar that knocked me over…" The prior held a finger to his lips to silence Massan, but he understood the boy's enthusiasm and decided not to have him banished from the room. MacDuff remembered the carnage he had awoken to, a little

136

embarrassed that such events could take place under his very nose. Dubhshuileach had saved him had he not? He also remembered with shame the fact that he had got very drunk that night and had passed out for some time.

"The boy may well have the rights of it," said the old Trinitarian. "Your scullion was butchered that evening was he not?" he continued. MacDuff nodded. How did the monk know that?

"He was about to kill me," he said.

"Said who?" asked the prior. "Your saviour, Dubhshuileach? Tell me, was 'Blackeye' your sole witness? Why would your scullion want to kill you? You treat your household well do you not?" Callum was calm, his voice gentle despite the gravity of his inference. "So many questions...so many unanswered questions."

"He had stolen a coin..."

"Ah! A coin! Would this coin come from a bag of coins perhaps?"

"I know not..."

"Keep you any coins here in red, silk bags?" Callum was on a roll now and sensed that although MacDuff initially did not know of what he spoke he was beginning to understand the questioning now. "Think, my lord," encouraged Prior Callum, "red, with a sliver of gold thread round the edge?" The bags of money hidden under the floor of the great hall were known to be there only by MacDuff so how could this Holy Man know of their existence?

"I have such bags, yes," said MacDuff, "but they are well hidden."

"Can I suggest you count the bags my lord, and tell me if any are missing?"

"Why would any be missing? Think you that some may be missing?" His eyes narrowed as his brain searched the archives of his memory desperately trying to find something that would make sense to him. And then it came to him! MacDuff remembered the bag he saw at Rossend Castle. That is why I recognised it! He thought. He leapt to his feet. "I shall return," he said.

"It seems young Massan here saw Dubhshuileach's men retrieving a red bag, full of coins, from a secret place near where the King's 'accident' took place," said Callum, but MacDuff was already on his way out of the door, pushing past a couple of servants in his rush to get to the great hall.

*   *   *

Mool had waited in for the return of Dubhshuileach to give him all the news that Walter de Balwearie had brought, pressing him to consider fleeing while still able to. Dubhshuileach had seemed unimpressed at the news and Mool guessed that he was in no mood to be harangued so he decided to leave it until the morning to continue the discussion. So it was that Mool found himself standing outside his master's room from the very first sign of light, uncertain as to whether he should waken him or not. He paced outside for a while before plucking up the courage to knock and enter.

"My lord, we really must leave," said Mool opening the shutters to Dubhshuileach's private room and letting in a rush of cold air. "We should have left last night on your return..."

"Aye, perhaps you have the rights of it, Mool," Dubhshuileach sat up in bed obviously in a better mood. "Run we should, but it irks me so to be skulking around in the shadows doing work that is deemed important enough for the Holy Church and the nobles to turn a blind eye, and yet too sensitive to allow us to get on with it unimpeded." He got out of bed and wrapped his plaid around himself securing it with the big black brooches.

"My lord, as I said last night we should take care to lie low for a time. It seems the Trinitarians have the boar's tooth – found at Claverley – and it is being linked back to us. Indeed it would seem that the pendant could link not only the death of Gatacre to us, but also the death of our king." Mool spoke, his voice a quiver. "MacDuff will be informed today of its existence by the Trinitarians along with the tale of the recovered coins, and all this will no doubt lead to him asking all sorts of awkward questions – it augurs no good for us."

"Indeed." Dubhshuileach seemed unduly concerned.

"Think you we should flee?" said Mool looking agitated by his master's apparent calmness. "We should flee, should we not?"

"Aye, but first we need security. We have to ensure that Fife is prepared to let sleeping dogs lie. It should not be in his best interests to awaken the Hounds lest he be bitten by the very legacy left him by his father. He knoweth the involvement his father had in the Hounds of Saint Andrew so we must remind him that to pursue us is as foolhardy as destroying himself."

"And how do we do that?"

"Simple my friend. we reveal to him a letter in my possession which details a pact by his father and mine committing themselves to our beloved and illustrious Andrew, brother of Peter the Usurper, and to the cause of recovering His remains at all cost for Scotland's posterity. This they vowed to do; and with the blessing of certain members of the Holy Church, Duncan MacDuff cannot afford to allow us to reveal his family's 'misdemeanours' so he must be wary of the Hound that bites..."

"Aye, but surely if Fife captures such evidence he can destroy it along with the Hounds," added Mool.

"Aye my friend, that is possible...but first he must find such evidence and I intend to keep him from finding – methinks we should remind him of its existence, not reveal its whereabouts." Dubhshuileach tied his belt round him, dirk and falchion as usual swinging in readiness from it. "Besides he knows not whether such a letter exists..." He smiled a wicked smile.

"And does it?"

"It would be remiss of me to go into details about the letter and its authenticity would it not? The less is known, the less can be told," he said.

"And what of his knowledge of the coins? He must know that we stole it if it is in our possession," said Mool.

"Then we simply give it him back."

"Give it back?"

"Aye, we give the coins back to him – simple. We have Beege take it back to him," said Dubhshuileach putting an arm round Mool's shoulder, "but first we send a messenger to deliver a note explaining how we found this bag in the possession of Beege and that we believe it to have come from Fife's castle at Abirdaur. We ask that Massan confirm that it was they he saw; the boy will no doubt recognise him as one of the men he saw sealing his fate. This note we send along with payment of one hundred marks and further correspondence mentioning the earl's family's involvement with the Hounds of Saint Andrew. We shall ask for his understanding: that by delivering the thief to him, by dealing with our rapist, by allowing him to maintain his dignity in the case of the boy and his mother, and by our leaving these parts for the time being, we are showing that we repent and thus should be allowed to melt away for the time being. This we are prepared to do for the sake of Saint Andrew, first-called of the apostles, Christ's martyr and our very own protector of Scotland." Dubhshuileach pulled the falchion from his belt and fingered the tip absent-mindedly.

"Rapist?" Mool feigned surprise.

"Aye, our friend Skate – I have dealt with him."

"Dead?"

"I will allow neither weakness nor stupidity to be an excuse for endangering the existence of the Hounds," he said looking out towards the sea from the window, "so yes, to answer your question, he is dead."

"I never liked the man," said Mool adding nervously, "I could not find the girl."

"No matter," replied Dubhshuileach turning to face him. "We should leave now. The girl is no longer of any consequence; neither is her mother." He waved a hand as if dismissing them from his thoughts. "The boy on the other hand," he said rubbing his chin thoughtfully, "I have plans for him. I admire his tenacity – when questioned at Ravenscraig he did not bow, he stuck to his story…and then he had the audacity to escape! He shows spirit."

"You have plans for him? But, we are to leave are we not?"

"Aye, we leave but I still have a plan for him," he said, gazing out of the window once more. "He reminds me of myself as a young man," he said. After a moment he turned to face Mool. "See to it that a messenger is dispatched to Abirdaur Castle with Fife's payment of one hundred marks, but first I shall write the note that has to be delivered with it. Once the messenger is dispatched we can send our falcon-eyed friend to deliver the stolen bag of coins, thus proving ourselves to be honourable."

"Yes, my lord," Mool bowed.

"And have our horses and bags prepared – we leave for Earlsferry immediately after the messengers are dispatched."

He watched Mool leave and once more turned to the window, to watch the sun; a huge orange ball struggling to creep up into the clear sky; it reminded him of the fruit he had seen on the trees near the Arab Baths in Runda when he had last seen his father in Iberia.

*   *   *

MacDuff knelt alone in the great hall having paced out carefully the correct combination of steps and turns. He pulled out a small knife which he normally used to eat with and fell to his knees, swiping furiously at the straw on the floor with his free hand until he could see the dull red hue of the flagstone. It appeared undisturbed – its edges tightly packed with grit, a veil of dust shrouding it. On closer inspection it seemed as if one edge had been disturbed, although seeing as he had just swept the flagstone clean with his hand he could hardly be sure. He held his breath as he eased the knife's blade under the edge of the slab working it round the edge. It seemed to gouge a furrow with ease, but MacDuff put this down to the quality of his blade rather than any recent disturbing of the stonework. He concentrated on his scratching and scraping until he was satisfied that he had done enough to remove the slab of sandstone. He dug the tip under the slab, rubbing the surrounding detritus away with his free left hand. The blade pushed its way in almost up to the hilt. MacDuff levered the flagstone up gently. It lifted easily. He held his breath once more. He dropped the knife and took the flagstone up in both hands hoisting it out of the way in one quick movement; it crashed down onto the floor next to the gaping hole and he leaned over peering in. His heart sank: he *had* been robbed! Gazing up at him were only three bags. He studied their beauty: intricate gold thread weaved its way along the top of each one; their soft, silken bodies bulged with the coins inside; their shiny red glow mirrored by MacDuff's cheeks as they turned scarlet with the realisation that one was missing. He was angry, but he was more annoyed with himself that he could have seen the bag at Rossend castle and not have realised it was his. In fairness, he told himself, he had not seen the bags for some time. It was not as if he checked on them on a regular basis; well, not too regularly anyway. How could he have lost one? Had it been stolen from him? After everything his father had gone through in finding them. These four bags had come a long way: his father had brought them from the Holy Land and they in turn were believed to have come from even further away than that: a land far away to the east that few people had seen and many more did not even believe in.

How could anyone have known about them? He was always careful. He glanced around the empty hall searching for ideas, for any small hint that would help him. How could he have been seen? His eyes searched the room. Suddenly he saw something move above him, up towards the roof. It was fleeting, but something moved. He looked again but could see nothing. He sat rooted to the spot, staring up towards the top of the far wall, above the dais. He sat for a moment, watching: nothing. And then he saw it again: a flash of movement like the swish of a mountain hare's tail as the hare, silent and unseen at first, suddenly leaps into action, scampering away into the undergrowth and safety. He studied the top of the wall once more and spotted the answer. He could not believe he had been so stupid. He sat, shaking his head in disbelief gazing up at the peephole in the wall – the very same as the one in the solar room at Ravenscraig Castle. If he had been watched from the solar room it could only have been by one of the household, he thought. Perhaps he did Dubhshuileach a disservice; perhaps Ewan the scullion was the culprit after all.

Drust sat cold and alone in his house, the fire that usually burned in the centre of the room nowhere to be seen. He sat head bowed turning the death of his brother over in his mind repeatedly. He could not understand why he had died but felt sure that it had something to do with him being punched. He wanted to avenge him but knew that realistically that would never happen. How could an old man like him manage to wreak his vengeance on men such as those who so violently snatched Christina from his home? Come to think of it, even as a young man he had never been one to get involved in any physical disputes. He was no coward, but he was not a fighter either. His brother lay on a cold slab in the nearby kirk at this very moment awaiting burial and all he could think about was his own loss, his own hurting. He felt ashamed of himself. He stared at his feet as he sat there, head hanging in shame. He should be thinking of others less fortunate than himself. He would pray for the soul of his brother, he decided. He would do it every day, and at the same time he would ask for forgiveness for the men who attacked his brother; they knew not what they did. The Lord would judge them ultimately. He thought of the others. What would become of Christina? Would she be executed? It was the only decision that could be made if the rumours of her guilt were to be believed; of course she would be executed. He would pray for her too – she had been misguided if anything and he felt strongly that the love of God was such that her soul would be cared for and allowed to rest in peace.

A cold wind blew round his feet causing him to shiver and reach for his overcoat. He wrapped it around his shoulders, pulling up the rabbit-fur-lined hood, and continued with his thoughts. Perhaps he would be allowed to look after the young girl, Aibhlinn. After all she was too young to look after herself and he was a friend of the family. Massan he was not so sure about – he was old enough to look after himself now, but it was no means certain that he would be cleared of any involvement in the King's death. Duncan MacDuff, the Earl of Fife would be the man who decided all their fates, he mused, so it behoved him to seek an audience with MacDuff to plead for clemency for his friends.

"It's the least you can do," he mumbled to himself as he struggled to his feet using his staff as a pole up which he could climb. His gnarled fingers wrapped around the wood, clutching fast as he pulled himself to his feet. "Aye," he said to himself, "I will appeal to my lord MacDuff." The shutters banged shut as he clasped them firmly together. "The least I could do," he nodded, lips pursed as he chewed the inside of his mouth. Picking his way across the rubbish strewn floor towards the door he stopped to scan the room and visualise what the room would look like and what he could fit into it if he was more organised. I could take up pottery; I could even collect David's stuff and use it here. He thought of how he had helped his brother move all the equipment from his father's workshop and reckoned that it could all fit in here. Perhaps, I am being silly, he thought, I am too old for taking up pottery. He opened the front door and turned once more to scan the room, shaking his head in disbelief that he could be so untidy. Then he finally turned to leave; I really must throw this mess out, he thought as he stepped out into the wind, closing the door behind him.

CHAPTER EIGHTEEN

MacDuff returned to his private room above the great hall and to his meeting with Prior Callum and the young lad, Massan. He sat at a table by the window which looked out over the sprawling dunes and across the Firth of Forth to where Edinburgh sat below the formidable escarpment known as Arthur's Seat. He asked his guests to join him; Callum did so leaving Massan on the comfy cushions. MacDuff seemed to be in a trance as he gazed out of the window taking in the view in all its glory. The sun was shining, it was a beautiful day and yet MacDuff's forehead was wrinkled with tension, deep in concentration. The old Trinitarian decided to say nothing, allowing MacDuff to fully digest and process all his thoughts, and also giving him leave to dictate the pace of the meeting. The grey appearance, the old robes, the worn features on the old man's face belied an active, intelligent mind; it was this dismal outward appearance that Callum often used to his advantage, lulling people into the impression that the lack of vigour externally was matched within. Of course, MacDuff knew perfectly well that the prior was an intelligent man; there was no misunderstanding here. Indeed there was mutual respect. MacDuff lifted an elbow up onto the table and rested his chin in his hand, sighing as he did so. His mind raced as Callum watched him aware that his face was being studied by the old man. He said nothing. Massan fidgeted on his cushion as if trying to catch Callum's eye but quickly realised that he was not going to be allowed to interfere.

"I found only three bags of coins where there should have been four," announced MacDuff to no-one in particular as he watched a seagull soar past the window, expertly gliding on the air currents until it settled on the curtain wall.

"Aye, as we thought," replied Prior Callum. "It seems we have a conspiracy on our very doorstep." MacDuff turned now to look at him, taking in the severity of what was being suggested.

"You think Dubhshuileach robbed me and killed the King? But why?"

"I said a conspiracy. I make no accusations. We needs must consider every clue, and your missing bag is in the hands of Dubhshuileach's men. It is a clue, 'tis all."

"A clue indeed. It is also the bag that I saw when at Rossend Castle…but," he rubbed his fingers into his eyes, pinching the bridge of his nose, "but how did it come about to be there? Who stole it if not the scullion? And if the scullion did not steal it then why was he killed?" MacDuff looked more confused than ever. He thought he had decided that Dubhshuileach was not involved. He had, after all, been watched by a member of his own household from the peephole as he checked on the bags; or when he hid the bags originally, perhaps. Now he was not so sure. Why were the Hounds of Saint Andrew involved? How come the boy's pendant – apparently, if the boy was to believed, given to the King by the lad – ended up being stuffed into the mouth of some English sheriff whom he had never heard of? Again, his mind raced; again Massan shuffled uneasily on his cushion.

"Begging your pardon, but what of my mother? She is no witch…"

Prior Callum shot him a scowl. Massan imagined that was the case, but seeing as the prior's face was part in shadow he dismissed the thought and just stared at the earl.

MacDuff looked up to where the voice had come from seemingly confused as to where he was. Suddenly, he grasped hold of the situation and what had just been said. "That is where we disagree, I am afraid," he said curtly. "I believe her to be a witch – as I said already it has been proven in front of my very own eyes…"

"But…" started Massan only to be hushed by Prior Callum.

"But," continued the earl, "I do not believe she is evil…I do not understand fully myself but I do not believe she deserves to die. She does not deserve fully the treatment which is normally reserved for such heretics." He glanced back to Callum to gauge his reaction. There was none, save for the upturned corners of the prior's mouth, which briefly betrayed his otherwise inscrutable stance. It was over in a split second but MacDuff was sure he had seen it – a smile! He felt a rush of adrenaline course through him as he realised that perhaps he was thinking the same as the Holy Man in front of him. He so wanted to make the right decision and knew what the punishment was for witchery, for *drùidheachd;* however, he had always felt uneasy about the way Christina had been dealt with. It had never felt right and he did not know why – she was a witch after all. Now he sensed that His Eminence, sitting across from him, felt the same way. "What say you, Your Eminence?"

Prior Callum closed his eyes for a moment. Massan and MacDuff, on tenterhooks, watched him until he opened his eyes and clasped his hands in front of him as if in prayer. He spoke slowly, deliberately. "I agree." His voice was kind. "I agree," he repeated nodding gently. Massan heaved a huge sigh of relief and unbeknownst to him or the prior, MacDuff sighed inwardly too. "You have the rights of it when you speak of the death penalty for witches," he said, "however I have reason to believe that this woman is not fully indoctrinated into witchcraft." Massan went to speak and thought the better of it. "It is my judgment that she should, if willing, be welcomed back to the bosom of Christ by living for a period of no less than ten years with the Carmelite nuns of Dysart…"

"If willing?" MacDuff did not understand.

"Aye, she must be willing to be welcomed back by Our Lord and to repent any such demonic spirits which may have infested her."

"She is willing," Massan offered, "I mean I am sure she will be…"

"It is also my judgment," continued Callum, "that her daughter, Aibhlinn should be cared for at the same nunnery, and for the same period of time." He unclasped his hands and turned towards Massan. "Massan, I believe is innocent of any crime, although…" he turned to MacDuff, "it is for you to decide as you are his overlord. Think you Massan is innocent?" MacDuff felt all eyes on him. The room fell into an uneasy silence. Massan's eyes were wide with fear. Prior Callum assumed that the earl had already made his mind up so he pressed on. "Think you, my lord, that young Massan here is guilty or innocent?"

Duncan MacDuff, Earl of Fife, turned to face the lad. "I believe him to be innocent," he said watching Massan close his eyes in relief.

"Then may I be so bold as to make a suggestion?" asked Callum.

"Please do."

"The lad should be taken into the care of the Trinitarians. He has shown an ability to learn whilst in our care. His is a very persuasive young man – too persuasive for the likes of Alasdair methinks. I should think that in the care of Malcolm of Scotlandwell he will learn much and can look forward to a life of fulfilment."

Massan looked to MacDuff who seemed to be weighing up the suggestion in his mind. "I agree," he said finally before they were all startled by a loud rap on the door.

"My lord! Visitors," came the shout from beyond.

"Excuse me," said MacDuff, rising from the table and opening the door. "Yes?" he said to the servant who told him a man from Kirkton had arrived to speak with him; he had insisted it was important and that he was a friend of the witch. "Show him to the great hall, I shall see him there," he said. The servant nodded. Also, he said, a messenger had arrived from Rossend, and that he had a letter for the earl along with a payment of one hundred marks.

*   *   *

The two men took their time packing only the most essential of items for their journey. Dubhshuileach insisted that they fill the wagon together, checking each item his myrmidon brought down, discarding those he deemed inappropriate. Mool said nothing, content in the thought that he, along with Bash, was being kept as one of Dubhshuileach's close confidants. He cared not for the fate of others – he valued his belief in the cause and its success above such trivialities as friendships; closely following behind the success of the cause was a grim determination to ensure his own safety. And it looked like he was safe for now. He just had to make sure that he followed his leader's instructions precisely. Mool gave the letter to the messenger who was dispatched well in advance of him speaking to Beege. Dubhshuileach took Bash to one side, gave him his instructions, and asked that he leave at the same time as Beege. Mool was informed so as he could arrange for the two men to be at the gatehouse at the same time. He got there first, instructing the porter to have the gate opened in readiness for the men's departure. Bash and Beege arrived soon after. He instructed Beege to deliver the red silk bag of coins to the Earl of Fife at Abirdaur. The request stunned him. Why was the bag to be returned after they had gone to such lengths to steal it, hide it, and finally recover it? Mool placated him easily. Beege was not the brightest, he mused. Watching Bash struggle up onto a horse borrowed from the stables, he laughed as the wee man's short legs laboured to hoist him up onto its back. He let out a loud fart as he finally settled atop the beast. He needs a smaller horse, thought Mool, still smiling as he watched the drama unfold before him. Beege, who worked at Abirdaur Castle, had his own horse (one paid for by the Hounds of Saint Andrew) which he mounted easily, his wiry frame fitting well with the wiry mare he straddled. He tucked the bag of coins into his bag.

"The flag Beege," said Mool.

"The flag?"

"Aye, give me it – I am to prepare a room for a meeting." He held out a chubby-fingered hand, wriggling his fingers impatiently for a response. "For when you have both completed your tasks." He ran a rough hand through his red hair, accentuating the old war wound on the top of his head. His eyes narrowed as he wagged his fingers impatiently at the man on the horse who seemed to be struggling to find the flag in the bottom of his bag. "Quick now!"

"There," said Beege, handing over the neatly-folded Saltire. "Take care of it," he added, "it is my responsibility."

Not any more, thought Mool wiping his red hair out of his eyes as he took the flag from him. "And you take care of those coins," he replied.

At that the two horsemen set off, one heading east along the coast road for Abirdaur Castle, the other west for St. Andrews; Dubhshuileach and Mool left shortly after them, their wagon rattling out through the main gate. They both knew that it was unlikely they would ever see Bash or Rossend Castle again in the near future, certain they would never see the sinewy Beege, ever again. They steered a westerly course, rumbling through Kirkton first of all and heading out on their way to the port of Earlsferry. It was here that they would sail to Northberwyk where they would charter a vessel to take them on to their final destination.

The journey, in a cold easterly wind, was uneventful and by the time their little wagon had jolted and rumbled its way up the coast circumventing Fife's castle of Ravenscraig, through Dysart, and arriving at Earlsferry, the two men reckoned that Bash and Beege would have reached their respective destinations. They paid to have some dockers help unload their wares onto a small, single-masted sailing ship, which was fortunately slightly larger than the normal ferry and which meant that their wares would be accommodated easily. Mool watched as the dockers hauled the cargo aboard whilst Dubhshuileach sought out the harbour master to arrange their swift departure. He returned not long after.

"We leave immediately," he said.

"You paid him or is he one of ours?"

"I paid him."

"What is to become of the Hounds?" said Mool in a whisper, careful that no-one was within earshot.

"Worry not, Mool," said his leader noticing his concern. "You are not privy to all my plans – you have no need to be. You are not witnessing the end of the Hounds, far from it. This is the beginning. Our presence will remain here in Scotland, even though I myself will not be here. We shall work in the shadows, as usual; we shall complete our task; and we shall rise once more. Only next time we shall be free from the shadows and we shall revel in Our Beloved Andrew's return; and the Pope in Rome, Peter's puppet will no longer hold sway in the land that is Andrew's."

"And what is to become of Bash?"

"Bash has an important part to play, as have you," he smiled. "Beege, on the other hand, has already betrayed one lord of his – I do not intend to allow him to betray another."

Mool returned Dubhshuileach's grimace; he instantly knew that loyalty would be rewarded and he was safe in the knowledge that of all the things that could be said about him one of them for certain was that he was loyal. Beege had demonstrated a weakness in betraying the Earl of Fife's trust, which even though to the Hounds' benefit, was still seen by Dubhshuileach and himself as just that: a weakness. If he could be disloyal to Fife he could equally be disloyal to the Hounds. Loyalty was vital, he thought; it was one of the things that would ensure their success.

A bell rang from the quayside, the harbour master indicating that the ship was ready to sail. "All aboard!" he shouted. The few passengers that were waiting to embark shuffled their way forward past a couple of packhorses, squeezing through some large barrels stacked on the wharf and up the gangplank onto the cog.

"Come Mool, let us continue with our quest – for Saint Andrew needs us and we must do His bidding."

"Aye," said Mool as he followed nervously onto the gangplank. The ship rocked gently on the calm waters of the harbour, but already he felt uneasy.

Noticing the other man's apprehension Dubhshuileach stepped aside on the gangplank to allow him to jump onto the ship's deck. "You have never travelled by sea before?"

"Aye, I have," replied Mool grabbing hold of a nearby rope to steady himself. "When I travelled to fight in Aragon against King Peter I sailed, but I must confess I spent most of the journey on my belly as if already dead!"

Dubhshuileach jumped down beside him surveying the sky. "We look to have favourable winds so I think this journey will be unremarkable enough. You will have the legs of an old sea dog by the time I am finished with you!" He laughed heartily and headed off towards the hold leaving the big, scarred beast that was Mool clutching on to the rope the way a newborn lamb clutches onto the underside of its mother.

*　　*　　*

Ten miles north of Earlsferry as the crow flies lay St. Andrews and at about the same time as the two Hounds of Saint Andrew boarded the cog a fair-haired stocky man was rapping on the postern of St. Andrews Castle, the official residence of Bishop William Fraser, Scotland's Primate. He waited nervously, holding his consignment in both arms, cradling the cloth-wrapped bundle as if it were his very own first-born. He was not used to dealing with matters of such magnitude and certainly had never met anyone of the Primate's stature, but despite his trepidation he felt proud that he had been selected, indeed trusted, for a task such as this. He would let no-one down.

The castle, comprised a huge, stone curtain wall, sat on a promontory on the northern reaches of the town not far from the cathedral, its northern and eastern sides also protected by steep cliffs which fell away to the crashing waves below. The south and west sides, those nearest the town, had a deep ditch for comfort along with the added bonus of a twelve foot palisade – one foot for every one of the Lord's disciples. This, in turn, was surrounded by an outer courtyard of various outbuildings which supplied the castle: Bash passed a brew-house, a carpenter's workshop, a blacksmith, a farrier, and stables where he left his horse with the ostler. The drawbridge leading to the Fore Tower which encompassed the gatehouse was down, suspended by chains to two giant beams jutting out from slots above the entrance, and it was across this that Bash now stood, shifting uneasily by the side door. The mace tucked into the leather belt on his breeches swung gently; he carried a dagger also. A slat in the oak panelling slid gently open and a pair of eyes tore into the back of the visitor's head. Bash's warrior instincts seemed to take over as he intuitively felt the presence and turning he introduced himself as a visitor seeking audience with His Grace. The figure behind the portal eyed him once more carefully before speaking in a gruff tone.

"Wait. I will fetch the constable."

"I have a letter…" The wooden slat slammed shut before he could finish and Bash was once more standing outside on his own shivering with cold. Or was it nerves? The biting easterly tore at his overcoat; his bare hands were numb with the cold, but still they clutched the bundle. He would not let anything or anyone stop him from gripping onto that; it was as if his life depended on it, which of course he knew it did. He fixed a stare on the peephole and waited, buffeted by the elements.

Eventually the slat opened and this time a different voice spoke, higher-pitched and nasal. "I am William Ben, the Bishop's constable. I believe you wish audience with Bishop Fraser?" He noticed the visitor holding what appeared to be a collection of old rags.

"Aye, that I do," said Bash pulling out a piece of parchment from the folds of his overcoat.

"And what would one, such as yourself, who skulks around a side door wish to discuss with His Grace?" It was a question Bash was prepared for. He handed the note of introduction through the small hole and waited for a response. He did not receive an immediate answer. He imagined the constable having to digest the contents with great thought such was the tone of importance in which it was written, but when it finally came it was the one he expected. "Welcome. You may enter, messenger." And at that he heard bolts being loosened and watched as the door swung open. "Follow me," was all the grim-faced constable said, securing the door behind Bash. Still gripping the note William Ben, a tall, balding man with aquiline features, strode off across the courtyard to the north range, leaving Bash lumbering some distance behind. The tall man waited by a yellow door until the squat visitor caught up and then they entered the building, stepping into a brightly lit corridor. "I will require you to surrender your weapons," he said. Bash handed them over and the constable showed him into the first room on the left. It seemed to be a reception room and was richly decorated with biblical representations across two of its walls. Lavish wall hangings adorned the others, straddling both the door they had come in and the glassed window adjacent to them. The constable motioned to the visitor to have a seat at the table in the centre of the room. Bash pulled up a chair and gently placed the bundle of rags on the table. The constable noticed the corner of a little wooden box before the visitor concealed it totally by wrapping the cloth lovingly around it.

"Who shall I say requests the audience with His Grace?"

"My name is of no consequence," said Bash without looking up, still clutching the bundle in front of him. "It is the gift that I carry which is of great importance; I am but the messenger," he looked up at the constable, turning slowly and deliberately to face him, "and it would please this humble messenger and the people I represent if you would see to ensuring Bishop Fraser is made immediately aware of my presence. As my note explains, it is a matter of the utmost importance that I am able to see His Grace without further delay." He turned away again from Ben and once again fixed onto the bundle in front of him. He pulled out a further sealed note and waved it gently in the air above the pile of rags in front of him. "You may want to give this to His Grace," he added.

"I shall announce you simply as 'messenger' then," was all he said in that weird, high-pitched tone of his, and at that he left the room, closing the door behind him.

Bash did not have to wait long this time. It was as if Scotland's Primate had dropped everything and rushed to see him straight away. The two men were left alone in the room; he imagined that the constable was in the corridor. He felt a sense of importance as Bishop Fraser introduced himself, almost stumbling over his words in excitement.

"Can it be true?"

"My Lord Bishop?"

"The letter; what it says…can it be true?"

"I am but a humble messenger, Your Grace. I know not what the letter says – I cannot read and the letter was sealed. However, if you will allow me to present to you a gift from Dubhshuileach, leader of the Hounds of Saint Andrew, I am sure you will make up your own mind as to the contents."

"The Hounds of Saint Andrew?" he said. The messenger unwrapped the little wooden box and held it out to the Primate, his hands still shaking slightly, this time they definitely trembled with nerves. Scotland's leading churchman took the box and placed it reverently on the table. It was just over a foot long, intricately carved with star shapes along the side, a crescent moon on top; it was from the Holy Land, he thought. He flipped the clasp and pondered for a moment. What had the letter said? *A relic all of Scotland deserved…entrusted to His Grace, the Bishop of St. Andrews, that town renamed in His honour…homecoming…quest to recover and return.* And who were these *Hounds of Saint Andrew*? He had barely understood it all, but realised that what was being delivered to him by this man was something of huge spiritual significance. He realised that he had too many questions, most of which would surely be answered by simply flipping the lid open. He took the edges of the lid in his trembling, bony fingers and stared into the eyes of his visitor, too excited, too fearful almost, to watch as he eased the lid up to reveal the contents. He studied the face in front of him for a few more moments, trying to reach into the man's soul, trying to figure out who this man was, and who these Hounds of Saint Andrew were. Then he looked down into the box. He gasped. It lay on a bed of purple silk so he knew it was exotic immediately. What lay on the silk was the cause of his exhalation. It was a piece of olive wood, the significance of which he knew instantly. It was common knowledge amongst the higher echelons of the Scottish Church that Christ's first-called apostle, Andrew, had been crucified not on an 'X' but on an olive tree.

*   *   *

MacDuff enjoyed nothing more than sitting looking down onto the great hall through his peephole. There was always something to watch; and today was no different. It was a hive of activity with household members going about their daily duties; laundresses, arms full of underwear, chattering as they did their rounds, accountants in animated discussion round a table, candles being refreshed, cooks heading back to the kitchen. He spied the old man and watched as he paced up and down with his staff, mumbling to himself. He seemed to be steeling himself, rehearsing what he would say when he finally met his overlord. The earl allowed himself a gratifying smile, knowing that if the man below was a friend of Christina and her family he would no doubt be pleased with what he would tell him: Christina was not to be executed; she will go with her daughter to the Carmelites; Massan was innocent of any involvement in the King's death. It made him feel good that he was going to be bringing someone good news, especially this visitor who had recently lost his brother. He thought about the messenger waiting in the lower chamber and decided that he should see him first. He would take the one hundred marks and find out what news he brought from Dubhshuilleach.

Soon he was standing in the lower chamber, ashen-faced and holding a rolled-up piece of parchment. "You may leave," he said to the waiting messenger. He read the note again, incredulous. It certainly was news from Dubhshuileach. It was news that he supposed proved Dubhshuileach had not been involved with the theft of the money; not directly at least. What about the pendant? he thought. No matter, the revelation that it was a member of his own household that took the money made him shake with anger. Dubhshuileach was right; Ewan had an accomplice; and he was being sent straight to him. He picked up a bell and shook it vigorously, bringing an attendant in almost immediately. "Inform the constable," he said. "Have the gallows prepared for a hanging. We shall be entertaining a felon guilty of theft."

"Yes my lord," the attendant nodded.

"I shall see the old man now. Have some food brought to us in the great hall – bread, wine and the like."

"Yes, my lord."

MacDuff wore a knee-length, red tunic over green hose. His linen chemise was turquoise in colour and corresponded in length and shape to his tunic. If he was going to meet one of his villains, he thought, he should look as fine as possible. He grabbed his mantle as he left the room and threw it over his shoulders; it was made of the very finest vair: variegated fur made from the grey-blue and white pelts of the Baltic squirrel. Such an expensive item of clothing he usually reserved for occasions where he would be mixing with his peers, but on a day like this when he would be demonstrating his authority to his vassals he felt it best to look as fine as possible. He considered fleetingly whether to fetch for his rollers and pomades, before deciding against it: he was never one to mess over-much with his hair.

Drust bowed reverently as MacDuff, a confident, fine figure of a man, came striding into the great hall.

"Sit! Sit! I beg thee," he insisted. "You will eat?" he asked.

"I should not, my lord. I have come on a very serious matter and feel that I will think better on an empty stomach."

"Hmm." MacDuff sat beside the old man, hands on his thighs. "Well, it sounds very important, so please tell me what it is you have to say," he leaned forward before adding, "then we can eat perhaps?"

Drust took the question as being rhetorical and nervously started to speak. "I seek your forgiveness on behalf of a woman and her family," he said. "This woman, Christina, is I believe being held at your castle of Ravenscraig," he continued. His mind fell blank. He felt uncomfortable being here; in his rags. Who did he think he was trying to petition the Earl of Fife? He must be stupid to think that anything he would say could change things. But he had to do it; he had to make the effort. He tried to force himself to speak, but no words would come. He looked at the earl who sat waiting for him to continue. "I...I..." He seemed to have just dried up, his mouth a desert; the flood of words that had rushed through his mind earlier as he prepared himself had vanished. They had been nothing but a mirage. He could not speak.

MacDuff watched the old man suffer in silence, struggling to speak and decided that he should put him at ease. "You come here with good intentions I think," he said softly after the awkward silence. "Have some wine," he offered, as his staff started to file in with food and drink for them. He took a pewter goblet and filled it to the brim with red wine, handing it to Drust. An attendant stood by his shoulder unsure what to do seeing as his master had just performed one of his duties. "Away wi ye!" MacDuff waved a dismissive hand. He tore off a lump of stodgy bread and stuffed it into his mouth.

"I mean no offence, sire," said Drust, head bowed.

MacDuff smacked his lips noisily as he chewed, gulping down the last of his mouthful before slurping down some wine. "Ah! That is better," he said, wiping his mouth with the back of his hand. "Your name is?"

"Drust."

"Well Drust, I think you should fear not..." He stopped and turned to another of his household who had arrived at his shoulder and was waiting patiently. "Yes?"

"Excuse me sire, but the gallows are ready."

"Aye," he nodded. "Well done. Have some guards sent in here. They will be required shortly." The messenger left and MacDuff turned back to an ashen-faced Drust. "Oh," he said, "worry not. The gallows are not for your friends, they are for a local felon." He smiled kindly to reassure the old man. "I have decided that despite having been tainted by evil spirits Christina is to be taken to the Carmelites at Dysart, along with her daughter, for a period of no less than ten years." Drust's eyes were wide now as he listened, transfixed. "Massan," he continued, "is to be looked after by the Trinitarians. He is guilty of nothing."

Drust's eyes welled up, his mouth suddenly salivating. "You are wise, my lord," was all he could say. He felt a rush of emotion come over him. He would still pray for Christina and her children, but he knew it was finished. They were safe; he could bury his brother and get on with his own life. A commotion startled him out of his daydream as a dozen men-at-arms filed into the hall taking up places near the door.

A thin, ginger-haired young lad approached them. MacDuff motioned for him to speak. "My lord, you have a visitor; come from Rossend Castle. He is known here: it is Gregor Johnstoun."

"Send him in."

Seconds later Beege strode through the door, unarmed he was pensive at the armed men in the hall; he was followed closely by two of them. He held out a scroll and a red, silk bag of coins which MacDuff took. He cut the twine around the scroll and broke the wax seal. The room fell silent as everyone stopped to watch their lord as he read, his facial expressions revealing that there was some unexpected news.

*　　＊　　＊

Lady Marjory, wife of the Earl of Fife did not have to knock on the door or wait before being asked to enter, but she did so anyway. She was able to go almost anywhere in Ravenscraig Castle without question. Her husband had requested that she not venture into certain areas of the castle, this she honoured; there were places, after all, that were definitely not appropriate for ladies. She had no desire to stumble across something which should not concern her. She knocked this time as she felt Christina should be given some respect back: the woman had lost all her self-respect because of the terrible ordeal she had gone through. The fact that Marjory was a lady and Christina was a peasant meant nothing to Marjory. Christina had been violently wronged; she needed help to recover; help to find her respect; and Marjory had already allocated two of her own maids to Christina. She is a woman after all, reasoned Marjory. She knocked gently once more. She could hear a voice; it was gentle, rhythmic. She recognised it: it was Faye, one of her maids, a good reader.

"Enter."

She went in. The room was awash with colour: blues, reds, oranges; it was like being inside a rainbow. She had chosen this room specifically for the woman's recuperation period as she believed its bright colours could inspire any tragic soul resting there. There was a yellow-painted wooden wardrobe in the corner to the right, a low, chest of drawers, again painted yellow, to the left, and near the window suspended from the ceiling was a wicker cage with a finch inside. Faye sat at the bottom of the bed reciting passages from the bible. She looked up without breaking her stride as Lady Marjory entered. Her Ladyship smiled. "Please Faye; would you leave us?" The maid stopped, closed the book and tucking it under her arm she curtseyed, leaving the two women alone. Lady Marjory felt vindicated as she approached the bed seeing Christina sitting up gazing out the window. The bruising on her face had gone down, hints of yellowish discolouration all that remained.

"How are you?"

"I am better," smiled Christina, "thanks to you."

"I come with news." The statement seemed to wipe the smile off the patient's face. "Good news," added Marjory sensing Christina's concern. Christina's eyes sparkled. Marjory realised that it had been the first time the woman's eyes had shown any sign of life; they had, up until now, appeared dull and lifeless, the eyes of the condemned. She also realised that this was the first time the woman had spoken since first telling her of her rape.

"I am to die swiftly? By the noose?"

"No, you are to live."

"To live?"

"Aye."

"But what of the witch-pricker? I have the Devil's Mark; it has been proven…" She was confused; she had never understood how she came to be sitting on a bed wrapped in linen sheets; she had never known why they would nurse a witch in such comfort; and now she struggled to understand why she was being allowed to live.

"You may have been tainted," offered Marjory, "but you are no witch. My husband has decided, and agreed by Prior Callum of the Redfriars at Cramunde, that you, if consensual, will go to the Carmelite nunnery at Dysart. There you will stay for a period of no less than ten years." She watched the tears rolling down Christina's face. "Your daughter is to accompany you."

"And Massan? What of Massan?" she sobbed.

"He will be looked after by the Trinitarians." She studied Christina's face trying to second-guess the answer to her next question. She felt she already knew the answer. "Are you willing?"

"I am," she replied, confirming Marjory's thoughts.

"You agree to all?"

"I agree to all. I wish to be cleansed; to be loved by God; to be forgiven by Him." Tears streamed down her cheeks. "I know I have forsaken God; ever since my husband died an agonising death of leprosy I have forsaken Him. But He has not abandoned me. I am no witch; the Lord, through your husband and the prior, has shown me forgiveness. I may be tainted, but I shall devote myself to Him at Dysart..." The words trailed away as she struggled with her emotions. She seemed happy; they were tears of relief, but mainly they were tears of joy. "I endorse your husband's decision with all of my heart," she gushed. "You are a lucky woman to have such a man," she added, making Marjory blush coyly.

"You are to be taken to the Carmelites immediately, now that you have shown willing. I shall inform my husband, the Earl of Fife, and he will arrange for you and your daughter to be taken there."

"Will we see Massan before we go?"

"No, but he will be allowed to visit."

"And my friends, David and Drust. Know you them?"

"No, but I am afraid to tell you that David is dead."

Christina stared at her. "Dead? How?"

"It is not known. I am told he had only a trickle of blood at his mouth. It would seem that it was natural causes."

"And Drust? How is he?"

"I know not Christina, but I am sure you will be allowed to receive visits from him also."

"Thank you, my lady," said Christina, spinning round in the bed and hopping out onto the floor. She curtseyed.

"You are welcome," said Marjory wrapping her arms round her in an affectionate embrace. They stood in each other's arms for a few moments; the peasant and the rich entwined, united in their humanity.

CHAPTER NINETEEN

The Earl of Fife looked up from the parchment he had just read. He had taken his time, soaking up every word, analysing every sentence, digesting every one of its three paragraphs. He gazed around the hall, looking at all the people assembled there. He turned to face Beege who was becoming increasingly nervous. He seemed to nod his head, just once, and suddenly Beege's arms were grabbed by the two guards behind him. They bent him forwards, twisting his arms straight out behind him causing him to shriek in pain.

"Gregor Johnstoun, it appears you have been disloyal," MacDuff said calmly. "*Caudex!*" he screamed, even though he knew the man in front of him would never understand the Latin for blockhead.

"Disloyal, my lord?" he squealed as the men twisted his arms further. Pain shot up his arms and he fell to his knees.

"Silence! You will speak when I say!" MacDuff stood up. "It appears that you have abused the trust and privilege given to you by me as a member of my household here at Abirdaur Castle. You deliver back to me *my* coins," his emphasis was loud and vicious. "You have the gall, the impudence, to rob me and then come back to present me with what is mine already. *Tu rattus turpis!*" The scarlet bag sat on the table now, a shining testament to the man's guilt. "You are delivered to me by my friend, Dubhshuileach of Rossend, who is sickened by your actions." Beege was snivelling now, still bent double on his knees. "Look at me!" screamed MacDuff. Beege lifted his head. He was knocked over, clean out of the grip of one of his captors, with the force of the blow from the back of MacDuff's hand. He was secured once more as MacDuff clattered his pewter goblet down into the man's skull, bending the drinking cup completely out of shape, red wine showering the guards and their captive as it crashed down on him. Blood poured out of a gash on the top of his head, his cranium damaged irreparably. He wobbled on his knees, supported by the guards. The pain was agonising. It seemed to sear through his brain; a red-hot poker of pain causing him to convulse and vomit on the floor. Drust looked on in amazement. MacDuff was incensed, filled with rage, his frustration and temper boiling over. He brought his pointed boot swiftly up square into Beege's bloodied face, his nose exploding on impact. Mucus, snot and blood streamed down the weather beaten man's face which now seemed to have taken on a distinctly pale hue. He coughed and spluttered, spitting out a yellow tooth along with a globule of red phlegm. For a moment the thought occurred to Beege to cry for mercy, to deny all knowledge of the theft. He had been tricked, deceived by his leader. He wanted to shout that it was Rossend; it was Dubhshuileach that stole the coins! But, the thought vanished as quickly as it had come. He knew that whatever the carl had planned for him it would be nothing compared to the furious wrath that would come from the fearsome leader of the Hounds of Saint Andrew. Bloody and broken, he resigned himself to fate.

"It is my vow," declared MacDuff to the assembled crowd, "that I shall be a champion of the Right and the Good against all injustice and all Evil. I took this vow at my investiture as Earl of Fife; it was one of many I swore," he spun round dramatically as he spoke. "It is with this vow in mind, and in my capacity of Earl of Fife, that I declare that my justice, to be done today, here and now, is for this felon to be taken and hung by the neck until dead." Beege made no reply, his head still bowed. "Take him away!" The men-at-arms hoisted Beege to his feet and dragged him from the hall which buzzed with conversation once more. "Attendant!"

The ginger-haired lad scuttled across from the door.

"Yes my lord?"

"Take this letter to the lad Massan and show it to him – have Prior Callum read it also. They will find it of great interest I am sure…"

The lad took the note and left. Drust watched him go, sensing that all that had been played out before him was not finished.

"The letter, my lord…it seemed to set something ablaze in you, and yet now you appear contented. Nay, you seem elated somehow."

"You wish to know the contents of the missive?"

"My lord, it is not for me to question…"

"I will tell you," Fife interrupted. "I will tell you what will no doubt be of interest to you. It is this: Dubhshuileach has asked permission to pass on his castle of Rossend to Massan."

"His castle?" Drust was incredulous. Again his mouth moved but no further words came. Did his ears fool him? Did he really hear what was just said?

"Aye," said MacDuff, "he wants his castle to be given to Massan and agrees that he should have it under the supervision of the Trinitarians."

Drust shook his head. "He truly is an enigma, that man."

"He feels for the lad, and believes he has been put through unnecessary pain. He cites the boy's mother's decline into witchery and her ill-treatment by one of his men as reason for his change of heart. He has dealt with the rapacious rebel within his midst: his justice dispensed by falchion. Another, Gregor Johnstoun, he has delivered to me to deal with as I see fit."

"But, to bequeath his castle…"

"He is a man of honour," MacDuff interjected, "and a *rich* man of honour at that. He is to leave us for a time and has no need for his castle. It is befitting he should act this way; it is honourable."

Drust used his staff to get himself onto his feet. "I shall pray for you also, my lord. You are a good man, and we are lucky to have you watching over us. May God be with you."

"And with you," said MacDuff, watching the old man hobble off towards the door.

*   *   *

The heat was almost unbearable outside and the two men were thankful for this haven in which now they rested. Wet and damp Scotland seemed so very far away now – both emotionally and physically. That windy day in Earlsferry seemed eons ago, not just a couple of months. They sat in the hot room along with half-a-dozen other people. Sweat ran down their naked bodies, but somehow it was cleansing. They sat with eyes closed soaking up the steam, listening to the quiet chatter reverberating through the large room. It did not matter to them that they could not understand Arabic; the Moors in here are too wrapped up in their own world to be talking about us, they reckoned. The bigger of the two leaned forward to grab a ladleful of water from a pail of cold water. He splashed the water over the floor, repeating this a few times. Steam sizzled up into his face which bore a black, swirling Celtic tattoo, Pictish in origin. The intricate design encircled his left eye sweeping out in a knotwork of double interlacing, which ended by his left ear. His damp, red hair hung over his broad shoulders below which, across the top of his back, were the words tattooed in blue, ANDREA SCOTIS. Underneath this was written DUX ESTO, and over his lower back COMPATRIOTES. Dubhshuileach turned to his friend. "Hot enough for you?"

His companion nodded, mopping his heavily scarred brow with a towel, dropping it back onto the pile on the floor behind them. The young masseur in the corner noticed the Latin inscription on the inside of his strong right arm; he could not read but knew it looked the same as on the other man's back.

"Aye, 'tis hot," he rasped. "I am for the cold room," he said standing up. He left his comrade who lay down stretching himself across the wall bench, one arm dragging on the floor. He groaned contentedly in the hot, moist atmosphere. A couple of Moors left at the same time. Shortly Mool returned, joining Dubhshuileach once more on the bench. "Ah! That is good!" he said as he sat down causing the relaxed Dubhshuileach to open his eyes slowly. "It *is* wonderful here," continued Mool. "My body feels so good, so relaxed, refreshed, and yet somehow I feel fitter. How did you ever find such a wonderful place?" He picked up a piece of soap, dipping it into a pail of water before lathering himself with it. When he realised that he was not going to receive a reply to his last question he decided to change the subject to one his leader may find more interesting. "It is over two months since we sailed from Scotland and we have found this place and settled in well. What next for the Hounds of Saint Andrew?"

"Patience, my friend."

"We are only two men – what can we do ourselves?"

157

"Aye, we are two men. Here we are two men, but when we return to Scotland we will join others. We have a presence still in Scotland; it is a silent movement, but one that awaits our return."

"When shall we return?"

"My dear Mool, you must learn patience; we return when the time is right. We have much to do before our return, but we should not worry ourselves meantime. Now is a time for relaxation and recuperation. We will know when the time is right to return, and that time is not now," he patted the other man's thigh as he spoke. "The Hounds of Saint Andrew sleep for the moment, but when they return they will return stronger, better prepared, and will complete our vow to our Lord." He lifted the pail of water next to him sloshing its contents across the hot floor in one sweeping movement. A huge steam cloud burst up from the wet tiles evaporating quickly, creating a dense, humid atmosphere. Two more Moors got up and left leaving just two old men in the corner. "Trust me," he said wiping the matted hair from his eyes, "we shall prevail."

"And what of this man you know?"

"Ah yes! He is a fixer; a collector of sorts. He collects not for himself, but for others who are prepared to pay him for his troubles. His father taught him well: Mehmet was his father's name. I knew his father; he was a good man. Indeed, it was Mehmet that retrieved our most recent relics for us."

"The one that Bash delivered?"

"Aye. Mehmet left a very young son when he died over ten years ago – I believe he was killed during some sort of brawl. His son is known as Tughrul. I believe he has discovered the whereabouts of certain items that we may be interested in. I know not what these items are, but have arranged to meet with him to discuss them."

"We meet him today?"

"Aye, today; but I shall meet him alone. It is best you leave when he arrives so I can negotiate with Tughrul. We will have much to talk about..." He reached under the bench and grabbing a towel he stood up and wrapped it around his waist. Then he leaned down and ruffled under the bundle. He pulled out his *sgian* and tucked it in the towel behind him. They chatted for a while until a tall, well-dressed man appeared in the doorway through the mist. He approached through shafts of light which beamed down through the star-shaped holes in the curved ceiling.

"I am Tughrul," he said with a smile.

"Leave us," Dubhshuileach said to Mool before introducing himself.

"I shall be in the cold room," said Mool, picking up a towel and heading out. They watched him leave. The two old men sitting in the corner stopped chattering. They watched the newcomer who looked out of place fully dressed in such a hot and humid room. He was aged about twenty and wore a gleaming white silk robe, baggy trousers orange in colour, and pointed boots. He wore a moustache like his father. Unlike his father however, a thick-bladed, curved sword hung from his belt. Dubhshuileach was amazed by the striking resemblance the man had to his father, Mehmet.

"I believe you are a fixer like your father."

"I am," he answered. "I work under the same circumstances as my father, with many of the same people. He left me a legacy you see; one that enabled me to take over his business." He smiled.

"Please, sit," offered Dubhshuileach.

"I prefer to stand."

Dubhshuileach noticed that Tughrul held a leather pouch in his left hand.

"You have something for me," he smiled.

"Yes. You are still leader of your 'Hounds'?"

"Aye." Tughrul looked confused. "I mean, yes," Dubhshuileach confirmed.

"I may be able to source relics pertaining to Saint Andrew," said Tughrul. "You would be interested in such items?"

"Yes."

"Then I will need to negotiate with your Hounds," he said, causing the seated man's eyes to narrow.

"Well here I am," he said. "Negotiate. Tell me what you know."

"I know this," said Tughrul throwing the pouch down at Dubhshuileach's feet. The leader of the Hounds of Saint Andrew bent down to reach the little bag which had slid further behind the bench than he realised. The large tattoo across his back caught Tughrul's attention, his eyes working down it until he noticed the small dagger tucked into the towel. Dubhshuileach kneeled on the floor raking about under the bench. At last, he got hold of the pouch; he smiled. "I know that you killed my father." Dubhshuileach froze. The two old men in the corner got up and left. Tughrul's words echoed through his head fighting with thoughts of how he could find himself in such a vulnerable position – on his knees on the floor, back turned. How could he have got himself into such an exposed position so easily? Where was Mool? He did not know that Mool had his own predicament to deal with: currently being engaged by four of Tughrul's associates, daggers at his throat stopped him from making any sound or movement. Dubhshuileach sat motionless. Rage started to bubble up from the pit of the big Highlander's stomach. How could he be betrayed by this man? How dare he! "It is time for you to repay," said Tughrul and at that, and before Dubhshuileach could move, he brought down the sword with all his might. It sliced through the kneeling man's thick neck with ease, spinning his head off across the floor. His sword embedded itself into the blood-splattered bench and it took Tughrul a while to ease and work the blade out, eventually putting a foot up against the wood as a lever and pulling it free. Underneath the bench lifeless eyes stared at the Turk, their disbelief at such betrayal etched for eternity like some sort of deathly tattoo.

*   *   *

Massan had grown fond of Malcolm, his tutor, over the last couple of months since they had moved into the small tower of a castle that was now his. Malcolm accompanied him whenever he left Rossend which the lad had found difficult to cope with at first. The Redfriar knew this and managed to bring Massan round by asking the lad's advice with fishing. Cautiously at first Massan showed the monk how he went about harvesting the sea. Soon he threw himself into the task with an enthusiasm that surprised Malcolm; and what surprised him even more was that under Massan's tutorage he was becoming quite adept at this fishing lark. And in such a short time too, he had laughed with Prior Callum who seemed to be taking very little interest in the pair of them anymore.

Massan visited his mother and sister at the nunnery once a fortnight, although he had been visiting them at least once a week back in April, and he told them of the things Malcolm was teaching him; Latin, French, astronomy, and religion were his favourites. He was particularly keen on religious studies; his tutor encouraging him wherever possible to view the world through the eyes of the Lord. Who would have thought my son would be learning such subjects, his mother had said. She was happy that he was being given the opportunity to understand the Lord; she too was revisiting old beliefs, and along with Aibhlinn, was discovering a renewed love of Christ.

Today's visit to see his mother had been brief; all his visits seemed to be shortening in duration, and Christina had commented on it.

"I have other things to do, Mother. I have my own castle now – I am busy…"

She butted in. "Yes, I know son, and I wonder and worry how you manage to run such a place…"

"I am not alone," he interrupted, "I have to live somehow and Malcolm helps me run things. We sell honey and vegetables at the market in Kirkton. He is a very good gardener; and we sell fish. I think Malcolm gets money from the Trinitarians as we never seem to go without."

"No?"

"No. I am no longer poor, Mother."

She wondered how a poor Redfriar was able to help the lad run a castle. It did not seem right. Mind you, it was just a small place after all – more like a tower really. They hugged as he readied himself to leave. Aibhlinn was given an extra special hug, Massan realising that he missed his little sister. She seemed to have grown since he had seen her last and had an ethereality about her he had never seen before; he put it down to her being with the Carmelites for the last two and a half months.

"God be with you," Christina hugged him again as if she was never going to see him again. A tear ran down her cheek.

"And with you, Mother," he said, "and may our loving patron, Saint Andrew, watch over you as one of his own, which is what you are."

She looked confused.

At that he left.

Malcolm was waiting across the way leaning against the stump of an old tree.

"Come, Massan. We shall sit by the shore today to eat," he said putting an arm around his pupil and heading off down the hill towards the little sheltered natural harbour. They sat for a while watching the gulls from the shelter of a large boathouse, Malcolm pointing out landmarks on the horizon; Edinburgh's Arthur's Seat and May Island were two that the lad knew; he had a good knowledge of local geography and history. It was time to expand that knowledge, thought Malcolm. They watched an old, grey man totter up from the shoreline. He carried a bag over his shoulder, which they decided was mussels. Or seaweed. He leaned heavily on a wooden staff, his posture crooked and seemingly not helped at all by the crutch.

"Are we to continue studies here while we eat?"

"Aye, son," replied Brother Malcolm. He pulled out some crabmeat from his bag. Massan's eyes lit up. Bread, cheese and honey followed and they settled down to eat. The old man picked his way carefully over some large rocks before stopping on the path downwind of them. He seemed to be catching his breath as he stood with his hands on the front of his thighs, staring at his feet. They continued with their meal, glancing up occasionally to make sure the little man was all right.

By the time they had finished eating the old man was on his way again, walking up the hill, stopping now and then to catch his breath. They exchanged pleasantries as he came abreast of them, the poor old man wandered in the mind, they decided, such was his inability to hold a rational conversation. However, their presumption did not take into account the whistling wind in which the old man stood, and from which they were sheltered. There was certainly nothing wrong with his hearing despite his age, and this old guy was no fool; he was, however, known locally as 'Nosy Niall'. Thus, he decided to stop round the corner out of the wind to find out if he could discover who the strangers were. He listened for a while, catching words on the wind here and there. *I have heard the most unusual conversation*, he would tell his wife later.

Shuffling as close to the edge of the boathouse as he could without giving himself away he listened, realising immediately that the Redfriar was doing all the talking.

"Now, what I will tell you will set you off on a path of righteousness, it will enable you to have a life that is purposeful, a life that is pure and one that secures your place at the Lord's garden in Heaven. My son, you have been chosen. You are a leader and from this day forth you shall be known as *Dubhshuileach*."

*   *   *

EPILOGUE

Kirkwall, Orkney Islands, 2nd September, 1286

"Get me a physician and a priest!" The Earl of Buchan screamed as he hurtled down the battered ship's gangplank onto the rain-lashed harbour. He cradled a young baby in his arms, but seemed not to know what to do or which way to go. Wind and rain tore at them as he stood there in a huge puddle bewildered, frightened and soaked to the skin. He glanced back at the remains of the *Golden Auk* – it was not a pretty sight. The ship was a shadow of its former self, its mast was gone, snapped in two by the furious weather; it listed badly, indistinguishable bits of timber were strewn across the deck, and bedraggled crewmen fought to save what they could from the hell of the ship's stores. The ship's bulwark had a gaping hole in it, caused by a combination of the relentless battering from the seas and the broken mast which had come crashing down onto the deck yards from the entrance to the harbour. How the captain, Bernard de St. Clair, had managed to tease the limping vessel into safety no-one knew. But he had, and no sooner had Buchan set foot ashore than the gangway behind him gave way crashing into the pounding waves. The lucky escape jolted him into action and he started frantically issuing orders once more.

"Get me a physician!" He glanced around not knowing which way to go when he saw a group of men racing towards him through the lashing wind and rain. They looked like the people they had left a few days ago back in Bergen and shouted in the same language. It was a language he could not understand, but he realised immediately that they wanted him to follow them. They surrounded him and the baby and shepherded him away from the water's edge towards the shelter of a small stone building.

"My God! My God! Have you a physician?" he screamed at the wide-eyed faces. Eight men and three women and no-one seemed to know what to do. "Blankets! Get me blankets for the Queen!" One of the women grabbed some sheepskins from a trunk in the corner of the room and threw them over the table top. Buchan lay the baby down, gently wrapping her in the soft wool. She made no sound. The Earl of Buchan's face was drained; the ship had struggled to make the harbour; he had thought they would drown out there; this he thought despite being used to travelling in rough waters. Two priests burst in as if thrown through the door by the force of nature. One of the locals forced the door shut behind them. They were from the ship; two of the few survivors from the night's horrific events. Oblivious to the others there they immediately set to prayer. Bernard de St. Clair flew in next. He explained that although they had managed to secure the ship it was now starting to sink. They had had to abandon it. As he watched the crumbling wreck give up to the relentless waves in the harbour he felt overcome with emotion as the prow's figurehead slipped out of site. It became apparent, as St. Clair was last off the ship, that more than half the travellers on board had been lost in the disaster: lords, ladies, dignitaries, clerics and lowly seamen – all had perished, the sea showing no prejudice when it came to choosing who she took. Locals attended to the wounded, shocked and disorientated survivors.

Scotland's Queen, the little Maid of Norway, was in dire straits; her health since birth had never been good and her father, King Erik of Norway had not wanted her to travel. He had even offered to have her sent to Scotland in one of his own ships, as did King Edward of England, the little girl's grandfather. Both offers had been politely refused; it was vital that the new Queen of Scots be brought to her people as soon as possible and that she be delivered by her own people. The crossing over the Norse Sea from Bergen was notoriously difficult, but this journey had proved to be the worst anyone could have experienced. They would just have to stay here nursing the little Queen until she was fit enough to travel; and the wind and rain conspired to allow them to leave.

As it turned out it would be months before the Earl of Buchan was able to leave, and he did so in sombre mood. The little Maid of Norway was dead. What was next for the country?

Scotland was a grand old lady. Her life seemed to be draining out of her with the slow decline of her Royalty. She was in a near fatal condition; her bloodline clotted, the only way forward would be to undergo surgery. The operation needed would seek to alleviate the clotting by releasing the bloodlines from elsewhere. But who could perform such an operation? Who was expert in Royal affairs? Who could be approached to assist this dying old lady? It would take some time but eventually a decision was made; a decision that the nobles of Scotland were to rue for years to come, for the honour of deciding Scotland's future monarch from the assembling contenders was to fall with Alexander III's future brother-in-law, King Edward of England. And he would turn out to be more of an expert butcher than caring physician. After all, the recent uncertainty Scotland's troubles were only just about to start.